DEATH OF A PORN STAR

MAGNOLIA BLUFF CRIME CHRONICLES
BOOK 43

C W HAWES

CWH BOOKS

ENTER THE IMAGINATIVE WORLD OF CW HAWES

Enter my world and you'll find that murder was never so good. Just click, tap, or scan the QR code below.

There's nothing like a good old-fashioned slow burn murder mystery. The quirky characters. The eccentric sleuth. The bumbling police detectives. The nefarious villain. And of course, the leisurely pacing until we reach the exciting climax.

If you are new to the Magnolia Bluff Crime Chronicles, then *Death of a Porn Star* is an excellent entry point into the series and into my world.

In addition to my books in the Magnolia Bluff Crime Chronicles, I write the Justinia Wright Private Investigator Mysteries, which are an homage to Nero Wolfe and Archie Goodwin. You'll discover exciting stories, eccentric and quirky characters, and wicked killers. And if you like

Magnolia Bluff, you're sure to like Justinia Wright's Minneapolis.

So just click, tap, or scan the QR code to enter my exciting world of mystery and mayhem. You will get a free copy of *Vampire House and Other Early Cases of Justinia Wright, PI* and you'll get my monthly email of news and curated contact. The game is a foot!

Book Cover Design: The Book Khaleesi

❀ Formatted with Vellum

For Susannah

PROLOGUE
BACK HOME

Monday, January 5, 11:37 pm

THE HOUSE IS QUIET. Being old, there is a creak here and there. The mumbling that old houses do. Like they are talking to themselves.

The wind buffets the windows, resulting in an occasional rattle.

Otherwise, there is no sound. The fire in the fireplace has died down to the point where it is mostly a pile of glowing orange-red embers. The tang of the oak lingers in the air.

We arrived back in Magnolia Bluff yesterday evening after being away for nearly a year. Ember, my lovely and loving wife, needed the time away to work through the trauma she experienced last January. So we packed up the kids, pets, and the nanny and went sailing around the world. We had a delightful adventure, and I'm glad to be back home.

Home is where the heart is, they say, and my heart is here in Magnolia Bluff. At least the part that isn't with Ember.

Everyone has gone to bed, and I'm sitting before the fire with Princess, my dog, curled up at my feet. Wilbur, Emmy's cat, is curled up in Em's chair. I think he's even gladder to be home than I am.

I'm smoking an old bulldog pipe I got from my dad and drinking a Corpse Reviver No. 1. This is about as relaxed as one can get. Savoring the diverse flavors of tobacco and alcohol, gazing at the glowing coals, with your best buddy at your feet.

By the way, my name is Harry Thurgood. I'm the proprietor of the Really Good Wood-Fired Coffee and Ice Cream Emporium. Yeah, that's a mouthful. Probably why the locals just call it the Really Good.

While away, I kept up with a few folks here in town. Principally, Graham Huston, owner and publisher of the *Magnolia Bluff Chronicle*, our twice-weekly newspaper.

The murder and mayhem have continued. Our able-bodied citizenry has gone on to help our constabulary solve many of those crimes, in spite of Captain Briggs's adamant stand against them doing so. He's the esteemed head of the MBPD, after the police chief.

But in addition to murder and mayhem, there's also been love and, as a result, a few new additions to our town. Who doesn't like that?

Tomorrow is a new day. And a workday. I'll be back at the Really Good, and Ember will be back ministering to her flock. And life goes on.

Turn the page, and a new day begins in Magnolia Bluff, Texas.

1

TUESDAY, JANUARY 6, 5:28 AM

SERGEANT INVESTIGATOR REECE SOVERN was halfway through his second cup of coffee and the egg sandwich his wife, Hetta, had made for him.

It felt good to be finished with his special assignment and back at his desk.

His temporary replacement, Palmer Kraus, had been busy and mostly successful, but there were three cold cases that in Reece's opinion shouldn't be cold.

The brutal murder of the Reverend Adelbert Humphrey, assistant pastor at Saint Luke's United Methodist Church. A copycat killing of the Full Moon Killer from a year ago. All the clues had eventually led to dead ends.

Then there was the gruesome murder of Pastor John Reston of the Flaming Light Gospel Tabernacle. What started out as a case with the promise of a quick resolution soon turned into a maze of dead-end leads and what appeared to be a quagmire of lies and deception. And so a year later, the case was still unsolved.

Finally, there was the drive-by shooting and attempted murder of Ember Cole. This one truly baffled Reece.

Who wanted Ember dead? She was a kind, caring, and loving person. She wasn't perfect. Who was? And he was very much aware she had parishioners who didn't like her. But didn't like her enough to kill her? He found that very difficult to accept.

Was her would-be assassin someone out of her past life in the porn industry? Maybe, Reece thought. But how would he find the person without Ember's cooperation? And he realized she was not likely to walk down that road willingly. In fact, she'd just as soon he not bother trying to solve the case.

Jesus had saved her, she'd said, and that was that. Pure Ember.

Reece drank coffee and followed the java with an emerald green perfecto, which he stuck in his mouth. He let his teeth gently gnaw the cigar. He never smoked one.

He leaned back in his chair, and put his hands behind his head.

Briggs was still ornery as ever. Reece's butt hadn't even warmed his chair when the captain reminded him no civilians were to be involved in any police investigations and then he wanted to know if Reece had cracked the cold cases yet.

"Back in Billings, these cases would've been solved, Sergeant. I don't want to see any grass growing under your feet. Got it?"

Reece told him he got it.

On the other hand, Chief Jager was as laid back as ever. Why he'd hired Briggs was a mystery. Those two were as opposite as the North Pole is from the Amazon.

Must've been something political was all Reece could come up with.

Then there was Turner getting a private investigator license. Brandon Turner. That arrogant, bossy, nasty retired New York City cop. Now a goddamn PI. He shook his head. At least he was still a civilian, and Reece could tell him to go jump in the reservoir.

He smiled. He liked that. He liked that a lot.

He brought his chair forward. There was a sticky note on the Humphrey case. In red ink was the word "Urgent." Urgent because Mary Lou Fight had made a big stink about a quick resolution to the case. Her absence for a good part of last year had given the MBPD a bit of a reprieve. But since her return, she'd been once again badgering everyone that justice needed to be done.

Justice. Funny word that. Once Reece had thought of it as an absolute concept. Not any longer. Too often "justice" was bought or overlooked. A sad state of affairs that, but he had no delusions about it being how things have always been. At least ever since people had become people.

Since Mary Lou was hollering, he decided he and GJ, his trusty assistant investigator, would do some poking around on the Humphrey case. Never know, might stir up some dust and find something of value underneath.

2

TUESDAY, JANUARY 6, 6:48 AM

REECE SOVERN, hands on hips, his cigar pipe, a gift from Harry Thurgood, set at a jaunty angle in his mouth, let his eyes roam over the crime scene. Room six at the Cozy Corners Motel. The owners, Arnold and Bette, were going to be pissed at having to do the cleanup.

He knew the victim. Who didn't? Patrice Bremen. Homecoming queen at age seventeen. Mother and wife at age eighteen. Divorced at age twenty. Snagged herself three wealthy husbands in the following fifteen years and robbed them blind in the divorces.

For the past two years she'd found a new way to make cash: pimping herself and her daughter on the Only For You website. A classic case of good girl gone bad.

"Notice the blood spatter, Sarge?" Investigator Georgia Jean Riggins asked her boss.

"Yeah. Somebody with a lot of anger was wielding that knife."

"Oh, Wylie's here."

Wylie Garrison stood in the doorway. He was a short,

somewhat portly man. Narrow face. Sandy hair slowly disappearing. Wire-framed glasses hanging crooked and desperately on his snub nose.

Since he was the local justice of the peace and county coroner, his word made the dead officially dead. Up until then, there was a chance the body might walk away.

"Reece. GJ. What do we have?"

Reece pointed to the bed with his cigar pipe. "Patrice Bremen. Someone decided they wanted to see what she looked like in red."

Wylie shook his head, stepped up to the bed, and let his eyes scan the mutilated and naked body.

"What a mess," he said. "Arnold and Bette are going to have to buy a new mattress." He looked around the room. "And get the room painted."

The coroner felt for a pulse, shone a penlight in the victim's eyes, and once more gazed at the length of her body.

"She was a pretty girl. Once upon a time."

"That she was," Reece said. "I assume she's dead?"

"I'm afraid so," Wylie responded. "I was going to have breakfast at the Spoon. Think I'll pass. You two have a good day."

Reece watched him leave, and a new figure occupied the doorway.

"What are you doing here, Huston?" he asked.

"What do you mean what am I doing here? I'm the local newsman, and this is news."

"Beat it," GJ said.

Huston smiled at the investigator. "Who's the victim?" he asked.

"A former citizen of Magnolia Bluff and the great state of Texas," Reece answered.

"Very funny, Reece. You realize the rumor mill will have the complete lowdown an hour from now. Give me a little something."

"Why? You putting out a paper in the next ten minutes?"

"Okay. Fine. Be that way. Just remember who buys ink by the barrel and sends out his eight pages to over four thousand households."

"All right, Huston. The victim is Patrice Bremen. Born and raised here in town. Spent time away marrying and divorcing rich. Came back home and opened up an online sex shop. Now she's dead. Someone knifed her really good."

"Did you say that on purpose?"

Reece let a smirk play on his lips. "Perhaps."

"Geez. So where are you at in the investigation?"

"Staring at a dead body and wondering who'd do such an awful thing?"

Huston took a deep breath and slowly exhaled. "Okay, Sarge. I'll get my information elsewhere. And that's too bad for you."

"Does this look like the face of someone who cares?"

"Come to think of it, no, it doesn't."

Reece watched Graham Huston leave and then turned back to the body.

"You know what's really odd about this, GJ?"

"Uh-uh."

"There's not a single cut on her arms."

3

TUESDAY, JANUARY 6, 7:18 AM

FERGUS WAS SITTING at a corner table in the Really Good, his back to the wall, telling me in his disjointed, almost mystical manner about dancing knives.

"They're dancing again, I tell you," he said.

"Where?"

"At the house of sin."

"And what house might that be?"

Estrelita brought him his eggs, bacon, biscuits and gravy, hash browns, and toast. Seeing his coffee cup was empty, she gave him a refill.

When she'd left, his watery eyes met mine. "The house of sin with twelve rooms."

I pondered for a minute. "The Cozy Corners Motel?"

He nodded and put egg in his mouth.

"There was a murder at the motel?"

He nodded and ate bacon.

"Last night?"

He nodded again and conveyed biscuits and gravy to his mouth.

"Not good advertising for Arnold and Bette. Do you know who was killed?"

"The sinner woman." He drank coffee.

"That might be half the town."

He sniggered and ate bacon.

"Come on, Fergus. The suspense is killing me. Who died? Do you know?"

"The one showing her body and her daughter's on the computer. Doing sin for money."

"Ah, I think I know who you're talking about."

The bell over the door jingled as Graham Huston entered the shop. He crossed the floor to where I was sitting, calling out an order for two egg sandwiches with extra bacon to go.

He pulled up a chair, sat, removed a pint of Old Forrester Blue Corn Texas Bourbon from his back pocket, and unscrewed the cap.

Fergus put down his fork, looked at the bottle, and licked his lips.

Graham poured what must've been a jigger's worth into Fergus's coffee cup. "What can you tell me about Patrice Bremen's murder?"

The old vet drank half the cup in one gulp, licked his lips, and said, "I was at the cemetery. Heard a lot of yelling. Arguing. Then silence. Saw a shadow get into a car and drive away."

"Did you recognize the shadow?"

Fergus drank the rest of his doctored coffee. "Nope."

"Someone local?" Graham asked.

Fergus shrugged and ate biscuits and gravy.

"That's more than I got out of Reece." He picked up Fergus's cup and caught Estrelita's attention. He set it back down, poured another jigger of whiskey into the cup, screwed the cap back on the bottle, and stood.

Estrelita arrived, gave Graham his sandwiches, and filled Fergus's cup.

She looked at the newspaperman. "You shouldn't encourage him, Mr. Graham."

Graham put the bottle back into his pocket. "I can't count how many times he and I have shared a bottle. Best newsman in town. He's earned it."

He turned and headed for the door, calling over his shoulder, "Thanks, Fergus. Harry." And was gone.

Fergus took a bite of toast.

"You could've told me that," I said.

"Told you what?"

"What you told Graham."

"Graham was here?"

I stood, shook my head, and walked back to my table in the opposite corner, snagging coffee and doughnuts on the way.

Only six days into the new year and we already have ourselves another murder.

I knew of Patrice Bremen — who didn't — but I didn't know her. She was the new wave of porn star. Capitalize on the internet and do porn right in the comfort of your own bedroom to a worldwide audience. The advantage of DIY porn is that all the money is yours. Some of these women were millionaires. It boggles the mind.

Fergus had finished his breakfast and was drinking coffee. How much did he really know? How much was fantasy? Was anything he saw real?

The bell over the door jingled, and in bounced Monika Crow, Graham's Gal Friday. I probably just dated myself.

Since the morning was chilly, she was wearing a coat and boots. Where I'm from, this was light jacket and sweater weather.

Under her arm was a rolled-up newspaper. She walked briskly over to my table and handed me the paper.

"Since you didn't stop in to get your copy, I thought I'd drop it off."

"Thanks. Appreciate it. I suppose there's nothing in here about the Bremen murder."

She shook her head. "Nope. We only just found out. Graham might do an extra edition tomorrow."

"Apparently he's already talked to Reece, and he was just in talking to Fergus."

"He texted saying he was trying to track down her daughter."

"Maybe he should just follow the police."

"Nah. Reece and GJ gave him the heave-ho."

"Briggs's influence."

"Yep. Just means we have to be more creative."

I chuckled at that.

"Got to go, Harry."

"Want coffee or anything?"

"Thanks, but I'm good. Catch you later."

She bounced back out the door. Man, to have that kind of energy again.

I drank coffee. Uluguru Mountains Tanzanian Peaberry. Made in my vacuum siphon pot.

A majority of the customers that frequent the Really Good want foo-foo coffee. You know, the banana split latte with a double shot of cherry-infused espresso. That kind of thing.

Then there is the smaller group that just wants a high-quality cup of java. Maybe with cream or sugar or both. I like mine with a little cream.

I watched Fergus get up and head for the door. He gave me a salute, which I returned, and was gone.

Who wanted Patrice Bremen dead? And why? Was it a shakedown gone bad? The rumor mill said she was worth around four million. I'd seen her driving around town in her top-of-the-line Cadillac, and that car isn't cheap.

Or was it a dissatisfied customer? Or perhaps someone who didn't like it that a sinner was profiting from her sin?

For once, Em and I needn't get involved. And that was a good feeling.

4

TUESDAY, JANUARY 6, 8:01 AM

THE REVEREND EMBER Cole sat behind her desk and let her eyes roam her spartan office. She'd spent almost twelve months away. Was she ready, truly ready, to resume her duties as the Lord's servant to His flock at Saint Luke's United Methodist Church?

She'd been shot and had a faint scar to prove it. She'd been kidnapped and almost killed to feed a group of vampire lifestylers gone haywire. And what was worse, her playing detective had almost gotten her friend, Joyce Blackstone, to share a similar fate.

Was she ready to become part of her faith community again? Part of her town again?

There was someone who wanted her dead out there. Watching her. Waiting. Waiting for the opportunity to try again.

Was she ready? Ready to start living again?

She took a deep breath and slowly exhaled. Then she lifted her arms, palms up, and said, "Yea, Lord, though I walk through the Valley of the Shadow of Death I will fear no evil, for Thou art with me."

Her arms slowly lowered, and her hands rested on her desk. She smiled. "Ember Cole, you got this."

———

The Reverend Chris Hayes, pastor of the First Baptist Church, stepped out of his office.

"Ember, it's so good to see you. Come in."

He waved her over to the sitting area next to his desk and, when she was seated, sat across from her.

Ember thought his office wasn't all that different from her own. He had many more books; otherwise, it was simply furnished. No frills.

"How are you?" he asked. "Was your time away therapeutic? I have to say, you're looking relaxed and refreshed. And the tan looks good on you. If you don't mind my saying so."

She smiled. "I don't mind. It was just what the doctor ordered, as they say."

"So what brings you here? Social call? Business?"

"I just wanted to check in with my fellow ministers. See how they are doing."

"Well, this fellow minister is doing well. Nothing much has changed in your absence. The usual mayhem—"

"All because of that writers group that had a retreat here. The murders and mayhem started then."

"Writers group?" A puzzled look descended on his face.

"Yes. About four years or so ago. When Neal Holland died and Graham took over the *Chronicle*. Can't remember their name. Something underground."

"Huh." He shook his head. "Don't recall. Although don't

forget, Rebecca had been killing someone every May for years."

"Yes, but now there's a new murder virtually every month. And we already have one for this year. Larrilyn, my secretary, told me as I was leaving the office Patrice Bremen was murdered."

"A troubled soul, that one. But murdered? When?"

"Apparently last night."

"Technically, she was a member here. But she hadn't been active for most of her life."

"Are you going to do the funeral?"

His face was skeptical. "Are they having one? There's only the daughter. I don't think there are any relatives left in town."

"I don't know. I just kind of assumed."

"The daughter's not a member here, and I doubt she's a Christian. So I'm assuming there probably won't be a funeral. Maybe a service at the funeral home. Or just a memorial. Or nothing." Hayes shrugged.

"I suppose. If there's no family, you're right, there might not even be a memorial. Patrice didn't have many friends."

"I don't think she had any friends. In town, that is. Why the interest?"

"Just curious. Then again, it might be my past. If I'd died when I was living like Patrice, there wouldn't have been anyone. I don't even know who would have made any decisions. Probably a judge."

"Well, that was a long time ago, and Patrice has her daughter."

"Possibly I'll pay the daughter a visit."

Hayes chuckled at that. "Ah, Sherlock, do I see a deerstalker on your head?"

Ember laughed. "No, just a servant of God desiring to comfort a fellow sinner."

She stood, and Chris did too. "Nice talking with you, Chris. We'll have to have you and Rhoda over for dinner soon."

"We'd like that. May you have a blessed day, Ember."

"And you as well."

He watched her leave and couldn't help but think she did indeed have on that deerstalker.

5

TUESDAY, JANUARY 6, 9:04 AM

A YEAR IS A LONG TIME. Plenty of time to lose touch with people. Maybe even forget their names.

Before we went sailing around the world, every morning (except for Sunday, because the Really Good is closed on Sundays) the Niners would meet for coffee, pastries, and gossip.

Jack Bonhoffer, my floor manager, said they kept meeting while Ember and I were gone. Nice to know the meetings and the place had become a habit.

The Niners, by the way, is my nickname for the group, because they always troop in at nine in the morning.

So, Estrelita and I had arranged the tables and set out coffee and some sweet goodies in anticipation of their arrival.

And sure enough, at nine o'clock on the nose, they started to arrive.

Chief Jager and Graham Huston.

Caroline McCluskey and Magnolia Nadine Roane. Caroline's the town librarian, and Magnolia Nadine is just another rich woman, except she truly does have a heart of gold.

The Reverend Billy Bob Baskin, he's the Presbyterian minister. Sometimes I kid him that he should take up pipe smoking because Presbyterian Mixture was made just for him.

Usually one of the Whitacres joins us. They run the pipe shop in town. Today, Terall was in attendance. And per my request, she brought me a pound of their Reservoir Blend. For payment, I gave her a pound of my special Puerto Rican coffee.

Sometimes Doctor Mike Kurelek drops by. He's a licensed therapist who used to teach at the college until the college board, in its infinite wisdom, farmed out the psychology department.

LouEllen Mueller also occasionally swings by to see what's cooking. She owns a nightclub on the edge of town.

Neither one joined us today, however.

Graham started things off by asking Tommy Jager about Patrice Bremen's murder.

There was a gasp from Caroline. "When did this happen?"

At the same time, Billy Bob said, "Oh, dear, they're starting already."

Tommy said, "Ask Reece."

"He said to ask you." Graham said this with his poker face on.

Tommy nearly spewed his coffee. "Like hell he did."

Graham persisted. "What can *you* tell me?"

"Nothing. Ask Reece. I haven't talked to him yet."

Magnolia Nadine said, "Francine Boedecker said her cousin told her that Patrice was killed in a bondage situation gone wrong. Francine's cousin got the information from a friend of the photographer who knows Mabel Willet."

Tommy jumped in while Magnolia Nadine took a breath. "That's a long chain of hearsay, Magnolia." He plowed on before Magnolia Nadine could chastise him about not using her full name. "And you ought to know better than spreading such rumors."

Magnolia Nadine gave him a scowl that could boil water.

Graham said, "Bondage? Huh. That'll sell a few papers."

"You planning on writing *Fifty Shades of Deviancy?*" Caroline asked.

"Maybe *Fifty Ways for a Good Girl to Go Bad and Why Not to Do It,*" Billy Bob said.

Tommy snorted. "That title would really sell books. Probably make the high school banned books list."

"What about the daughter?" I asked.

Magnolia Nadine put down her Danish. "Heard tell she was the worst of the two. Was actually pimping out her mother."

Billy Bob shook his head. "Does depravity know no bounds?"

"No, it doesn't," Graham answered.

At that point, my lovely wife walked in.

Graham said, "How come you're late, Mrs. Rev? The coffee's almost gone."

"Wow, Ember, that tan looks good on you," Caroline said.

Ember sat. "Thanks, Caroline. I was talking with Reece."

6

A HUGE SMILE spread across Graham's face. "Do tell, Mrs. Rev. Do tell."

Em made the zipper motion across her lips. "Promised him I wouldn't say a word."

"You're kidding, right?" Graham insisted.

"You ought to know Ember by now," Caroline said.

"You could stand her on a pile of live coals and she'd just smile at you," Magnolia Nadine said. "Downright frustrating it is."

Laughter erupted from the table as though Krakatoa were attempting a repeat performance.

Graham shook his head and complained, "Reece will talk to everyone but me."

Terall said, "Perhaps he's trying to tell you something."

Graham continued, "And after all the good press I give him."

"Well, Huston," Tommy began, "maybe you ought to send Monika to talk to him. Looks to me like he prefers the ladies."

Graham whipped out his phone and fired off a text. "Thanks, Tommy," he said when finished. "Can't imagine why I didn't think of that."

"Maybe you don't like to delegate," Caroline said.

Tommy chuckled. "Librarian, one. Newspaper editor, nothing."

"Go ahead and laugh," Graham said. "Just remember—"

"Yeah, we know. You send that rag out to four thousand households," Magnolia Nadine said.

At that moment, in marched the Crimson Hat brigade. The Niners departed faster than dry leaves before a wild hurricane fly. All except for Terall Whitacre.

———

While Estrelita took the orders of the Hats, I bussed the tables abandoned by the Niners. When finished, I grabbed coffee and a doughnut and joined Terall at my table.

"More coffee?" I asked her.

"No, thank you. I need to be getting back to the shop. But before I go, I'd like my curiosity about those women satisfied."

"What do you want to know?"

"What's so special about them?"

"They're Mary Lou Fight's eyes and ears."

"And she's the one who has it in for you and Ember, right?"

"As well as the entire town."

"Doesn't she have a life?"

I chuckled. "Yes, she does. Her purpose is to cause as much misery and mayhem as possible. That's her life. And take a good look at the one seated to her right."

"She's a beautiful young woman."

"That's Oralene Fight. Mary Lou's adopted daughter. And if it's possible, she is more of a menace than the Queen Bee herself."

"She's so young."

"Depravity knows no age. My belief is that she's Magnolia Bluff's Moriarty."

"What do you mean?"

"Whereas Mary Lou does evil deeds because she wants power, Oralene does evil because she is evil. She is a cold-blooded killer who manipulates others into doing her killing for her."

"Killing? As in murder?"

"Yes. I believe she manipulated her siblings into killing her father and his business manager. There are several other murders and Ember's attempted murder that I'd lay at her feet. But she's clever. The trail of blood never leads back to her."

Terall slowly shook her head. "I hope I never have the bad fortune of making her acquaintance."

"That might not be enough to avoid the laser's red dot."

7

TUESDAY, JANUARY 6, 10:02 AM

REECE SOVERN SETTLED in behind his desk. He took a sip of coffee and wrinkled his nose. *Damn that Thurgood. I can't drink normal coffee anymore.*

He took another sip. *I guess I can drink it. But it's just a hot bitter liquid compared to Harry's brew.*

GJ was out interviewing the Bremen woman's daughter. He'd spoken with Arnold and Bette Weiss, the owners of the Cozy Corners Motel.

Arnold, arms folded across his chest, denied any knowledge of what had gone on in Room 6. "Sure I own the place. Doesn't mean I snoop on my customers. They have a right to their privacy, you know."

And Bette had nothing more to contribute except for a scowl that creased her face and made her look like a walnut.

The Bremen woman was a rich slutty whore. There was no other way to put it. And her daughter wasn't any better. A chip off the old block, as they used to say.

Reece drank coffee, made a grimace, and set his mug down.

Hopefully GJ would be able to get the customer records. That would give them a place to start.

But if she wasn't killed by a customer, then the case would probably go unsolved.

To his knowledge, the woman had no friends in town, and there were a whole lot of folks who thought she was Mary Magdalene's evil twin.

Most people think things and never act on those thoughts. But in Patrice's case, someone had.

Was the motive money?

Who wanted hers?

A dissatisfied customer?

Why kill her instead of slapping her around a bit?

Someone who abhorred whores?

Reece considered these questions for some time. Given the virulence of the attack, it could very easily be someone who hated harlots.

But why no cuts on her arms? That was exceedingly unusual. Either someone held them out of the way, or she hadn't fought back. And if she hadn't fought back, why hadn't she?

The autopsy might answer that one.

Reece closed the folder. He was fairly certain no one cared, not even the daughter, if Patrice Bremen's murderer was found,.

Quite honestly, his time would be better spent on the cold cases. Especially the one marked "Urgent."

There was a knock on the door and he told the person to enter.

"Hey, Sarge," GJ said as she walked in.

"Please tell me the brat confessed."

GJ snorted a laugh. "Don't we wish. No confession and has no idea who would kill dear old mom."

"Did she give up the client list?"

"No. I asked if she'd make a copy for us and she said she'd think about it."

He tapped the folder. "No one is going to give a damn if we solve this one or not." He held up the folder marked URGENT. "Now this one? Yeah, someone will be breathing down our necks on this case sooner or later."

"What case is that?"

"The Reverend Humphrey case."

GJ shuddered. "God. A radicalized Christian or a homophobe did that one."

"So how many suspects does that give us? Under a thousand?"

GJ snorted a laugh. "Good one, Sarge. Yeah, we have our work cut out for us. We gonna work it?"

"Yep. As I said, someone will be breathing down our necks on the case, or Mary Lou Fight's husband ain't a banker."

"Gotcha. So where do we start?"

"By re-interviewing every single person at Ember's church who interacted with him on a daily basis."

8

TUESDAY, JANUARY 6, 10:42 AM

REECE DECIDED he might as well start with the top banana at Saint Luke's United Methodist Church. The Reverend Ember Cole herself.

He and GJ sat opposite Ember, who was seated behind her large oak desk. Her hands were folded on the blotter.

Reece found himself wondering about that. Why a blotter? He was pretty sure Ember didn't use a fountain pen and no pen set was visible.

Ember's quiet voice interrupted his musing.

"So how may I help you?" she asked.

He studied her for a moment. *Almost looks like a nun. Just needs a habit.*

GJ said, "We want to talk to you about your relationship with the late Reverend Adelbert Humphrey."

Reece noticed Ember's lips tightened just for a moment before her face relaxed.

"I wouldn't say we had a relationship. He wasn't with us long enough for one to develop."

"How did the two of you get along?" Reece asked.

"I was on maternity leave for much of the time he was here."

"So you had no interaction with him at all?" GJ asked.

"Of course I had some interaction with him. I didn't particularly like him. He was a conceited, self-important, foppish prig. And I was pretty certain he was a puppet of Mary Lou's. So I didn't spend much time with him. However, he got on very well with most of the more mature women in the church. Particularly our senior women."

GJ scowled. "There was talk that he was gay."

"There was talk," Ember agreed.

"You don't think he was?" Reece asked.

"Do you remember Liberace?" she asked.

"I do," Reece said.

"He was our Liberace."

Reece nodded. "I see."

"And in case you're wondering, I had no need to kill him. The bishop had agreed to move him."

Reece raised his eyebrows. "Really?"

Ember nodded.

"How soon?" he asked.

"There was a church he could have gone to immediately."

"So if the perp had waited…" GJ mused.

"Precisely. He would've been gone."

"Bad news for Humphrey," Reece said. "So who, if anyone, in your congregation might want him dead? Someone who wasn't aware he was leaving."

Ember shrugged. "I can't think of anyone who'd resort to murder. And, as I've said, he was quite popular with older women. The seniors loved him."

"So you've said," GJ quipped.

"So I have." Ember favored her with a smile.

Reece had the impression that the smile was hiding a stiletto. *No love lost between these two.*

He stood. "Thanks, Ember. You know the drill. If you happen to recall something, anything, let one of us know."

She and GJ stood.

"I will," Ember assured him.

———

Sitting in his car, which was parked on the street in front of the church, Reece studied the front of the building for a moment or two and then shifted his attention to the parsonage.

"What are you looking at, Sarge?"

"According to the neighbors, a van was parked in front of the parsonage for the better part of an hour before Humphrey showed up. Then a little while after the deceased got home, the van leaves. So where did it go? And who drove it?"

"We don't know."

"No, we don't. But if the van was driven by our perp, I'm guessing he drove down the alley, parked long enough in front of the garage to take the body out the back door and put it in the van. Before we tackle the rest of Ember's congregation, we might want to talk to the folks on the other side of the alley to see if anyone can confirm my guess."

"Good thinking, Sarge."

Reece started the car and put it into drive.

9

TUESDAY, JANUARY 6, 12:01 PM

REECE AND GJ sat in his car eating lunch. He had nothing against the booth cushions or the padded seats of the straight-back chairs of Storm's Drive-In.

It was ears. Too many of them.

Ears he didn't want to overhear the discussion of the case.

"That was kind of a bust, wasn't it, Sarge?" The words were said around and partially through GJ's double pickle burger with cheese and bacon.

Reece shrugged, not wanting to run the risk of his tongue tripping over his loaded triple-decker cheeseburger.

After he swallowed the bite of burger, he said, "It was certainly disappointing. I was hoping someone would have seen something."

"So we're back to interviewing the churchies."

Reece chuckled. "Yes, we are." He sucked on the straw in his paper cup of Dr. Pepper. "What would be very helpful is if we could find a motive. Why was he killed?"

"He was gay. Some homophobe at the church most likely."

Reece chewed on his bite of burger and on GJ's comment. When he'd swallowed, he said, "I'm not convinced."

"Why not?"

"According to Ember, she lost a dozen families in the denominational split. Which means it is likely the folks most opposed to homosexual ministers had already left the church."

"There could've been a sleeper."

"Possible. But I don't think probable. The viciousness of the mutilation is telling me the killer was probably a rejected lover."

"If that's the case, why are we talking to the churchies?"

"Because they saw him, talked to him, worked with him, maybe fought with him. Perhaps one of them will tell us something that holds the key to solving the case."

GJ popped a fry into her mouth and chewed on it thoughtfully. She swallowed and said, "If one of those churchies might hold the key, perhaps we should talk to those old women who were fond of him. He might've told one of them something that's important for us to know."

Reece, burger halfway to his mouth, held very still and pondered what his partner had said. Then he smiled. "I think you're onto something there, GJ." An enormous bite of burger disappeared into his mouth.

———

Reece had called Ember, who'd routed him to Larrilyn Hammer, the church secretary. From Larrilyn, he got a list of twenty-four members Reverend Humphrey regularly called on.

The first six had been a bust. Two were so deaf, conversation was all but impossible. A third started snoring four minutes into the interview. Another thought they were her grandchildren paying her a visit. Number five talked about her tiny vegetable garden and showed them the seed catalogs that had come in the mail.

"Oh, to be sure," she'd said, "Reverend Humphrey loved his vegetables. That's why we got on so."

Number six told them she'd once been a ballerina and Reverend Humphrey so loved the ballet. She tried to demonstrate to them she had actually been a ballerina, and if it wasn't for GJ's fast reflexes, Miss Catalina Dalrymple would have gone *en pointe* with her nose instead of her toes.

Consequently, it was without enthusiasm that Reece and GJ trudged up the walk of 843 Monroe Street to talk with Henrene Boseman.

The woman who answered the door was short. Reece guessed no more than five-two. Her silver hair was in a short, loose cut that was combed to the right but with no defined part. Her dark chocolate brown glasses went well with her deep brown eyes.

She must've been a beautiful woman in her younger years, and at ninety-seven she's still pretty good looking.

"Are you Henrene Boseman?" he asked.

"I am." Her voice was steady and clear.

Reece smiled to himself. *At last, now we might get somewhere.*

"I'm Reece Sovern and this is GJ Riggins, we're—"

"I know who you are." She focused on GJ. "I knew your parents, Georgia Jean, and I know your cousin Waymon and his wife, Burdette." She faced Reece. "And you're the sergeant investigator on the police force. I'm assuming this isn't a social call. So which investigation do you want information on?"

Reece and GJ looked at each other and then turned their attention back to Henrene.

Clearing his throat, Reece said, "Uh, all of them?"

Henrene put her hands together and laughed. "Okay. C'mon in and we'll talk. You prefer coffee or tea? A bit early for whiskey, don'tcha think?"

"Coffee would be fine," Reece said.

Henrene deposited them in the small living room while she went off to the kitchen.

They sat on the sofa.

Reece let his eyes roam the room. The furniture was about sixty years out of fashion, but it was well cared for. There wasn't a cobweb in any of the corners and not a speck of dust was to be seen anywhere.

Henrene appeared with a tray containing a tall coffee pot, sugar bowl, pitcher of cream, spoons, cups and saucers, a plate of cookies, and a decanter. She set the tray on the coffee table situated between the sofa and two rocking chairs.

Telling them to help themselves, she sat in one of the rockers and picked up her knitting.

"By the way, the decanter is there if you want some brandy in your coffee instead of cream or sugar."

"Would you like coffee?" GJ asked.

"Why you're such a sweetheart. Yes, please. Half brandy, half coffee."

GJ did as she requested and handed her a cup and saucer. She then poured coffee for Reece and herself.

Henrene took a big swallow of her doctored coffee. "Okay, which murder shall we talk about first?"

"What can you tell us about the Reverend Adelbert Humphrey?" Reece asked.

"A pleasant young man for the most part. Gossipy. Obviously a swish. Rather stuck on himself. Apparently came from a family with lots of money and men in high places. Had he remained alive, Mary Lou Fight would've pushed that adopted daughter of hers into a marriage with him."

Reece and GJ looked at each other.

"What? You didn't know that? If you didn't know that, you haven't been talking to the right people."

"Obviously," Reece said.

"Didn't Mary Lou know Humphrey was gay?" GJ asked.

Henrene shook her head. "I don't think it mattered to her. She's looking to push that ne'er-do-well into high society. Power and money. That's all that matters to Mary Lou Fight."

"But if he was homosexual…," Reece began.

"You youngsters don't know anything anymore. Lavender marriages we called them back in the day. The point was to protect the homosexual person from ostracism. I'm thinking that's what Mary Lou was trying to arrange. A lavender marriage would eliminate any stigma coming to the Reverend from his sexual proclivity and would get wealth and power for the ne'er-do-well."

"What did Humphrey and Oralene think about this?" Reece asked.

"Don't know. He was murdered before Mary Lou had a chance to get things arranged is my guess. She might have mentioned what she was thinking to the girl, and that was probably as far as it got."

Henrene drank brandy-laced coffee, then asked, "What's the next murder? The Bremen woman?"

"You know something about that?" GJ asked.

"Not much. Made her millions from divorce and sex. She was getting too old, though, to have wide appeal."

"Do you think her daughter killed her?" GJ asked.

"Lord, no. Why would she do that? Like killing the goose that laid the golden eggs."

"So who would gain from her murder?" Reece prompted.

"I don't think gain had anything to do with it. Some bondage crap gone wrong, or a psycho customer, or someone deciding it's time to start eliminating whores. Like Jack the Ripper."

"That's a pretty wide field," Reece said.

"It is," Henrene agreed. "You'll have to figure out which one of those three is the most likely and go from there."

"What about Pastor John Reston?" GJ asked.

"The younger one?"

"Yes," Reece said.

"I'm guessing that ties back to whoever killed his father and that business manager."

"A family affair?" Reece asked.

"Y'all thought so at the time. Any evidence surface to change your thinking?"

Reece shook his head.

"Then you know where to focus your efforts."

"What about the attempt on Reverend Cole's life?" Reece asked.

"Don't know on that one. She has enemies here in town, but none that I'm aware of who'd actually want her dead."

"What about Mary Lou?" GJ asked.

"Oh, she wouldn't mind seeing the reverend dead, but I don't think she'd do anything to bring it about. She'd rather just have her leave."

Reece finished his coffee and picked up a cookie. "You've been very helpful, Ms. Boseman. We appreciate it."

"Just my musings on the gossip that passes my way. Of course since the swish is gone, a lot less comes my way."

Reece handed her a card. "Call if you happen to think of anything else. Please."

Henrene took the card, told him she would, and he and GJ left.

Sitting in the car, GJ said, "She sure had an opinion about everything."

"Yes, she did." He took a green perfecto out of his pocket, removed the cellophane, and shoved the stogie into his mouth. He sat there chewing on the cigar and stared out the window.

After a few moments, GJ said, "Sarge?"

"Axe, knife, tent peg."

"Huh?"

"Purnell Tully was killed with an axe or a hatchet. Reverend Humphrey, multiple stab wounds. John Reston, tent peg through the skull."

"Yeah, so?"

"All sharp instruments. Which makes it a strong possibility they're all related."

GJ sank back into her seat, lost in thought.

"And what's more," Reece continued, "there is one or more of those Restons connected to each one."

GJ nodded. "And Patrice Bremen was knifed to death. Maybe a Reston was there as well."

"Maybe," Reece agreed.

10

THE REVEREND EMBER Cole knocked on the door. The houses on Oak Street looked no different from those on most other streets in Magnolia Bluff. Neat. Clean. Well-kept yards. All on quiet streets. The homes on Oak were a bit newer. Only fifty or sixty years old.

Kind of difficult to believe this bungalow is, or was, home to a multi-millionaire, she thought.

Ember knocked again. She heard the deadbolt draw back, and the door opened. Her nostrils were immediately assaulted with the strong stench of marijuana.

"Can't you read the sign?" The young woman's dark hair was a mess and the light robe did little to conceal the fact she wore nothing under it.

"What sign?"

"This sign." The young woman turned and started to point to the door. "Oh, shit. I forgot to put it up." She turned her focus back to Ember. "Okay. I'm here. What do you want?"

"I'm Ember Cole and—"

"Nope. Not interested. I like doing porn and I'm not interested in Jesus."

"Okay. I'm not asking you to be interested in Jesus."

"You aren't?"

Ember shook her head.

"So why are you here?"

"To see if you need someone to talk to. Or need help with anything."

"Oh, I see. You want to become *friends*. So you can clobber me with Jesus when I'm not looking. As I said, not interested. Bye."

The door slammed shut and Ember heard the deadbolt slide back into place.

She made her way down the walk and got into her car.

"I'll give her another day or two. Reality will sink in eventually. And when she realizes she's totally alone, I have a feeling she'll be more interested in talking."

———

Even though the temperature was only fifty-two degrees, with the wind making it feel like it was forty-seven, Scarlett Hayden took her cabin cruiser out onto the reservoir. The temperature guaranteed she had the water to herself.

She ran the cruiser full out to the southern end of the reservoir, slowed to half speed, and made a sweeping turn. Then pushed the throttle wide open and flew back north.

Most of last year she'd spent traipsing around the globe with Harry's lawyer, Stanton Lauderbach.

They had a wonderful time.

She enjoyed Stanton's company.

She enjoyed it very much.

But Stanton wasn't Harry.

And that was a problem.

A further problem was that Harry was besotted with a skinny shapeless bitch named Ember Cole. And that was the actual problem: Ember Cole.

She needed to get rid of Ember.

The solution was that simple.

Scarlett slowed the speed of the cabin cruiser, executed a wide sweeping turn, and opened up the throttle. The boat blasted down the lake, bow elevated out of the water, with the spray flying thirty feet to starboard and port.

Ember Cole had to go.

It was simply a case of how and when.

———

The bell over the door rang. I was pleased to see Brandon and Joyce standing in the doorway. I got up from my table and joined them, shaking hands with Brandon and giving Joyce a hug.

"You here for lunch?" I asked.

"That we are," Brandon answered.

"Grab yourselves a table. Do you know what you want?"

Joyce said, "I'll have the soup of the day and a grilled cheese."

"I'll have the beef tamale pie," Brandon said.

"Grab a seat and I'll get your order in."

I relayed the meal requests to Miguel, grabbed two glasses of water, and returned to their table.

"How have you two been?" I asked while setting the water glasses on the table.

"Doing well," Brandon answered.

"I hear you started a detective agency."

"That I did. It looked like the MBPD was giving the Spatch kid the runaround. And, well, you know me."

I laughed. "That I do."

"As it turned out, they weren't. But by that time the damage was done, and I was a private detective."

"I have a feeling it's not something you regret."

"It isn't," Joyce said. She took a sip of water, and then asked, "So how was your trip around the world? Is Ember okay?"

"The trip was glorious although by mid-point that yacht was feeling a bit too small. And I think Emmy is back to her old feisty self."

"Good."

"No aftereffects from the ordeal for you two?" I asked.

"Nothing long term," Joyce said. "I had a few sessions with Mike Kurelek, but other than that business as usual." She lightly smacked Brandon's chest. "And Mr. Macho here doesn't even have a nightmare."

Brandon put his hands up. "Hey, I was a cop. What can I say? What happened to us?" He shrugged. "All in a day's work."

"And what about that ego of yours?" Joyce asked.

"Okay. I had a bruised ego." He shook his head. "Walked right into their trap."

I chuckled. "Those women were crafty. According to Graham, they'd been killing people for five years."

Brandon nodded. "Sixty-seven victims."

"That's a lot of experience in evading detection," I said.

"Yep. If it hadn't been for you, I'm not sure Sovern and Blanton's crew would've figured it out."

"You give me too much credit."

Estrelita arrived with their lunches.

"I'll let you eat in peace. Em and I will have you over soon."

"We'd like that," Joyce said.

I returned to my table, snagging a coffee and doughnut on the way.

The Full Moon Killers were good at killing. Not good enough to continue evading the consequences of their crimes.

In my time, I've had to kill a few men in self-defense. I don't like killing. Life is precious. However, there are those who will never be rehabilitated. For them, I agree with British criminologist Mrs. F. Tennyson Jesse: *it's best if they are permanently taken out of the gene pool.*

And we have one such reprobate in Magnolia Bluff. I'm sure of it. Miss Oralene Fight. The former Miss Oralene Reston.

The question I wrestle with is this: do I have the right to remove her from the gene pool to avoid her doing likewise to me and my family?

11

TUESDAY, JANUARY 6, 3:29 PM

REECE HAD DROPPED GJ off at the station to prepare the paperwork requesting a warrant to obtain the Bremen woman's business records. And where he was going, it was best if GJ wasn't along.

He pulled into the driveway, put the car in park, and shut off the engine. He got out and let his eyes take in the property.

A nifty little cabin on the reservoir. Plenty of trees to block the summer sun, and with their leaves gone to let in the winter sun.

The dog knew he was there and was barking an alarm.

Stranger, Will Robinson, stranger!

Reece chuckled at his joke, while the green stogie made its way to the other side of his mouth.

He headed for the door and hadn't moved ten feet when it opened.

"What the hell do you want?"

"Is that the best you can do, Turner, after not seeing me for a year?"

"I was hoping they'd keep Kraus and force you into early retirement."

Reece stopped when he was a couple arm's lengths away from Brandon Turner.

"I hear you've become a private dick, instead of, or maybe in addition to being an arrogant one."

"Look, Sovern, you're interrupting my day. And don't go spitting cigar juice on my grass."

"Wouldn't think of it. Wouldn't want to sully the spit."

"I'm going back inside. It hasn't been nice seeing you."

"Hang on a minute, Turner."

"What?"

"If you have any insights into the Bremen, Humphrey, or Reston murders, or the attempt on Ember's life, I'd appreciate you sharing them with me."

"Wait. *You* want *my* help?"

"Nope. I said insights. Help and insights are two different words. Look 'em up."

"Wow. The flatfoot knows English."

"Haven't been one of those in years. And I'm still a cop. Haven't had to retire."

"Go to hell, Sovern."

"I might talkin' to you."

"I don't have a client, and I don't have any insights, and if you aren't out of here in five minutes a little birdie is going to tell Briggs his sergeant investigator is seeking help from civilians."

"That would be a bother. But just remember: private dicks can always use a helping hand on the police force. Remember that, Mister *Former* New York Cop."

Reece turned around and headed back to his car. As he was getting in, Turner spoke.

"All right, Sovern, I'll let you know if I get any insights on those cases."

"Thanks… Brandon."

Reece got behind the wheel of his SUV, turned it around, and headed back to the station with a grin spread across his face.

12

TUESDAY, JANUARY 6, 4:41 PM

THE SHOP WAS EMPTY, which isn't unusual for the last hour of the business day.

Jack was counting the day's take. Estrelita was running the floor sweeper to pick up crumbs and such. From the sounds emanating from the kitchen, Miguel was taking a cleaver to something.

I was nursing a coffee and nibbling on a cinnamon roll while drawing up menus for next week.

Graham Huston came through the door, said hello to everyone, and picked up his order of tamale pie and garden salad.

"I'll gladly pay you Tuesday," he said, "for a tamale pie today."

"Today is Tuesday," I replied.

"Next Tuesday."

"Sure. And tomorrow plan on joining Em and me for supper."

"Deal."

He vanished through the door. Five minutes later the bell rang again. This time announcing Reece Sovern. He ambled over to my table and sat.

"How's the world traveler?"

"I'm fine. How's the undercover detective?"

"Not undercover any longer and I have to say I enjoy being back at my desk."

"That's good. No place like home. At least according to Dorothy."

"I'm with her one hundred percent. You glad to be home?"

"I am. And so is Em and the rest of the family. A hundred-and -thirty-two-foot yacht gets pretty small after a while."

"I can imagine. If you have a minute, I'd like to run something by you."

"Did Briggs leave?"

"No. He's still here and still a pain in the ass."

"I see. He'll probably want our hides."

"Probably."

"I guess we're living dangerously. Shoot."

"Tully was killed with an axe or a hatchet. Reverend Humphrey was stabbed multiple times and then had his wrists slashed. The coroner wasn't sure if he died before he bled out and had his liver removed, or not. Pastor John Reston, the young one, was knocked unconscious by a blunt instrument, possibly a mallet, and then had a tent peg driven through his skull."

"Okay. Go on."

"All three murders involved the use of sharp instruments, and all three involved the Restons."

"Humphrey's murder involves the Restons?"

"We've heard, and will have to verify, that Mary Lou Fight wanted Oralene to marry Humphrey."

"You don't say. Well, that's interesting."

"Isn't it? So I'm just running this by you to make sure the connection to the Restons isn't just wishful thinking."

I sat back and thought a minute before answering. Then said, "We know they were involved with the murder of the father and Tully. In my opinion, based on what Oralene told Em, Lofton was thrown under the bus. He was the scapegoat. He was probably involved but certainly didn't act alone. Oralene was undoubtedly the mastermind, and her brothers simply did her bidding."

"I'm beginning to see that."

"Good. As for Humphrey, if Oralene was being pushed into a marriage she didn't want, she may have orchestrated a repeat performance. I'd even go so far as to say probably orchestrated. Considering John, Junior, I'm not sure. I don't have a problem with Oralene killing him. I just don't know why she would."

"Yeah, I don't either. Isn't that tent peg thing from the Bible?"

"Jael killed Sisera that way. Book of Judges. "

"There seems to be a religious theme with all of these murders and I'm wondering if there isn't one with the Patrice Bremen killing."

"Yes, there is. At least with the first two, that is, and possibly the third. It's the religious motif that makes me think Oralene is behind these killings. Who knows? Maybe she's also behind the Bremen killing as well. They all would fit someone eliminating sinners."

"She's a psycho."

"A very dangerous psycho."

"Yeah. I'm beginning to see that. I think GJ and I will pay her a visit."

"Good luck with that. I don't think you'll get a straight answer."

"All I can do is try."

"True that. On a different subject, Em will be calling Hetta to pick a date for you to be our dinner guests."

I watched him smile. "Looking forward to it." He stood. "Thanks for your thoughts. Catch you later."

He left. Noting the time, I got up and walked over to the sign, flipping it to closed.

Estrelita and Jack said goodnight and left.

I walked to the kitchen.

"Tomorrow morning I'll start at four to get the coffee roasting done," Miguel said.

"That's awfully early. Be sure to note it so I pay you for the extra time."

"Don't worry, I will. Otherwise, I'll never hear the end of it from the wife."

I laughed.

Miguel said goodnight and left.

There was nothing remaining for me to do, so I got my coat and hat, slipped the snub-nosed revolver into my pocket, and walked out the back door after setting the alarm.

With all the murders and the attempt on Em's life, I decided carrying a weapon was good policy.

I was almost to my car when I noticed a figure standing by the front grill. The person was dressed in a black ankle-length cape with a hood that left the face in darkness.

"Hello, Mr. Thurgood."

I'd know that voice anywhere. "Hello, Oralene."

"You should not have come back."

"This is my home."

"Mother is not pleased. She is, in fact, very unhappy that you and the harlot returned."

I decided to ignore for the moment the name-calling directed at Em. Instead, I said, "Why did you kill them? You call Em a harlot, but you're a murderess."

"I have killed no one. The Lord giveth, and the Lord taketh away. Blessed be the name of the Lord."

"You mean to tell me God killed your father and Tully and Reverend Humphrey and your brother?"

"God smote the sinners. You and your wife are sinners. God will smite you at a time that you know not. All sinners shall be smitten, for God hates sin and hates the doer of sin."

"Doesn't that apply to you, as well?"

"I am the Handmaid of the Lord. He is my Belovéd. I am the fairest among the maidens, and He has chosen me. I only do His bidding, for I am His to command."

"Does your mother know you're a killer? Does Mrs. Fight?"

"You have been warned, Mr. Thurgood. You should have stayed away. Far away."

She turned and walked down the alley, eventually disappearing into the evening gloom and shadows.

I felt the revolver in my pocket. I could have killed her. I could have rid humanity of a monster. No one is about. Who would have seen? No one.

Unfortunately, perhaps, I'm not a killer. She probably had no weapon. At least none was displayed. Words. Just words. And they can't kill you.

But words can be the beginning of the road to action. I've

been warned. Thank you, Oralene. I will now be ready for you whenever you decide to strike.

I got in my car and noticed the envelope under the wiper. I retrieved it and took out the note. The message was one sentence:

God will strike at a time when you know not.

13

TUESDAY, JANUARY 6, 7:28 PM

MBPD OFFICER LOGAN YTZEN had just pulled into Storm's Drive-In to get a burger when the radio came alive.

"Logan, are you there?"

"I'm here, Vivian."

"Home invasion is in progress. Six-two-four Oak Street."

"On my way."

Ytzen put on the flashing lights, pulled out onto the street, and let the siren do its job. Not that the streets of Magnolia Bluff were crowded with traffic.

Six minutes after he'd flipped on his lights, Ytzen was in front of the house.

He got out of his car, drew his service pistol, and approached the open front door.

Neighbors started collecting on their front lawns.

Ytzen stood by the open door. "Police. If you're armed, put your weapon down and put your hands on top of your head."

No response.

There was a light on in the small entryway as he entered the house, letting his pistol lead the way.

He checked each of the ground-floor rooms. The lights were on throughout the house, which was a relief as no one could surprise him by coming out of the dark. However, he had nothing to fear. All the rooms were empty.

A trail of blood led from the entryway to the staircase leading to the second floor.

The sliding glass door leading out to the patio and back-yard was open. There was no blood near the door.

The perp probably left that way. So where is the homeowner?

Ytzen noticed blood on the carpet covering the stairs. In fact, quite a bit of blood.

Looks like I may have my answer.

He slowly climbed the stairs. When he reached the second floor, he saw four open doors. The rooms to his immediate right and left were bedrooms.

Looks like all the bedrooms are on this floor. And the closed door straight ahead is probably the bathroom.

"Police," he called out. "Is anyone here?"

There was no answer. He slowly moved to the closed door, checking each of the rooms as he passed them.

When he reached the closed door, he tried turning the knob and found it didn't move. Locked.

He decided the best course of action was to break down the door. He slammed the flat of his shoe just below the knob. Wood splintered and cracked. He slammed his foot again, and this time the strike plate tore away from the door and the door frame.

The bathroom wasn't large, but it contained a tub, and in the tub was a very bloody young woman.

———

Reece Sovern looked down at Tansy Tucker Truitt, the daughter of Patrice Bremen. The doctors had decided to keep her overnight for observation, as she'd lost a fair amount of blood.

She had a nasty slash across her left cheek. Thirty-seven stitches worth. Another on her right calf. Twenty-nine stitches for that one.

Both worthy of scars. Probably end her porn career, Reece thought.

The doctor had given her something to make her sleep. He watched her eyes close and her breathing slow; the breaths coming more evenly.

He looked at his notes. Tansy had ordered a pizza to be delivered. When the doorbell rang, and she opened the door, the young woman threw the pizza at her and rushed into the house. In the process, Tansy's cheek was slashed.

She managed to get away from the intruder by hitting her in the head and kicking her in the shin.

However, the attacker caught up with her on the stairs, slashing Tansy's leg. A rearward kick connected, and Tansy made it to the bathroom, locking the door.

She called 911 and then passed out.

Reece chuckled. *Who has a landline in the bathroom? Porn stars, apparently. And it's a good thing she did, because she'd dropped her phone during the initial attack.*

He closed his notebook and studied the sleeping woman. Whoever killed the mother had come back for the daughter. A knife wielder in both cases.

The difference being the killer had help with Patrice.

Someone had held the arms, so they hadn't gotten cut. At least that was Reece's guess.

So why the solo attempt on Tansy?

Where was the partner?

And why not wait for the partner?

What was so important about killing Tansy that couldn't wait?

Maybe the partner had gotten cold feet and wanted no part in a second murder. That was a distinct possibility.

Tansy hadn't recognized the woman posing as the pizza delivery person.

Which indicated the attacker wasn't a relative, friend, or regular customer.

Which further meant Reece was looking for a woman.

A young woman.

One who'd decided to start killing sex workers.

And that begged the question.

Why?

14

TUESDAY, JANUARY 6, 11:42 PM

GRAHAM HUSTON, having finished his supper and feeling a bit claustrophobic in his room at Nell Walker's boarding house, took his bottle of Blue Corn whiskey and went for a ramble.

He let his feet do the walking. He knew from practice they'd end up where they and he needed to be.

Every so often he took a swig from the bottle.

At some point in his ramble, he realized his feet had taken him to the cemetery on the opposite end of town. He was standing at the grave of PFC Freddy Millstone. The place where he'd buried the dog tags of Harley Spooner.

"Hope you fellas are having a pleasant conversation," he said.

From out of the shadows, a familiar figure wove its way to Huston's side.

"Evening, Fergus."

"More like night."

"Very true. Evening sounds a bit better. Less final." He handed the bottle over, and Fergus took a swig.

"Come to join the conversation?" Fergus asked, handing the bottle back to Graham.

"Mostly just to listen, if they'll let me."

"Probably will."

Graham took a swig and passed the bottle back to Fergus. "Come here often?"

"More often than not," Fergus answered. "Dead folks have a lot of wisdom."

Graham nodded and took the bottle back. He put it to his lips, let the fiery liquid fill his mouth, and slowly swallowed. He held the bottle out to the old vet, who took it.

"So you were here when the Bremen woman was murdered?"

"Don't know. I was here when there was yellin', and I was here when it stopped."

"Why would someone kill her?" Graham asked. "Just can't see a local customer doing that."

He took the bottle from Fergus, looked at it, and handed it back. "Finish it, my friend." Fergus didn't object.

The old vet wiped his mouth with the back of his hand. "Another dead soldier." He set the empty bottle next to the grave.

Graham nodded. "Plenty of them, aren't there?"

"That there are." After a pause, Fergus said, "Don't think it was a customer that killed her."

"Who was it then?"

"A sinner who doesn't like sin in others."

"Plenty of them around."

"There are."

"Someone in town killed her?"

"Seems likely."

"Has this person killed before?"

Fergus nodded. "Seems likely."

Graham chewed on that for a while.

"It wouldn't be someone from the Reston family, would it?"

"Cursed."

"The Restons are cursed?"

"Bred in sin. Live in sin. Die in sin."

"We're all sinners. Aren't we?"

"According to some. More like we're just primates with big brains, opposable thumbs, and a penchant for making tools. We ain't in the jungle or the savannah anymore. But we still act like it. Everything we do is just the old survival instincts in action. These streets, they're the savannah now. The concrete jungle. Our killin' might be metaphorical, but the instinct is the driver. And some of us decide, the rules of society be damned, and we act like we did half a million years ago. Our fingers and our teeth drip blood. And some call that sin."

Graham let the old vet's words roll around in his mind for a time.

"I think," he started to say, and then realized sometime during his cogitation, Fergus had silently departed. Almost like a ghost.

Graham smiled at that. A ghost. He focused on the grave. "Goodnight Harley, Freddy. If you're out wandering about, I hope you're having a good time."

He left the cemetery, walked past the Cozy Corners Motel, gave it a lingering look, and continued on his way.

I think Fergus was talking about the Restons. Might be worth my while to see what they have to say about Patrice Bremen's death, as well as the unsolved murder of Ember's assistant pastor and that of

*the young Pastor John. And the attempt on Ember's life. Can't forget
that.*

He walked on, headed towards the boarding house,
letting his mind go over what he knew and didn't know
about the Reston family.

As he mounted the steps of his one-room home, he'd
come to at least one conclusion. The Restons were indeed
cursed.

15

WEDNESDAY, JANUARY 7, 6:01 AM

EMMY WAS PRAYING when I left the house. She usually gets up at five and spends close to an hour in prayer.

I'm not a praying sort of guy. If there is a God, and he is sovereign, then he controls all things; and if my prayers can sway him, then to my mind he's not sovereign. There is, of course, the argument that he destined me to pray for whatever — not for his benefit, but mine. And I'd have to admit that's a valid argument. But I feel little to no inclination to pray. So I don't. Maybe I wasn't destined to do so. And I don't see the need if he's omniscient. Even the good book says I don't know how to pray. The holy spirit takes my utterances and appropriately presents them to God.

But Emmy finds comfort in her time of prayer, and that's all that matters.

I find comfort in the contemplative smoking of my pipe. And there you have it.

Now Elder Smythe, whose farm supplies the Really Good with vegetables, fruit, eggs, and poultry, pastors a Primitive Baptist church, which is the polar opposite of Emmy's church. Yet I've seen the elder and Em go on and on about how wonderful they find the sweet hour of prayer.

But then God and Jesus are real to them. I'm agnostic about God and don't believe Jesus ever existed. I probably shouldn't be a Methodist, and I definitely wouldn't make it in Smythe's church. In the end, though, how I live and treat people seems to me to be what is most important. Which is why I didn't shoot Oralene. Do to others... You know the rest.

Miguel did indeed come in early to roast three batches of coffee beans. A delightful Kenyan, a magnificent Java, and an exquisite Ethiopian.

The Kenyan will be used for the foo-foo drinks. The others are for those connoisseurs who just like coffee.

I use the vacuum siphon method for brewing coffee because it produces a very smooth and richly flavored coffee. Cold brew also produces a superior drink, and I have that available in the summer.

Noonan from Bluff Bakery dropped off four boxes of doughnuts and pastries.

Miguel and I also produce our own baked goods, but we can't do everything, so I'm glad I have Noonan available to round out our selection of sweet goodies.

I didn't tell Em about Oralene's threat because she's been through a lot, and burdening her with Oralene's madness isn't something I want to do. Besides, she knows that nutcase harbors a deep-seated malice towards us and will be watchful. At least I hope she'll be.

The question I keep asking myself is, what can I actually do to short-circuit the woman? To nullify her evil intentions? And the answer I keep coming up with is — nothing.

There's not a thing I can do except stay vigilant.

The problem with that conclusion is no one can be vigilant twenty-four hours a day, seven days a week, three hundred and sixty-five days a year. It's just not possible.

If someone wants to kill you, truly wants to kill you, you're a dead man walking. That's reality in the face of a determined killer. Thank God, most killers aren't that determined.

But Oralene might be. She's certainly crazy enough to be.

I'm pretty sure she orchestrated the deaths of her father and Purnell Tully. Was likely involved in Reverend Humphrey's brutal demise. And may have had a hand in the Bremen woman's death. Oh, and there's her brother. Can't forget him.

If I were Mary Lou, I'd be quaking in my boots that I might be next.

Don't piss off Oralene.

However, we all have our weak spots, our vulnerabilities, our Achilles heels. And so does Oralene. I just don't know what it is.

Perhaps I need to call Elmore and have him keep an eye on our little killer.

16

"I'M LEAVIN' this town," Tansy Truitt nearly shouted.

Of course she'd described the town using a word that rhymed with truckin'.

What's with young people nowadays? Reece asked himself. *They don't know how to communicate without loading their sentences with obscenities.*

"Not today you aren't," he responded.

"And why not?"

"Because I need you here to identify your attacker."

"And what if you never find her, then what?"

"We'll find her."

"Yeah, right."

"We'll assign an officer to watch your place to make sure there aren't any more attacks."

"Go right ahead. I have money. I'm going to L.A. I'll have plastic surgery on my face and leg and maybe get me a big ol' pair of titties to round out the package. And then I'll be back in business."

"Don't make me arrest you as a material witness."

"Look, someone tried to kill me. I'm getting the hell out of here."

"I don't blame you for wanting to leave. And you can. But not right now. That's why I'm assigning an officer to you for your protection."

"Oh, thank you, Officer. I feel *sooo* safe already."

The sarcasm was dripping off her statement like grease off a pig on a spit.

Reece just about chewed through the stem on the Zeppelin pipe so as not to respond in kind.

"You are welcome, Ms. Truitt. And to make sure you arrive at your home safely, Officer Helen Beauregard will drive you there."

"Is she a dyke?"

Reece took a deep breath and slowly exhaled. He would have loved to slap her. "No, she isn't. But ask her yourself. Either way, she'll probably whack you a good one when no one is looking and in such a way it won't leave a mark."

"What about her body cam?"

"Cameras are so unreliable, you know? Circuit board goes bad. Something just happens to cover the lens. Who knows? So when Officer Beauregard takes you home, stay put. You don't want to be considered a flight risk so I have to jail you. Got it?"

Tansy gave him the stink eye. Then grudgingly said, "Got it."

Reece left her room and walked over to the nurse's station. "Hi Lois. Keep an eye on our charge in room seven. Truitt. She's not to leave the building unless she's with Officer Beauregard."

"Sure thing, Reece."

"Thanks. Appreciate it."

He walked out of the hospital and got in his car. He fired off a text to GJ telling her to keep watch at the hospital to make sure Tansy left with no one but Helen.

What are you doing with your life? he asked himself. *You're fifty-one. Maybe it's time to forget this crap, retire, and go fishing.*

———

Oralene Fight lay in bed thinking. She was naked, nestled between pink silk sheets and underneath a heavy quilted comforter.

She'd caught that little sneak, Eliška, returning the diary to its hiding place in the toilet tank.

It's a good thing I took the precaution to write most of it in code.

She chuckled recalling the look of fear in the Czech maid's eyes, when she'd gripped the young woman's blonde hair at the ears, and said, "You are a dead woman. God has marked you as the object of His holy wrath."

The maid had responded, "It is your mother. She told me to spy on you. Talk to her."

"Very well. I will. Perhaps God won't strike you dead just yet. Perhaps."

She'd let go of the maid's hair, and the young woman ran out of the bathroom.

Oralene smiled at how readily the maid gave up the information that Mother was spying on her.

But that information made Oralene frown.

I am going to have to do something about Mother. But what?

That was the question. And the sooner she answered it, the better.

17

WEDNESDAY, JANUARY 7, 9:32 AM

GJ, leaving the left wrist in the handcuff, snicked the other ring closed around the bedrail.

Tansy Truitt opened her mouth, and GJ's face was suddenly two millimeters in front of the girl's.

"If you scream, I'll gag you."

"You wouldn't dare."

"Try me. You obnoxious little whore." GJ stood up.

"I bet you're a dyke. Look like one."

"If I was, I'd go straight looking at you."

"You wouldn't say that if I hadn't gotten cut."

"There's plenty of you not cut, and I'm sayin' it."

"I'm worth over a million dollars."

"There are a lot of sad-sack men out there if that's the case, because you're flat-out ugly."

Tansy's face scrunched up and GJ, voice sharp, said, "If you start crying, I'll gag you. Take it like a woman. And if you can't, quit dishing it out."

"My mother was murdered," the young woman nearly shouted.

"You haven't shown any sign of grief, so stop the sympathy ploy."

"I don't like you."

"Ditto. And if you hadn't tried to escape before being released, we wouldn't be talking now."

Tansy stuck her tongue out at GJ and then faced the wall, at least as far as her city-provided bracelet allowed.

———

Oralene saw her brother Lofton leave the house and tooted the horn of her car.

She also saw that he ignored her. Not accidentally but on purpose. She watched his head turn in her direction and then turn back to the sidewalk.

Does he think he can ignore me? Oralene muttered under her breath.

She put the big Caddy in drive and pulled up next to him, keeping pace as he started walking faster.

When he didn't stop, she rolled down the passenger window.

"Lofton," she yelled. "Stop walking and get in this car."

He hesitated and then walked towards the Cadillac.

Oralene stopped and he got into the car.

"What's the meaning of you ignoring me?"

Lofton, not looking at her, said, "I have nothing to say to you, O."

"What do you mean you have nothing to say to me? I'm your sister."

"Why did you do it? Why did you kill John-John?"

"What are you going on about? I didn't kill him. God struck him dead for his sin."

"God doesn't strike anyone dead, O. We do. So I ask you again, why did you kill him?"

"The Almighty struck him down for his sin. The same sin that caused our Lord and Savior to destroy your father."

"Jesus saves, O. He doesn't destroy."

"He, with a scourge, drove out the moneychangers from the temple. And when He returns, He will be on a white horse with eyes of fire, and a sword shall come out of His mouth, and He shall smite the nations. He shall break the sinners and the godless with a rod of iron. Our God struck down the sinners. And He will strike down you, my brother, if you aren't careful."

"I'm going, O. We have nothing to talk about. You shouldn't have done it. You've gone too far."

Lofton opened the door and exited the car.

Oralene screamed, "Lofton. Get back here. I'm your sister, don't leave me."

But Lofton ignored her and started walking on down the sidewalk.

Oralene prayed: "Oh, God. Your Son taketh away the sin of the world. He breaketh the sinner with a rod of iron. Some to salvation and some to damnation. I am your Handmaid. You've kissed me with the kisses of Your mouth. For Your love is better than wine. I am the Rose of Sharon. I am the Lily of the Valley. You, my Belovéd, are mine and I am Yours. Do not forsake me. Let me be Your right hand, and we will slay Your enemies."

She watched her brother disappear around a corner and knew what she had to do.

18

WEDNESDAY, JANUARY 7, 1:04 PM

THE REVEREND EMBER COLE, having learned of the attack on Tansy Truitt and that she'd been discharged to her home, decided to pay the young woman a visit.

Hopefully, I'll have better luck getting her to talk to me after all that's happened to her, she told herself.

Ember's Bronco pulled up behind the police car parked in front of the house. Not seeing a police officer, she got out of her vehicle.

The neighbor across the street was standing at the window watching her. Ember waved. The woman waved back and continued to watch her.

Smiling to herself about the stereotypes of nosey neighbors, she started up the walk, just as Helen Beauregard came around the corner of the house.

"Are you keeping an eye on the place?" Ember asked.

"I am, Reverend."

"If it's all right, I'm going to talk to her."

"Sure. You can try. She's a nasty one. Entitled brat."

"She's not very pleasant, that's for sure."

Ember continued up the walk, and when she reached the front door her finger pressed the doorbell.

When there was no answer, she rang the bell again, waited a minute, and then pounded on the door with both fists.

The door flew open, a wave of marijuana stench assaulted her nose, and Tansy, clad in a see-through negligee, said, "What the hell do you want?"

Ember smiled sweetly and answered, "There's no sign, so I thought you might be up for visitors."

"Oh, it's you, the stealth-pusher of Jesus. Sorry, don't feel like getting clobbered when I least expect it. I've already been knifed. Goodbye. And don't come back."

The door slammed shut.

Helen chuckled. "Sorry, Reverend. Don't mean to laugh, but…"

Ember smiled. "She'll want a friend one of these days."

"She has one. Mary Jane."

"But Mary Jane isn't going to hug her when she's in need of being hugged. I'll be back."

Ember returned to her car.

"I'll give her a day or two. She might want to talk by then, because eventually she'll run out of weed and then she'll want that hug."

———

Reece Sovern answered the ringing of his desk phone.

"Sovern."

"Sergeant Sovern, Doctor Arthur Weber here. I'm one of the assistant medical examiners. I conducted the autopsy of Patrice Bremen."

"Thanks for calling. What can you tell me?"

"Ms. Bremen received seventeen stab wounds. The killer probably used a standard kitchen butcher knife. I'd say a seven-inch blade."

"When did she die?"

"Somewhere between one and three in the morning. Immediate cause of death was most likely when her lungs were punctured. But when that occurred in the stabbing frenzy, I can't tell you."

"Jesus."

"Yeah. The attacker was strong enough to drive the knife in all the way to the handle. And I'm guessing the blows were delivered fast and furious."

"The killer didn't play with the victim."

"Not after the stabbing started. From the bruising, someone held the victim's wrists very tightly."

"That explains why no cuts to the arms."

"Yes, it does. Her legs were tied at the ankles with twine. There were fibers in the abrasions on both ankles."

"Tied, you say?"

"Yes."

"Funny. They weren't tied when we showed up."

"That is a bit strange."

"The whole affair is strange. Any dope in her system?"

"No. She was struck on the head. Cylindrical object. Rolling pin or baseball bat. Not enough force to crush the skull, but certainly enough to stun her or render her unconscious."

"Anything that might ID the attacker?"

"No. The perp, probably perps, at least two, wore gloves."

"That's unfortunate."

"Yes, it is."

"Anything else?"

"A lot of medical mumbo-jumbo. I'll email the report over. You can read it and if you have questions, give me a call."

"Thanks, Doc."

Reece cradled the phone, pushed his glasses back up to the bridge of his nose, and got from his desk drawer an emerald green perfecto. He removed the cellophane and stuck the stogie in his mouth.

"As I thought, at least two assailants. So why only one with the daughter? That just doesn't add up."

He rolled the cigar to the other corner of his mouth and gently gnawed the tobacco.

"I wonder what the Fights are up to on this Wednesday afternoon? Perhaps GJ and I should brighten up their day."

19

WEDNESDAY, JANUARY 7, 2:31 PM

REECE PUSHED THE BUTTON, and in the distance came the muffled tones of the chimes.

He looked at the security camera staring at him and GJ. He was tempted to wave with just one finger showing.

A voice came over the intercom. "How may I help you?"

"Sergeant Reece Sovern and Investigator Riggins to see Mrs. Fight and Oralene."

"Do you have an appointment?"

"No."

"I will see if they are receiving."

"You can let them know," GJ said, "that if they aren't receiving, we'll be back with a warrant for their arrest."

"Please wait."

"Think they'll call your bluff?" Reece asked.

"It wasn't a bluff, Sarge."

Reece chuckled. "I doubt even Judge Jones would issue an arrest warrant."

"Well, that may be. But if they aren't receiving, and Jones

won't issue a warrant, I can always talk with my cousin Waymon."

"He has influence over Mary Lou?" Reece's voice was laced with incredulity.

"No, but he does chair the Finance Committee at Saint Luke's, and if Mary Lou wants to control the budget, she needs Waymon on her side."

"Huh. That's pretty doggone good thinking, GJ. I better watch it. You'll have my job before I can blink."

GJ giggled. "Ah, Sarge, you know I'd never do that. I like working for you."

The door opened. The young blonde woman in the black maid's uniform said, "Mrs. Fight and Miss Fight will see you."

She stepped aside to allow them to enter, closed the door behind them, and said, "Follow me."

Reece let his eyes take in the foyer. Even to his lower middle-class eyes, he could see that while expensively decorated, the Fights had absolutely no taste.

Must've got this crap at some rich person's Ikea, he noted to himself.

He and GJ followed the maid through several tastelessly decorated rooms until they stood before a door. The maid knocked and opened the door in response to the word, "Come."

There he found Mary Lou and Oralene seated on a burnt orange loveseat. Across from the loveseat were two Chesterfield chairs, also in burnt orange, and in between the loveseat and chairs was an ebony coffee table.

The walls were painted maroon, with gold trim. Gold and black curtains covered the windows.

"Have a seat, officers. Eliška, bring tea, please."

"Yes, ma'am." And the maid disappeared.

Reece and GJ sat.

"This is called the Billiard Room," Mary Lou said. "But as we do not play billiards, we have no billiard table. There is the card table where we play bridge every Wednesday with Theodore and Clemmie Zollerndorfer. Do you know them?"

Reece smiled. *Show off. Of course she knows we wouldn't know them.* Out loud, he said, "Not personally, no."

"They own Zollern Cellars," GJ said. "I've been out there a couple of times."

"I wouldn't think you could afford their wine on a policeman's salary," Mary Lou said.

"Oh, no, I can't," GJ replied. "Not on what the city thinks I should be able to get by on. I was collecting donations for the Police Benefit Fund. You know, the fund that helps the families of poorly paid cops who get killed or severely injured in the line of duty."

Reece barely choked back the guffaw that wanted to explode from his mouth. Thank goodness Eliška appeared with the tea.

She poured for them and explained that the sandwiches were arugula and Brie, and the two types of cookies were oatmeal fig and orange.

While the maid was performing her duties, Reece studied Oralene, who was staring at him and GJ.

The lights are on, and someone's definitely home, he told himself. *But how many cards are missing from the deck?*

When Eliška had departed, Mary Lou drank tea, and when her cup returned to the saucer, asked, "So what brings you here, Sergeant?"

"I'm going through the Reverend Humphrey case—"

"It's about time someone did. Your substitute, that Kraus

fellow, was completely worthless. Never lifted a finger to stem the tide of violence sweeping our fair city."

"Sorry to hear that. In any case, I'm going over the testimony that was collected and have been looking for evidence we may have missed. I'd like to get this case wrapped up. I'm sure you agree, Mrs. Fight."

"Definitely. Ask your questions, Sergeant."

Reece noticed out of the corner of his eye GJ was chowing down the sandwiches and cookies. He wondered if she was trying to make a statement.

"Would you mind, Mrs. Fight, recounting your movements from the afternoon he was kidnapped until his body was found the following morning?"

Mary Lou stayed to script, repeating virtually verbatim what was in the case file. That allowed him to focus mentally on Oralene.

Only there was nothing to focus on.

With the saucer in her left hand, cup in right, she'd raise the cup and take a sip, her eyes darting from Reece to GJ, and then she'd lower the cup to the saucer and repeat the performance. Aside from those motions, her body was a statue.

Mary Lou came to the end of her monologue.

"And I hope you quit wasting my tax money and arrest someone soon."

"And who do you think we should arrest?" GJ asked, licking her fingers.

"Whom, dear. Why the lounge lizard, of course. The body was found on his land."

"Refresh my memory as to who is the 'lounge lizard'?" GJ asked.

"Harry Thurgood," Oralene said.

"He's the one who reported the body," GJ said.

Mary Lou smiled. "Very clever of him to do so. How better to throw you all off from suspecting him."

"We suspect everyone until we have a solid lead," Reece said. "Even you," he added after a pregnant pause.

"How dare you!" Mary Lou exclaimed. "He was my pastor."

"Look, Mrs. Fight, in today's world, people kill strangers for a five-dollar bill. Men kill their best friends, just to take their wives. It's a pretty ugly world out there. We have to suspect everybody. So, your best option is to tell us why we shouldn't suspect you and why we should suspect someone else."

"I told you, he was my pastor."

"Not good enough. We need to know you had no motive, means, or opportunity."

"Someone was with me for the entire time period you asked about. Didn't I make that clear in my previous statement?"

"Okay. That's good. No opportunity. How about you, Miss Fight?"

"She was—"

Reece held up his hand to stop Mary Lou.

"I asked Miss Fight. She can answer for herself."

Oralene set the cup in the saucer and set them down on the table. She folded her hands in her lap. "I was here. Eliška will verify."

"She's employed by Mrs. Fight," GJ said. "How do we know she won't simply agree with whatever you say in order to keep her job?"

A faint smile touched Oralene's lips. "You don't. And it is very difficult to prove a negative. Should I call her so you can ask her?"

"Not necessary," Reece said.

Oralene, the little smile still on her face, picked up her cup and saucer and drank tea.

Reece stood, and GJ followed. "Thank you for your time. Aside from Harry Thurgood, any suggestions as to who might want Reverend Humphrey dead?"

"He was a sodomite, you know," Oralene said. "A sinner before God. A sinner in the house of God. A sinner in the pulpit of God. And God hates the sinner."

"What are you saying?" GJ asked.

"God struck him dead. But you can't arrest God."

"I can arrest the human agent," Reece said. "And I will."

20

WEDNESDAY, JANUARY 7, 3:04 PM

REECE GOT behind the wheel of his big black SUV. GJ occupied the passenger seat.

"Is she nuts, or what?" GJ said.

"I think there are a few cards missing from the deck, that's for sure."

"So what did she mean?"

Reece shrugged. "My guess is that Humphrey was a sinner and deserved to die."

"Did she kill him?"

"That is the big question, isn't it?"

"Did you see Mary Lou's face when Oralene called him a sodomite?"

"Yeah. She wasn't happy."

"Does that tell us anything?"

Reece repositioned his glasses. "I don't know. Maybe. Maybe Mary Lou knows, or at least suspects, that Oralene was involved."

"Or it could mean Mary Lou doesn't like her attitude towards homosexuals."

Reece nodded. "Yeah. That's probably more the case."

"So now what?"

"What we've got thus far from the old women was that he was a chameleon. Told them what they wanted to hear."

"And very little about himself."

"Apparently."

"So we're back to why he needed to die."

Reece nodded, readjusted his glasses, which had slid back down his nose, and took the cellophane off of an emerald green lonsdale. "Once we have the answer to that question, we'll be on the road to finding his killer."

"It doesn't appear to be for money."

"No, it doesn't."

"A lover's quarrel?"

"Possibly. But no one seems to think he had one. A lover, that is. Of course, that doesn't mean he didn't." Reece put the cigar in his mouth and sank his teeth into it as if it were going to run away. "So that leaves us with he was killed because he was a homosexual in God's pulpit. And someone didn't like it."

"Then that leaves us with…"

"The Restons. And Oralene."

———

On the Green there is a bench close to the Really Good that I often sit on and smoke my pipe. I might ponder the day's events. I might contemplate life and my place in the universe. Or I might simply enjoy the weather.

This afternoon the temperature was sixty-four, but the sun made it feel much warmer.

I was smoking Presbyterian Mixture, even though I'm a

member of the Methodist Church. A bit of iconoclastic rebellion? Could be. Then again, perhaps I just like the taste.

In any event, this was a day when I had nothing on my mind. I was just enjoying the Texas Hill Country weather when I caught a whiff of an all too familiar perfume. Before I could turn to confirm the identity of the wearer, she was sitting next to me. And I do mean next to me.

"Hello, Scarlett."

"Hello, Harry."

"The bench isn't crowded, you know."

"I know. I'm filled with desire, Harry. I'm *wet* with desire."

"Probably too much information. How's Stanton these days?"

"Very well." She moved over three millimeters. "He's fine. I can't ever thank you enough for bringing us together."

"It was your idea."

"Yes. But you made it happen."

"So I did. What brings you to my bench?" I put the pipe in my pocket.

"No. Keep smoking. I love a man who smokes a pipe. It's a sign that he's intelligent. Thoughtful. Stable. Mature. And sexy."

"Hugh Hefner I'm not."

"And I'm very glad. Because I want you all to myself."

"Maybe you have me. In another timeline."

"Lucky that me. But not this me."

"Sorry. Sometimes life is cruel." I continued smoking my pipe. "How's the resort?"

"Doing well." She put her hand on my thigh. "Very unfortunate about Patrice."

"It is. A lot of people didn't like her because of the way she chose to make money. But was she a bad person?"

"No worse than most of us." She inched her hand up my thigh.

I puffed on my pipe. "So who disliked her for what she was doing so much they had to end her life?"

"You think Reece will figure it out?"

"Probably. Except he's working on the Humphrey case."

Her hand moved another inch up my thigh. "I'm not a Hat, but I know almost all of them."

"And?"

"They think it's one of the Restons. But they don't say that to Mary Lou. She thinks you killed Humphrey."

"She would. Why the Restons?"

"They're new and therefore immediately suspect."

"I see. But did one of them kill him? And perhaps Patrice, too?"

"She must take good care of you." Scarlett withdrew her hand.

"She does."

"I guess lil' ol' me doesn't stand a chance."

"Not in this dimension."

"Pity."

"Which Reston?"

"All of them."

"Surely not Jearlene."

"Depends on who you talk to."

"Why? Why would they kill people they don't know?"

"Sin. That family is a cesspool of sin. Adultery. Incest. One or more of them has a screw loose. Being the victims of sin, they seek to exterminate it in others."

"You a psychiatrist?"

"I'm a student of life. Human behavior. That's why I know that even though you love me, because you're an honorable man, you won't make me yours alongside your wife."

My pipe was out. I turned to Scarlett. "I have to get back to the shop. Tell Stanton I said hello."

She kissed the tip of her index finger and touched my lips. "I will."

"Hope you have a good rest of the day."

I stood and headed back to the Really Good.

The town was lining up against the newbies. The strangers. But in this case, maybe they were right.

21

WEDNESDAY, JANUARY 7, 4:00 PM

SERGEANT INVESTIGATOR REECE SOVERN, hands on hips, an emerald green lonsdale jutting from his mouth, eyeglasses halfway down his nose, studied the whiteboard he and Investigator GJ Riggins had set up in his office.

There was the victim: the Reverend Adelbert Humphrey. And there were the suspects. The major players were all on the board.

GJ said, "Oralene Fight with the knife in the kitchen." And laughed.

Reece shook his head. "She may have pulled the strings, but it was someone else's hand on the knife."

"So that means we really need to find two perps."

"In a perfect world, yes. We'd get them all. But in this world we'll be lucky to get the hand on the knife."

"That's what I love about you, Sarge, you're so pragmatic."

"Glad you think so. Most days I'm not so sure."

"So do we start bringing the Restons in for interrogation?"

"Yeah. I think so. There're a lot of fingers pointing their way. Might as well see where the trail leads."

————

Oralene Fight, a Fight by adoption, a Reston by birth, sat in one of the folding chairs and stared at the lectern her brother John-John used to stand behind and preach the Word of God every Sunday. Although, like Pa, he spent as much time in the center aisle and in front of the first row of seats as he did behind the lectern. And like Pa, he took to sinnin' at an early age.

Like God, she loved her brother and hated his sin. Unlike God, she could only destroy the sin by destroying the sinner. She was confident, though, that God would sort out the wheat from the chaff. He was a good God, rewarding the righteous while destroying the wicked.

And Oralene was proud that God had chosen her to be the rod of His wrath. She'd have preferred to be a vessel of mercy. But one doesn't argue with God. When called, it's "Yea, Lord, I hear and obey, for You are the Almighty, the Just One, and the All Knowing. I am less than a maggot at Your feet."

She was leery of the interest the police had in her and Mother Fight. And she suspected the interest was mostly in her. She was fully aware of the rumblings in the Society. The Crimson Hats. They wanted to see her gone. They were afraid of her power. Particularly Pearline Appelwhite. The woman had been displaced as number two in the Hats, and she didn't like it. She didn't like it at all.

Oralene knew Pearline was a sinner. They were all sinners. The members of the Crimson Hat Society. That was the hold Mother Fight had on them. Their dirty little secrets. They did Mother's bidding to keep those secrets hidden. Secrets that would destroy them.

Pa had preached that all had free will. But Oralene knew that free will was an illusion. God was the potter. And He made some vessels to honor, and some to dishonor.

Preach the gospel, and those with the good seed grew into saints. Those with the bad seed rejected the Word of the Lord and reveled all the more in their sin — to their destruction.

Oralene had received the Word of the Lord.

I am to destroy sinners. God will sort them out.

22

WEDNESDAY, JANUARY 7, 5:32 PM

I LIKE GRAHAM HUSTON. Some see him as a gruff curmudgeon. I see him as our Diogenes. A man who values simplicity and the truth. A man afraid of nothing because he's already good friends with Death.

Besides Graham, I'd invited Telford and Terall Whitacre to dine with us, and they'd accepted.

They own T & T Tobacconists. Transplants from Massachusetts because the draconian tobacco laws in that state were greatly impacting their business, which is their livelihood, they picked Magnolia Bluff to be their new home and place of business. Mostly because they fell in love with the Hill Country scenery and felt this area would be a great place to enjoy retirement. And Texas has far fewer intrusive laws than their former home.

Telford is short and round. His wife, Terall, is tall and slim. They are in their mid-forties, and are well educated, intelligent, and articulate. They have no children, but opted instead for a Standard Schnauzer. Mitzi by name. She was curled up by the fire.

Wilbur, Em's cat, had vanished. He is not at all fond of strangers. Princess accepted the visitors, but aside from Em and me, Graham is her person. She was curled up at his feet.

We were all in the family room. Em and I in our wingback chairs. The Whitacres were on one loveseat, and Graham was on the other.

The sound of the wood quietly hissing and crackling in the fireplace was an ostinato to our conversation.

Graham was nursing a tumbler of Texas Blue Corn. Telford had a glass of Sercial Madeira. Terall, a fino sherry. Em, a French 75 Mocktail. And I, a hot pink gin.

"I have gifts for our host and hostess," Telford said. He reached into his suit coat pocket and took out two boxes. He handed one to Ember and one to me.

"Go ahead and open them," Terall said.

I untied the bow and opened the box. In it was a pipe. Dark yellow with a black stem. The shape was an apple. I looked over at Em. She also had a yellow pipe with a black stem. Hers looked something like a prince shape.

She turned it over in her hand. "It says 'The Smoke' on the side."

Mine had the words "the pipe" on it.

Telford explained, "They were all the rage back in the mid-sixties to mid-seventies and then just disappeared."

Terall added, "Their popularity was mostly due to vigorous marketing to women to buy them for the pipe-smoking men in their lives."

Graham snorted. "Makes it sound like women are suckers."

"Those pipes were quite expensive back then," Terall said. "Made for an impressive gift."

"There's a trick to smoking them," Telford said. "I'll fill you in later."

Graham swallowed Blue Corn. "I have a question for the amateur detectives."

"What? No gift?" Em said, then laughed when she saw Graham roll his eyes.

"You get plenty of gifts. I give them to you in the *Chronicle*."

"So you do," Em replied. "What's your question?"

"Have you solved the murder, or I should say murders, yet?"

Ember laughed. "My better half and I aren't even trying."

Graham set his glass down. "Wait a minute. You don't expect the MBPD to solve this latest killing, do you? Or the unsolved cases that have been sitting around."

"Reece is very capable," Em answered.

The newspaperman snorted in derision and picked up his glass. "Fancy training. Secret missions. But he's still Reece."

Raylene Reston called us to supper. I'd hired her to serve our meal so her mom, Jearlene, could go home and take care of the younger children.

With Joetta married and taking care of her own little one, and Oralene living with the Fights, Raylene was now the second mother to her numerous younger siblings.

The young woman stands around five-nine, is slender, and her face could launch a thousand ships. Her dark honey blonde hair touches her waist, but she had it in a bun so it wasn't in the way for serving.

With the murder of Pastor John Reston, Senior, I've been helping the Reston family. Aside from charging them very low rent, I employ Jearlene, who goes by Jerri, as our housekeeper and cook. I also employ young Samuel and Elisha at the Really Good in the summer and sometimes after school during the winter. And if they need it, I help out Landon and Joetta. Landon works at the paper for Graham, but the job doesn't pay much.

When we were all seated, Raylene served the first course. Texas Caviar Dip and corn chips. Why it's called caviar is beyond me, as there are no fish eggs in it.

After Em said grace, Graham loaded up a chip and shoveled it into his mouth.

While he was chewing, Telford asked, "Graham seems to think you are going to don your deerstalkers, break out your calabash pipes, and solve this current murder."

Graham swallowed. "Not just the current murder, but that of Reverend Humphrey, too."

"You're sure asking a lot," I said.

"You took care of those wannabe vampire nuts."

"Reece was there. I didn't do it alone."

"All right. You had help. Reece is good with firearms."

"That was an awful affair," Terall said.

"Yes, it was," Ember agreed.

Graham piled caviar on another chip.

"Go easy on that, my friend," I said. "We have four more courses."

"I'm eating for two." And the chip disappeared into his mouth.

Ember giggled at the comment. "Come again?"

"Very funny," he replied, "coming from you."

Ember turned fifty shades of crimson.

"That was bad, Graham, even for you," I said.

"I know. I'm sorry, Ember. Forgive me?"

"Yes, I will. But don't do that again."

"I won't."

Everyone in town knows, but if you don't, my sweet Emmy used to be a porn star.

"So what do you mean by 'eating for two'?" Terall asked.

"I'm eating for two days into the future. Saves on the food bill."

Em shook her head. I rolled my eyes. But he got chuckles out of the Whitacres.

I signaled to Raylene to bring the second course. A roasted beet salad.

"Ah," Telford said, "I love beets."

"Are you truly going to sit on the sidelines, Harry?" Graham asked. "Am I going to have to solve those cases by myself?"

"Are you forgetting Reece and GJ?" I asked in return.

"As I said, am I going to have to solve those cases by myself?"

"I wasn't planning on solving them. I have my coffee shop and hard money loan business to run."

"What did you do with all the books from the vampires?" Terall asked.

"They're in storage," I answered. "Don't have a clue what to do with them."

"They did do us a good turn," Telford said.

"Just softening us up for their next meal," Terall replied.

I couldn't help but laugh at that, even though I put a bullet into the head of one of those beautiful women. I did it to save Em.

With everyone having finished their salad, I signaled Raylene to clear the dishes and bring the soup. Cauliflower. I also served a fino sherry with the soup course.

Graham looked at the small glass of amber liquid, smelled it, then dumped it into the soup.

We all burst out laughing. Graham looked at us, shrugged, and spooned soup.

The conversation drifted away from murder to the weather, local politics, the assault on tobacco and other infringements of our freedom, and the local wine scene.

While talking, we ate our way through a luscious pork roast, apple pie, and then a cheese plate. We drank many glasses of Texas Gewürztraminer and finally retired to the family room with our coffee.

"That was amazingly good, Harry," Telford said. "Kudos to your chef."

"I'll pass your compliment on to Jearlene. She'll be pleased."

"Why do you care about them?" Graham asked.

"The Restons?" I asked in return.

He nodded.

"They were strangers. And in need. With no one to help them."

"Like us," Em said. "That's partly what brought Harry and me together. We were strangers."

"We're all strangers in this town," Terall said. "Thank you for befriending us."

"Our pleasure," I said.

"Strangers in a strange land," Graham said. "It fits."

I excused myself to check on Raylene. She'd cleaned up, put the dishes in the dishwasher, and boxed up the food to take home. I love leftovers, but I thought the Restons might enjoy them more than I. And they would certainly help Jerri with her food bill.

"I'm all done, Mr. Thurgood."

"Very good, Raylene."

I handed her a hundred-dollar bill for her time. Her eyes were like saucers.

"Thank you very much."

"Thank *you*. Is your mom picking you up? Do you need a ride?"

"No, I'm fine. I'm getting a ride from O."

Oralene. The thought of Oralene contaminating her beautiful sister soured my stomach.

But what if Oralene had already poisoned the young woman standing before me?

What if?

23

THURSDAY, JANUARY 8, 4:24 AM

I COULDN'T SLEEP. Oralene picking up Raylene last night wasn't sitting well. So I got up, threw on some clothes, donned my coat, grabbed my dog, and went for a walk.

It was the general belief of those in the know that Oralene had orchestrated the murder of her father and the family's business manager, Purnell Tully. She didn't actually do the killing. Her siblings did. At least, that was the speculation.

Her brother Lofton had been thrown under the bus. He was the scapegoat, according to what Oralene told Em.

I hired Stanton Lauderbach to defend the young man. The trial ended in a hung jury, and the DA decided not to push for a retrial.

In my opinion, and that of many others, the killers had gotten away with murder.

Since then we've had other murders, and they've been solved. Murders Oralene had not orchestrated.

However, I couldn't help but sense the hand of Oralene in the murders of Reverend Humphrey and her brother, John-

John. Then there was the attempted murder of Em, the killing of Patrice Bremen, and the attempted murder of Tansy Truitt, Patrice's daughter.

Did Oralene's hand pull the strings on those killings and attempted murders as well?

I don't know.

While pondering these things, I smoked my new Bakelite pipe with the pyrolytic graphite liner.

The Presbyterian Mixture tasted pretty good in the thirty-eight degree early morning air.

Princess was on her leash, and we walked with no intended destination. My mind turning over what I knew about the Restons.

All of a sudden, Princess stopped. Her ears perked up, and a low growl rumbled in her throat. She turned around, and charged off into the darkness behind me, yanking the leash out of my hand.

I heard a cry, grunt, and savage growling. I whipped out my phone, tapped on the flashlight, and ran after my dog.

Coming to her aid was not to be. Someone jumped out of the darkness and slashed me with a knife. I felt a stinging burn all across my chest.

I tried to grab him or her, but missed.

My reward was a slice across my fingers.

And then it was over.

Princess was whining. Somewhere in the dark.

When I found her, she was pawing at her face. The bastard had maced my dog.

I scooped up all seventy pounds of her and carried her back to the house.

I didn't know who'd attacked us, yet I knew who'd attacked us. And there was going to be hell to pay now.

This morning she was toying with me. Like a cat.

Macing Princess was cruel and mean-spirited.

Ruining my thousand-dollar Brooks Brothers coat? Unconscionable.

Davis Briggs or no Davis Briggs. I just put on my deer-stalker.

24

EM INSISTED I go to the ER and drove me there.

I got patched up by the nurse practitioner. She said I was lucky the wounds were fairly shallow.

On the drive home, Em said, "We're in the soup now, aren't we?"

"What do you mean?"

"We're back in the detective business."

"Did we ever leave?"

"We did for a year."

"Yeah. Not much to investigate on a yacht."

"But now we're back in Magnolia Bluff."

"Yep."

"I hate that writers group. They started it all. It's like we're characters in some crazy writer's murder mystery."

I shrugged. "Maybe we are."

"Very funny. Pinch me."

I pinched her and she yelped.

"Nope," she said. "We're real and they started this."

"But we're going to finish it."

"Amen to that."

"I'll see if Telford has any calabash pipes."

"Sherlock Holmes didn't smoke one."

"I know."

"What's an oily briar?"

"I don't think I want to know. Anyone who keeps tobacco in a slipper and smokes yesterday's dottles first thing in the morning... Nope. Don't want to know."

"In any event, we're now on the case. Correct?"

"Correct."

"Poor Princess. Should we take her to the vet?"

"Probably."

"I'll do that. You have the Really Good to run. My schedule's more flexible."

"Okay."

When we got home, I put Princess in the car, and Em took off for the vet's office. And I drove to the Really Good.

At the shop, I updated the staff on the morning's events.

Estrelita asked me a dozen times if I was all right.

Jack said, "Sounds like another normal day."

And Miguel said, with a great big smile on his face, "We are going to have a lot of customers."

The thing of it is, Jack and Miguel are more right than not.

I told them I was off to the *Chronicle* office and would be back shortly.

Jack said, "Of course."

Miguel and Estrelita laughed.

I shook my head and left.

Crossing East Main, the Green, and West Main brought me to the door of our town's twice-weekly newspaper.

There was a light on inside. Monika wasn't at her desk, so

I assumed the light was on for Graham. I pulled on the door and entered. He was sitting at his desk in the back of the room.

"Morning, Harry. Didn't get enough of my wit and charm last night?"

"No, I didn't. But more than that, I have some news for you."

"Great. Shoot."

"I got attacked by a knife-wielding maniac this morning and my dog got maced."

His eyebrows shot up. "That why your hand is bandaged?"

"It is."

"Sit down and tell me about it."

I did.

When I was done, he leaned back in the old swivel chair he'd inherited from Neal and put his hands behind his head.

"That's some story," he said. "You think it's our perp?"

"Definitely."

"Dressed all in black, you probably can't ID the person from just their eyes."

"No. Don't have to. I know who it is." I told him about Oralene's threat.

He nodded his head. "I'd say that clinches it. Talk to Reece?"

"Not yet. I will after I'm done here."

"But Oralene's threat was verbal."

"Yes. The note under the windshield wiper was unsigned. So she can easily deny authorship."

"Of course. What are you going to do?"

"Get a holster and start openly carrying my revolver."

Graham laughed. "I'll have to start calling you Bat Masterson."

"I'd laugh, except this is no longer funny."

"Sorry. No, it's not. I'll run a special edition. Might get it out tonight, otherwise tomorrow morning."

"I'll pay for it."

"Might not need to. I'll let you know."

"Okay." I stood. "Now to update Reece. Catch you later."

I made my way back to the Really Good.

Fergus was at the corner table opposite mine. He waved and said good morning. I waved back.

I grabbed a coffee and a couple of doughnuts, sat at my table and texted our sergeant investigator. In twenty minutes he was sitting at my table.

"Give me the lowdown," he said.

While I gave him the story in full, Estrelita served him coffee and apple pie. A substantial wedge of cheddar was next to the double slice of pie.

"So what do you want to do?" he asked. "Not much for me to go on."

"Graham's putting out a special edition."

He snorted a short laugh. "Must be nice to control the press."

I chuckled. "Let's say I just have a bit of influence."

"A big bit." He took a bite of cheese. "Thanks for the update. I'll open a file, and I'll factor this into all of our ongoing investigations. It's all I can do."

"That's fine. Just wanted to let you know."

"What in blue blazes is this town coming to?"

"It's starting to get out of hand."

"We just might be earning ourselves the title of Little Sin City."

"Or the Murder Capital of Texas."

25

REECE HAD DEPARTED, and the regulars were coming in for coffee and a bite of breakfast. All eleven of them. They were local retired folk who'd started dropping in because of Em's and my sleuthing escapades or my joining the church.

Four of those regulars were Claiborne Allen and his wife, Blondene, and Benton John Widdon and his wife, Urleen. Claiborne being the current chair of the church council at Saint Luke's and Benton, the former chair.

Both men are pipe smokers. Claiborne, of humbler economic status, owns but three old Medico pipes and smokes nothing but Half and Half.

Benton has some money, but lives fairly simply. He owns four Weber and three Kaywoodie pipes and imports Rum and Maple from Germany. He can afford to.

Amazing how so many old American pipe tobacco blends are made in Germany and sold to Germans, but not exported to the US.

After they sat down and Estrelita took their orders, I

walked over to their table, greeted them, and chatted for a few minutes.

Blondene and Urleen asked about Ember and the twins. I said they were all well. The guys asked about the yacht and whether we had run into pirates.

"We had a run-in while in Indonesia. They beat it out of there in a hurry after they got a taste of our firepower."

"What did you have?" Benton asked.

"A couple guys up the masts using thirty-aught-sixes to snipe. Four shotguns with rifled slugs. And a couple M sixty machine guns. One fired ball ammo and the other, armor-piercing rounds."

"I bet the armor-piercing rounds did a number on the pirate boat." Claiborne said.

"You bet. They didn't stick around for long once those rounds started hitting."

"Sounds dangerous," Blondene said.

"It was a bit nerve-wracking, but the entire episode was over in ten minutes. Once they saw we weren't easy pickings, they wanted no part of us."

When Estrelita showed up with their food, I moseyed on back to my table after picking up a fresh cup of coffee and three doughnuts for myself.

Somehow, Oralene or her minions were cognizant I was out walking. That can only mean one thing: they have the house under surveillance. Which means we aren't safe. And that's not a pleasant feeling to have.

If Oralene is watching us, then I'm going to have to watch her.

I retrieved my phone from my pocket and sent a coded text to Elmore.

Five minutes later, I got a text back. 817. He was on a job and would contact me later. And when he did, it was going to be turnabout is fair play.

26

REECE SOVERN RANG THE DOORBELL, rolled the corona to the other side of his mouth, pushed his glasses back up to the top of his nose, and pressed the button a second time.

The door opened, and he and GJ were looking at Lofton Reston.

"Hello, Lofton," Reece said. "Remember us?"

"I remember you."

"Mind if we come in and talk?" Reece asked.

"My mama says that nobody can come in without her being home, and she isn't home now."

"I see. We just want to ask you a few questions. We could talk out here on the porch. How about that?" Reece said.

"What's this about? I've done nothin' wrong."

"We didn't say you did," GJ said. "We're looking for information, and you just might have it."

"I know nothin'. About anything. Leave us alone."

And the door banged shut.

"Now what do we do, Sarge?"

Reece removed his hat and ran his fingers through his

hair. He thought for a moment, replaced the hat, and said, "We get arrest warrants for the whole damn lot of them."

———

Once again, Ember was pushing the doorbell button of 624 Oak Street, the home of Tansy Truitt. For the third time.

The door swung open with a bang. The stench of marijuana rolled out of the open doorway and assaulted Ember's nose.

"You again!"

"Hi, Tansy. I was hoping you would join me for a cup of coffee or tea."

"Why won't you leave me alone? I don't want you or Jesus in my life."

"That's fine. Have you had breakfast?"

"No, I haven't."

"Come on, then. Get dressed and let's get breakfast."

"If I go with you for breakfast, will you leave me alone?"

Ember smiled. "Maybe. Maybe not."

"Shit. Okay. Give me a minute. I'd invite you in, but the place is a disaster."

"That's fine. It's a nice day. I'll wait outside."

The door closed, and Ember sat on the step.

Helen Beauregard got out of her squad car and walked up to the sitting minister.

"Hello, Reverend."

"Hi, Helen. I hope it's okay if Tansy and I have breakfast."

"Are you serious? She actually talked to you?"

"Briefly. Hopefully, she'll talk more over some good food."

"I have to tag along, but I'll give you space to talk."

"I understand."

The door opened, and another shockwave of marijuana stench rolled out.

"Is she going with us?" Tansy asked, her voice laced with acid.

"Helen has to keep an eye on you for your own protection," Ember said.

"Fabulous," Tansy replied.

"But if you don't shower pretty soon," Helen began, "I definitely won't be needed because your stench will kill everyone who gets within fifty feet of you."

"Ha, ha. Very funny, Officer. Okay, Reverend. Let's go."

"We're going to the Spoon," Ember said.

Helen gave a thumbs up and headed for her car.

When the police officer was out of earshot, Tansy asked, "Do I really stink?"

"You aren't too fresh."

"God. I can't even smell myself. Do you mind waiting a bit longer while I run through the shower?"

"Nope. Not at all."

"Thanks."

Tansy dashed back inside, and Ember walked down to Helen's cruiser.

The window slid down. "She change her mind?"

"No, she's going to take a shower. Said she couldn't even smell herself."

"That is bad. It must be worse than the city dump in there."

"It probably isn't Flo's Floral, that's for sure."

Helen let out a laugh. "How can people live that way?"

"I'm not an expert, but I think her mom's death really affected her. Then there was the attack she was lucky to fight off. I don't think she's coping well."

"So how did you get her to go to breakfast with you?"

"I didn't. Jesus did."

"Okay. Stop right there. No Jesus woo-woo here. Not after last time."

"Sorry. I'll go wait up at the door."

Ember returned to the front door, recalling while she walked how Helen had fled her office when she'd told the police officer some things about her life and how Jesus was calling her to come back to Him.

She'll come around. She can't resist Jesus. Ember smiled at the thought, recalling her own experience of Jesus calling her to Himself.

She started humming "Jesus loves me, this I know" when out came Tansy with a wet head of tangled dark hair, a pink blouse, light blue slacks, and a pair of sandals on her feet.

"Couldn't find my comb, or any fresh underwear. I'm going commando. Hope you don't mind."

Ember turned and headed for her car. "I don't, if you don't."

Tansy jogged to catch up with her. "Oh. Okay."

"And I have a comb in the car."

"Uh, thanks."

As they reached the car, Ember leaned in close and half-whispered, "I was in porn. Nothing shocks me."

Tansy said nothing, but Ember thought she detected the cattiness beginning to slip.

———

Ember asked Lorraine for a booth that was out of the way, and she got one in the back. Officer Beauregard was four tables away and between the two women and the door.

"Order what you want. My treat."

"I have money, you know."

"So do I. We can each pay our own if that makes you feel better."

"Nah. And, um, thanks."

"Don't mention it. My pleasure."

In a moment, a waitress took their orders, and when she was gone, Tansy said, "Okay. Clobber me with Jesus. I'm ready."

Ember laughed. "I'm not clobbering you with Jesus."

"You're not?"

"No, I'm not. I'm here to listen. You lost your mother, and you've been attacked. I'm here to help you. To be your friend."

The young woman stared at Ember for the longest time before her face crumpled and she burst into tears.

27

REECE HAD JUST GOT BACK to the station from the DA's office. He hadn't seen the district attorney himself. Reece just wasn't important enough to see Ham Hamilton in the flesh, except at campaign time, of course. Instead, he saw Assistant DA Amanda Horton. An attractive woman. Blonde. And as pleasant as a prostate exam. Reece hated lawyers.

At least she liked what he'd shown her and said she'd see Judge Jones to get the warrants. He entered his office and closed the door.

As much as he'd grown to like Harry Thurgood, he still didn't fully trust the man. There remained his unidentified means of support. Because everyone knew he didn't make enough from that coffee shop to even pay for a slice of pie from Bluff Bakery.

If he were independently wealthy, why not say so? If he had a business somewhere else, why not say so? What was the big secret? And he took an awful lot of trips out of town. Why?

"Because," he'd say. And that was it. You couldn't get him to elaborate to save your soul.

If it were truly business, what kind of business?

Whatever was the actual source of Harry's money, it appeared to be a regular El Dorado. Because he was flush. Made the Fights look like ne'er-do-wells. Not that they didn't need to be taken down a peg or two.

And because he didn't fully trust Harry, he had to keep the Reston arrests quiet as long as he could. He didn't want that smarmy Lauderbach gumming up the works. That wouldn't be easy or for long because Jearlene Reston worked for Harry. Maybe he could save her for last.

GJ was working with Briggs to get as many officers together as she could so that all the warrants would be executed at the same time.

The tricky part would be the juveniles. They ranged in age from sixteen down to six. CPS would probably assign someone to be with them while they were questioned, since they'd also be arresting their only parent.

He got a cigar from his desk drawer, removed the cellophane, and sank his teeth into it.

Sure wish I'd been a cop in the old days. Things were so much easier. None of this bull crap we have to deal with today.

There was a knock at his door, and he told the person to enter.

The door opened, and GJ stuck her head in. "Got a minute, Sarge?"

"Sure. C'mon on in."

She entered, leaving the door open.

"Everything is set. For the young kids, who'll be in school, the School Resource Division will take them into custody."

"Good. Now we wait on Judge Jones."

———

Ember, with the help of Clara Relish, the nanny, put Tansy Truitt to bed in one of the spare bedrooms, and she was soon asleep.

"The poor thing is distraught," Clara said.

And Ember agreed.

While Tansy slept, Ember sat in the room with the twins. She was holding Monette in her lap, Max was on the floor playing with a truck, when Tansy woke up.

"Where am I?" she asked.

"In my home. You've just had a twenty-minute nap. Feel better?"

"I do. Thanks. I guess I kinda fell apart."

"Perfectly understandable. You've been through a lot in a very short span of time."

"Yeah. I guess so. Sorry I spoiled breakfast."

"We'll do lunch instead. How's that?"

"Okay. I'm kinda hungry."

"Good. Jerri prepared mac and cheese and a salad for us. How's that?"

"Sounds great. Are these your kids?"

"Yep. Monette and Maximilian."

"They're darling. I'd like kids someday."

"They're wonderful. Raising them is a big undertaking, but hey, millions have done it before us, so we can do it too."

Tansy laughed. "I guess so."

"C'mon. Follow me to the kitchen. We'll sit in the breakfast nook."

Ember sent a text to Clara informing her that she and

Tansy were going downstairs. In a moment, the nanny took charge of the children.

On the way to the elevator, Tansy said, "Must be nice to have a nanny."

Ember laughed. "It does make things easier."

When they reached the first floor, Ember led her guest through several rooms before entering the kitchen.

"What a house!" Tansy exclaimed. "This place is enormous."

"Built by a rail baron. They liked showing off their wealth in those days."

"I guess."

"Lunch is on the table, Reverend."

"Thanks, Jerri."

Ember and Tansy sat.

"Help yourself," Ember said.

"So why did you give up the porn business?" Tansy asked while dishing up mac and cheese.

"I saw old hookers and old porn stars. Quite honestly, they were pathetic. Nobody wanted them. If you aren't young and beautiful, there isn't much demand for you."

"It's a lot different on Only for You."

"Possibly. But that didn't exist back then. And all I know is that I didn't want to be a washed-up whore. Then I heard a radio preacher talking about the love of God and that Jesus's yoke is easy and His burden is light. That was it. I told Jesus I was His. And when He actually appeared to me, I knew I had the real deal."

"Wait. Jesus appeared to you?"

"Yep. In a dream. But it was so vivid, I think it very well wasn't a dream. Anyway, He told me I was His, and that I needed to leave Vegas. So I did."

"No regrets leaving?"

"None. None whatsoever. I'm a new person in Christ. I am His and He is mine."

"I think it's different when you do your own porn. When you have your own company."

"From the money end, sure. You're in a better position. But there is still all the marketing."

"That's true. Took up a lot of Mom's time. Now, I'll have to do it."

"And you're still going to get old. And let's face it, men, and I suppose women too, want to see young women. Your value continues to drop the older you get."

"I suppose. Never thought about it. Although that might be why Mom was focusing more on me."

"Could very well be." Ember paused a moment, and then asked, "If you weren't doing porn, what would you like to do for a living?"

"This will sound really crazy, but I'd like to be a stay-at-home mom taking care of my man and our kids."

"That's absolutely fabulous. Why don't you do it?"

"I don't know. Where would I find a guy who wanted me and not my money?"

"Get a job and don't tell him about the money. Or better yet, give the money away."

"I'm not doing that. But I wouldn't have to tell him about the money. At least not right away."

"True. But I would tell him eventually, and probably sooner rather than later."

"Why aren't you preaching Jesus at me and calling me a sinner?"

"Because we're all sinners, and I did tell you about Jesus. I told you my story when you asked."

"So you did. That was rather painless."

Ember smiled. "Wasn't it?"

The conversation drifted to other topics, and when lunch was over, Ember was pretty certain she'd made a new friend.

28

THURSDAY, JANUARY 8, 2:42 PM

REECE CHUCKLED. The Honorable Rutherford B. Jones was quick, very quick, in signing the arrest warrants.

Must need to get down to the Pickle-Dilly Bait Shop. The cigar moved to the other side of his mouth. *Although I'm not sure why. Not much fishin' done hereabouts in winter.*

He shrugged. And smiled. To avoid a repeat of the singathon the family gave when previously arrested, Reece had arranged for the family members to be separated.

The young children were at a juvenile detention center with a child protection worker and the two school resource officers.

Jearlene Reston was in Interrogation Room One. Oralene, in Room Two. Lofton was in a cell. And Raylene was in an empty office, handcuffed, and under the watchful eye of Officer Kristine Combs.

Reece had separated Samuel and Elisha from the younger children as they were almost eighteen. And they worked for Harry Thurgood.

He entered the room where Samuel was sitting with a child protection worker. GJ followed.

Reece began. "Well, Mr. Reston, you can thank your brother Lofton for your arrest. If he'd talked to us civil like, we wouldn't be here."

"What do you want? I haven't done anything wrong."

"You haven't done anything wrong that we can *prove*. But we know you are as guilty as Judas."

Samuel said nothing. Just turned his face away.

"To make this short and quick," GJ began, "tell us all that you know about the murder of Reverend Humphrey."

"I didn't kill nobody."

"Didn't ask that," she said. "What do you know about it?"

"Nothing."

"Did your sister, Oralene, convince you to kill him?"

"I killed nobody."

"What about the attack on Reverend Cole?" Reece asked. "Did you do that?"

Samuel's face frowned in puzzlement. "She's nice to us. Why would I want to kill her?"

And so it went. After twenty minutes of getting nowhere, Reece let him go.

It was the same with Elisha. Except for the praise he heaped on Harry and Ember.

"Almost like the little bastard worships them," Reece said.

"Except he's not so little, Sarge. Unless you think a bull moose is little."

Reece snorted.

"Let's get downtown and question the others. The school resource people can handle the real young ones."

Reece decided to tackle Jearlene first. He entered Interrogation Room One, followed by GJ, and the two sat opposite the forty-ish woman.

He began, "We'd like to ask you a few questions about the murder of Reverend Humphrey."

"I didn't know the man."

"Perhaps. But you might know something and not realize you know it."

"That may be, Sergeant. But I am not going to talk to you."

"Look, Ms. Reston, Jearlene," GJ began.

All Jerri Reston did was make the zipper motion across her mouth, fold her arms across her chest, and sat back in the chair.

Reece pursed his lips, making the corona jut out of the corner of his mouth, shook his head, and told the officer on guard to take her to a cell.

He stepped out of the room, looked up and down the hall, stepped back in, and told GJ to find Raylene Reston and coffee.

While GJ was gone, Reece kept shifting his eyes to the door. Any minute now he expected that smarmy Lauderbach to show up. And then it would be over. He might as well release the whole lot of them.

And he'd be back at square one.

29

THURSDAY, JANUARY 8, 3:27 PM

GJ BROUGHT Raylene Reston into the interrogation room and sat her in the chair opposite Reece, and sat herself in the chair next to him. She set a mug of coffee in front of her boss, one in front of Raylene, and kept one for herself.

"Why am I here?" Raylene asked. She pushed the coffee away, and GJ took it.

She's exquisitely beautiful, Reece thought. *That dark honey-blonde hair. Skin like porcelain. And the grace of a ballet dancer.*

"We have a few questions for you," GJ answered.

"About what?"

"Let us ask them and then you'll know," GJ replied.

"Tell us what you know about Reverend Humphrey's murder," Reece said.

Raylene leaned forward, put one hand by her mouth, like she was telling a secret, and whispered, "He was a sodomite, and God hates sodomites."

"So God destroyed him?" Reece asked.

Raylene slowly nodded her head. Her eyes large. The pupils almost swallowed up the irises.

Then she added in a whisper, "Just like Sodom and Gomorrah."

"Were you there when Reverend Humphrey was killed?" Reece asked.

She slowly shook her head.

"Do you know who was?"

She slowly nodded.

"Who?" GJ asked.

"God."

GJ buried her face in the palm of her hand.

Reece bit down so hard on his cigar, the end fell into his lap. He took the wad out of his mouth and, with the rest of the stogie, hurled the mess into a corner of the room.

He took a deep breath and slowly exhaled. "Where were you when Humphrey was murdered?"

"Home."

"Was anyone else there?" GJ asked.

"Everyone except Joetta and Oralene."

"Did you try to kill Reverend Cole?" Reece asked.

"Why would I do that? She's nice to us."

"What about Patrice Bremen? Did you kill her?"

"God did. She was a sinner. And God hates sinners."

Reece looked at GJ. "Who do we have left?"

"Lofton and Oralene. She's in Two."

"Let this one go and bring in the boy."

"Let her go?"

"Yeah. Get her outta here."

GJ left with Raylene in tow.

Reece got up and paced the room. He was sick of these Restons. Either they didn't have a clue or God did it.

Must be one busy God they have.

The problem was he knew they were guilty. And they knew he knew.

As long as they hang together, we don't have an in. We have to get one of them to spill the beans. Which one is the weakest link in the chain?

GJ brought in Lofton and sat him in the chair his sister had just occupied.

The two investigators resumed their seats.

"Hello, Lofton," Reece said.

"Hello."

"Here we are again."

When the young man said nothing, Reece continued, "What are you doing now that your brother is dead? Weren't you helping him at the church?"

Lofton, eyes down, nodded his head.

"Now that he's gone, what have you been doing?"

"Helpin' Mama."

"Doing what?"

"Whatever she wants me to do."

"Probably difficult to get a job when people think you're a killer."

Lofton raised his head, looked Reece in the eye, and lowered his head again.

"Why did your sister kill him? Was he a sinner, too? Like your father?"

"Pa was a real bad sinner and deserved to die. John-John was not Pa."

"So why did your sister kill him?"

"She didn't."

"Yeah, I know. God did. That's a load of cow dung. Last time God directly killed somebody was way back in Old Testament times. So why did Oralene kill your brother?"

Lofton raised his head. "Ask her. I didn't do it."

"For once, I believe you. I don't think you killed your brother. But you helped kill Reverend Humphrey. Didn't you?"

Lofton licked his lips. "He was a sodomite."

"So I've heard. Did that give you and your sister license to kill him?"

"God hates sodomites."

"If God hates them, shouldn't you let Him deal with them?"

"He did."

"Nah. He didn't. You did. You and Oralene."

"No, I didn't. I didn't kill him. Talk to O."

"That's your sister, Oralene. Right?"

Lofton nodded.

"We will talk to her. But you'd make it a lot easier if you'd tell us what you know."

"I didn't kill him. Talk to O."

"Okay. We will."

Reece turned to GJ. "Get him outta here. He's free to go."

GJ got up and escorted Lofton Reston out of the room.

"Talk to O," Reece muttered. "I definitely will, young man. I definitely will."

30

THURSDAY, JANUARY 8, 4:16 PM

REECE AND GJ relocated to Interrogation Room Two. Before them sat Oralene Fight.

"Well, young lady," Reece said, "seems as though everyone is telling us to talk to you. Why would that be?"

"Talk to me about what?"

"The murder of Patrice Bremen, the murder of your brother, the murder of Reverend Humphrey, the murder of Purnell Tully, and the murder of your father. That's a whole lot of killin' that your family is sayin' we should talk to you about. Why is that?"

"I have no idea, Mr. Sovern."

There was a knock on the door. The guard in the room opened the door a crack, spoke with someone, closed the door, and said to Reece, "Ms. Fight's attorney is here. Wants to speak with his client."

Reece shook his head. "Now we get nowhere. Goddamn lawyers. Get her outta here."

"You're just going to let her go?" GJ said.

"Once lawyered up, it's worthless trying to get any info out of them."

The guard opened the door, and Oralene Fight, smiling sweetly, left the room.

"I think we should've talked with her, Sarge."

"The lawyer would say we're fishing and put an end to it. I'd rather not give the bastard the satisfaction."

GJ shrugged.

"No, we have our weak link. Lofton Reston. The same as before. Possibly Raylene. But definitely Lofton. So we go to work on him. Before we do, I want to get the reports from the school resource officers. Maybe the kids spilled the beans."

———

I was not a happy camper when I found out Reece had hauled in the entire Reston family for questioning. On arrest warrants, no less. A call to Stanton told me he was in court and wasn't available. A text to Reece went unanswered.

Reece had made so much progress. I hope this isn't a sign of the return of the "bad" Reece. The Reece who freely threw Em and me in jail.

On the other hand, I'm not always going to be around, and until the Reston family deals with the skeletons in their closets, they are going to be open to never-ending trials and tribulations. And the same goes for Oralene.

If they don't deal with that monster, I swear not even God will be able to help them.

So maybe this action by Reece was the best thing for the family. A wake-up call. After all, Reece has a job to do: help keep law and order in Magnolia Bluff. Sure, he's a bit rough around the edges. Probably his Marine background. But what you see is what you get. And I'd rather deal with that kind of person than one who was dishonest right down to his soul.

I suppose the biggest reason I was ticked with Reece is that he hauled off my cook before she'd finished my dinner preparations. Yeah, I know. Petty of me. And selfish.

My phone dinged. I took it out of my pocket and looked at it. Elmore. He was ready for my job. Now the fun would begin.

31

THURSDAY, JANUARY 8, 7:18 PM

I PICKED up pizzas at Olivia's for our supper. It always amazes me how she knows what we want without my communicating the order to her. A pepperoni for me (she was surprised I didn't want anchovies); veggie for Ember; and bacon, mushroom, and black olive for Clara (who had not had pizza from Olivia's before this).

We sat in the family room. A fire was singing merrily along in the fireplace. Max and Monette were in the playpen. They'd chowed down at the chuck wagon prior to the pizza delivery. Wilbur was curled up in front of the fireplace on the hearthrug. Princess was at my feet, hoping I'd drop something for her.

I was in my wingback, Em in hers, and Clara was sitting on the loveseat nearest Ember.

"Mr. Thurgood, sir, if I may ask, do you know why the police took away Mrs. Reston?" Clara asked.

I swallowed my bite of pizza and tossed a pepperoni to Princess. Her jaws snapped shut on that as if it were her last meal. I answered Clara's question: "Reece Sovern is currently focusing on trying to solve the murder of the Reverend Adelbert Humphrey. It's my understanding he hauled the entire family in for questioning today."

"I see," Clara replied. "So she didn't do anything wrong."

Ember said, "Jerri? No, she's done nothing wrong. I imagine Reece was throwing a wide net, hoping to catch some fish. Don't you think so, dear?"

The last question was directed at me, and I nodded, as I had pizza in my mouth.

"She's such a nice woman," Clara said.

Pizza no longer in my mouth, I concurred: "Jerri's the best. A hard worker and devoted to her kids."

"So," Ember began, "do you think Reece got anywhere with any of them?"

"Depends on how fast the lawyers got there," I answered.

"I thought you said Stanton was tied up," Em said.

"I did. But Oralene may have had a lawyer, and perhaps Stanton was able to get in touch with someone to help them. I don't know."

"May I ask, sir, did someone in that family kill the minister?"

"No proof, Clara, but there is suspicion."

"Oh, dear. It's like they're cursed."

"It is." Ember's voice was laden with sadness.

"The bad one is Oralene, but we haven't been able to get anyone in the family to turn on her," I said.

Em nodded. "It's almost as if she has everyone hypnotized."

I was taken aback. But it made sense. "You know, Emmy, you might be on to something."

"Really?"

"Yes. Think about it. Lofton willingly goes to the guillotine rather than point the finger at any of his siblings. And those same siblings didn't lift a finger to save him. They were willing to let him hang, so to speak."

"That's awful, Harry. But how can she do it? It's beyond belief."

"Is it? In the brief span of six years, the National Socialists completely changed the culture of Germany. If a person is willing to be convinced, willing to be controlled, then that person is already a slave. A master simply needs to present himself. Or herself. This is especially the case with people who are not self-responsible. And especially the case with many religious people."

Ember gave me the stink eye over my last sentence, but I held up my hand and she allowed me to continue.

"In the case of the Restons, you have a family that is into snake handling, which is almost cultish in and of itself. They used religion to fleece people. So the dynamic of control was already a family dynamic. The family business, as it were. Then add in the fact they were rife with adultery and incest. The parents were cheating on each other. The father was abusing his daughters. The daughters, in turn, came to hate the father. One daughter decides to do something about it. She uses her father's charismatic religious aura of prophets, prophetesses, and speaking in tongues to turn her siblings against the father. And they kill him. They also kill his sidekick, who is having an affair with the mother, while having sex with her daughters."

Ember nodded. "Yes, I see what you mean. Add to that mess, that Oralene is the natural leader in the family. She's the one all the kids look up to. So, I guess it makes sense she'd have extraordinary control. But it just seems so, so diabolical."

"It is diabolical. She's obtained a control over the family that not even her parents enjoyed. When she says, 'God killed them,' I think she truly believes it. And has convinced her siblings to believe, actually believe, the same. All the while duping their mother."

"It's group control," Clara said.

"That's right, Clara," I replied. "Hypnosis. Propaganda. Simple repetition. Claiming to receive the word of the Lord. The means are irrelevant. The results — a group belief and solidarity — are everything."

"You'd better tell Reece," Ember said, "because this might help him break the family."

"I'll talk to him first thing in the morning."

The information might help Reece. Give him a different perspective. But if it comes to naught on the official front, I think I'll find use for it on the unofficial front. Or more accurately, Elmore will.

32

THURSDAY, JANUARY 8, 7:51 PM

REECE SAT BEHIND HIS DESK, holding a loaded triple-stack cheeseburger in his hands. GJ sat on the other side and put a french fry in her mouth. Both were studying the whiteboard, which was laden with suspects and clues.

GJ looked down at her notes, and Reece took a bite out of his burger.

"You know, Sarge, the second youngest kid, Mary Jean, she's almost ten, what she told Officer Tupelo was rather significant."

"What was that again?"

"She told Tupelo that they have to follow what Oralene says because God speaks to her."

"*They* meaning the family?"

"Yes. The family follows Oralene, or O, as they all call her, because she's God's anointed and he speaks to her."

"Doesn't Ember say the same thing?"

"Reverend Cole?"

Reece nodded.

"Yes, the rumors all say she thinks Jesus talks to her."

"She doesn't go around calling everyone a sinner."

"No, she doesn't," GJ said. "Scared the crap out of Helen, though."

Reece chuckled. "Yeah, Helen ain't talkin' to her alone anymore."

"Helen said Cole knew stuff only Helen's mother would know. Said Jesus told her."

"That's spooky. But who knows? It could be that Jesus does talk to Ember."

GJ rolled her eyes. "Yeah, right. A kook. That's what she is. And now she's latched on to Tansy Truitt."

Reece shrugged. "Ember might do *that* kid some good."

"Another Hooker for Jesus. Or Whore for the Lord."

"I think you're too harsh." Reece sucked Dr. Pepper up the straw. "What's wrong with going from a life of sin to a life of benefiting others?"

"That's assuming showing your body or having sex for money is wrong."

"You don't think prostitution or porn is wrong? That it doesn't demean women?"

"It's just sex. Is sex wrong?"

"No, sex itself is just sex. But it can be used wrong. It's like a hammer. There's a right way to use a hammer and a wrong way."

GJ doubled over in laughter.

"What? What did I say?"

"Only a guy would compare sex to a hammer."

"I thought it an accurate comparison. Look, people get urges and have to scratch the itch. But I believe God created sex as part of the whole man-woman bonding thing. When a man and a woman only scratch that itch with each other in marriage and hopefully have kids from scratching that itch —

it's what our entire civilization is built on. It's the bedrock. The family is that important."

"Wow, Sarge, that was pretty eloquent. You've been talking too much to Thurgood."

"Go on. I have not. It's how I feel."

"Okay. If you say so. Meanwhile, back with our religious psychos."

"Yes. So the kid, what's her name?"

GJ looked at her notes. "Mary Jean."

"So Mary Jean is the only one who tells us that the family has to do what Oralene says because God talks to Oralene."

"Right. None of the other kids mentioned it."

"Why?"

"They're all older? More guarded?"

Reece chewed his bite of burger and chewed on what GJ speculated. When he swallowed, he said, "We need to get one of the other kids, hopefully more, but at least one, to say Oralene told them they had to kill someone because God wanted them dead."

"That's a pretty tall order, Sarge."

"It is. But it's our job to figure out how to get it."

33

FRIDAY, JANUARY 9, 6:14 AM

I WAS PUTTING pastries and pies under the clear dome covers when a tapping at the door made me look up.

The person was Reece, so I crossed over to the door, unlocked it, let him in, and relocked it.

"What's on your mind, Reece, or do you just want to get a head start on a good cup of coffee?"

"Both. Got a minute or two?"

"Sure."

I poured us each a cup of pure Kona coffee, put a cheese Danish on a plate for Reece, two raised glazed doughnuts on one for myself, and walked to my table, where Reece was already sitting.

"Here you go, good sir," I said, giving him his coffee and pastry.

"Thanks, Harry. A little bit of heaven."

"I have a bone to pick with you."

Reece held up his hand. "I know. I know. I ruined your dinner by arresting your cook. Sorry about that. These Restons are driving me crazy."

"Yes, I was ticked. I wish you had talked to me first."

"You know, sometimes I do have to think and act on my own. That is what this city pays me to do."

"Okay. You got me there."

"And I wanted to talk to them before they lawyered up."

"Did you get anywhere?"

"No. However, one of the school resource officers did. She was told that the family has to do what Oralene says because God speaks to her."

"Really? That's interesting. Because it dovetails with an observation Ember made."

"Do tell."

"She said it's as though Oralene has the family hypnotized so they do her bidding."

"Huh. So you think she's using this God thing to brainwash her siblings into doing what she wants?"

"Seems like it."

"Well, her control might at last be starting to lose its hold."

"That would be a blessing."

Reece drank coffee. "This is really good, Harry."

"Pure Kona. From Hawaii."

"Have you had this before?"

"I have, but not often. Too expensive for most people's wallets. But for you, it's on the house."

"Can't thank you enough."

"My pleasure."

Reece chowed down the rest of his pastry and upended the cup to finish the coffee.

"Okay, gotta run. Good insight on Ember's part. I think she's on the money." Reece stood.

"Hope you get that maniac behind bars."

"Working on it. Catch you later, Harry."

I stood. We shook hands, and Reece was out the door.

I sat and drank coffee.

Interesting news. If the wall of solidarity is indeed crack-ing, I'm willing to wager the first crack is Lofton. Perhaps I should have a talk with the boy. He might tell me things he wouldn't dream of telling the police.

34

FRIDAY, JANUARY 9, 7:30 AM

THE REVEREND EMBER Cole locked the front door and started down the walk.

Even though the morning temperature was only forty-six, the weather forecast was promising a high of seventy-four.

I'll take the moped this morning. The ride will be invigorating.

She stopped for a moment and looked up at the sky. It was bright blue with only a wisp of cloud along the horizon.

This is the day the Lord hath made. Rejoice and be glad in it.

She was about to head for the garage when she noticed a fast-moving object in the sky.

"What is that?"

Her left hand went up to shade her eyes so she could get a better look.

"It's a drone. And it's heading right for me."

She reached into her handbag to get her handgun, couldn't find it, and looked up to see the drone almost upon her.

Diving to the pavement, she felt the rush of air as the

machine passed above her, and then heard it crash into the door.

Thank you, Lord. That was close.

She stood up and walked to the wreckage just as Clara opened the door.

"Oh my goodness, Reverend. What's this?"

Ember looked at the wrecked machine and watched Clara pick up a two-foot length of saw blade.

"I guess I'm still on somebody's hit list, Clara. That's what this is."

———

The squad car pulled into the driveway, followed by a big black SUV. Sergeant Andrew LaPorte and Officer Logan Ytzen stepped out of the squad moments ahead of Reece and GJ exiting the SUV.

Ember was sitting on a lawn chair and stood as the police approached her.

LaPorte directed Ytzen to check out behind the mansion. He then asked Ember the direction from which the drone approached her.

He nodded when she told him and slowly walked in that direction.

GJ ignored Ember and walked past to examine the drone.

Reece stood before her and said, "Another attempt."

"Given the piece of saw blade on the front of that thing, I'm going to say yes."

"Didn't see anybody around, did you?"

"No one obvious. The operator must've been hidden and quite a ways off."

"Easy to do. Even for us ordinary folk these days."

"I just can't figure out who has it in for me."

"If it's the same person, they changed weapons. Which is a bit unusual in and of itself."

"How so?"

"Criminals are creatures of habit. They rarely deviate from their modus operandi. If they use guns, they always use guns. If they like baseball bats, they always use baseball bats. But with you, we have a drive-by and now a drone. Not that I want another attack, but if there is one, I wonder what he or she will choose to use."

"I hope we don't find out."

"Ditto, Reverend, ditto."

Sergeant LaPorte returned. "Didn't notice anything out that way. Of course, using a drone, they could have been anywhere."

Officer Ytzen rounded the corner of the house. "Nothing suspicious," he shouted.

GJ finished her examination of the wreckage and joined the group. "Pricey drone. At least four or five grand. Seventy-pound lift and a top speed of eighty."

"Eighty?" Reece said.

"Yep. It's a high-end model."

"How about you and Logan load that wreck into the back of the SUV so we can get it to Forensics."

GJ intercepted Officer Ytzen, and the two hauled the drone to the vehicle.

"Well, Reece, this is all yours. Logan and I will get out of your hair."

"Catch you later, Andrew."

Sergeant LaPorte marched over to his squad and got in.

"So now what, Reece?" Ember asked.

"Write a statement and drop it off at the station. And be careful."

GJ returned with a whisk broom and a plastic bag. She swept up the tiny bits of debris in front of the door and then took pictures of the damage done to the door.

When she was done, she said, "Nice to know your steel-core door could stop the thing."

"I guess that's good to know," Ember replied.

"Do you mind my asking," GJ began, "do you have transparent aluminum windows on your ground floor?"

"Why do you ask?"

"Curious more than anything."

"Yes, that's what we have. Harry wants us to be safe."

"Wow. He must be fabulously wealthy, because those things aren't cheap."

"He has money. How much, I have no idea."

"Doesn't that bother you?"

Reece cut in. "C'mon, GJ, we need to be going. Catch you later, Ember. And stay vigilant."

"I will, Reece. But even if I'm not, Jesus is always vigilant."

"For the sake of the little ones, I'm glad," he said.

Ember watched him and GJ get into their vehicle and drive away.

She looked at her watch. *That shot an hour. Now let's get to the church and, Lord, I'd appreciate a much less exciting rest of the day. Amen.*

35

FRIDAY, JANUARY 9, 7:51 AM

JUST GOT a text from Em telling me someone tried to take her out with a drone.

I told her I was on my way home. She told me not to bother. The police were on their way, and she was all right.

And as I was making for the kitchen to get my car, which was parked in the alley, she texted:

> And I mean it, Mister. Don't come home. I'm all right.

What could I do? I texted back a kissy emoticon.

So instead of driving home, I poured myself another cup of Kona coffee, splashed in a little cream, and grabbed three doughnuts.

One of these days, my metabolism will suddenly slow down, and overnight I'll have the physique of Santa Claus.

However, until that time comes, I'll enjoy my doughnuts.

But how to protect Em? That's the actual issue at hand. First, someone tries to gun her down and fails to kill her. The second attempt is with a kamikaze drone. And that attempt also fails.

The question is, who is behind these attempts? Is this Oralene making good on her threat? If so, then that means she's changing her weapon of choice just for us. Well, just for Em. And if that's the case, why? That's not SOP for criminals. Variety is not usually their gig.

Curious. Very curious.

Elmore arrives today. Once he sets up surveillance on Oralene and her family, then the answers should start rolling in.

And I can't wait to get those answers.

———

Scarlett Hayden was furious.

"Five thousand dollars down the toilet. It's like the hussy leads a charmed life."

Her mammoth Land Rover pulled into the driveway. She parked in front of the front door of her home.

"At least the cops shouldn't be able to trace it to me."

She'd paid cash for the drone in Denver, so there'd be no credit card statement. And so there'd be no transit record, she paid cash for a used car in Denver and then sold it in Waco. She used Uber to bring her home.

"And all of that for nothing."

Getting out of her car, she flipped the bird to the universe, stormed into the house, kicking the door shut behind her.

She marched to the living room, threw her purse onto a chair, stripped out of the black jumpsuit, and at the portable bar made herself a martini.

Downing half the glass in one swallow, she moved to her bedroom, glass in hand, where she put on a transparent white ankle-length negligee, and returned to the living room.

She sprawled out on the sofa and sipped her drink.

It was obvious she'd have to change her tactics.

"The long-distance approach just isn't working."

She put the glass to her lips and let gin wash over her tongue and slide down her throat.

"I guess I'm just going to have to risk getting up close and personal."

She finished her drink in one long swallow.

"Nothing ventured, nothing gained. And what is the risk? Nothing. Except a little added excitement to the game."

36

FRIDAY, JANUARY 9, 9:03 AM

THE NINERS WERE right on time. Graham Huston and Tommy Jager pulled out chairs for Magnolia Nadine Roane and Caroline McCluskey. Reverend Billy Bob Baskin poured coffee for everyone. Terall Whitacre and Ember were chatting and drinking coffee.

Estrelita and I deposited two large plates of doughnuts, kolaches, Danish, and cinnamon rolls on the tables.

I sat next to Ember.

"Okay, Tommy, spill the beans," Graham said. "What's going on?"

Pointing his cheese Danish in Ember's direction, he said, "Ask that young lady."

"Ember?" Graham said. He focused on my lovely wife. "Did you have another escapade?"

She raised an eyebrow. "Escapade? No, I don't think I'd call it that. Someone, however, tried to send me to heaven before my time."

"What?" Caroline exclaimed. "Someone tried to kill you?"

"Again?" Magnolia Nadine added.

"Yes. But as you can see, the person failed."

"What did they do this time?" Graham asked.

"Tried to crash a high-speed drone into me that had a two-foot section of saw blade positioned in front of it."

"Good Lord," Terall said.

"How can you be so calm?" Magnolia Nadine asked.

"I'm not afraid of death. I am the servant of the Lord, and I am in His hands."

"You are a shining testimony of faith," Billy Bob said.

"I hope so," Ember responded.

"What do you have to say, Harry?" Graham asked.

I shrugged. "We've been lucky so far. I hope it continues to hold."

Ember shook her head. "It isn't luck, dear. It's the hand of the Lord."

"Ah, yes, of course. His sovereign destiny has protected you, because in his will you still have a mission to perform in order for his eternal plan to come to fruition."

Billy Bob laughed. "A Calvinist Methodist. Didn't think there were any in existence anymore."

Tommy said, "What are they talking about?"

"Theology," Terall answered.

Tommy rolled his eyes and took a big bite out of a cinnamon roll.

"So what exactly happened?" Graham asked, his pencil poised over his notebook.

Ember relayed the events of her morning.

"That was harrowing," Caroline said. Turning to Tommy, she asked, "Did you catch the culprit?"

He shook his head. "Nope. I'm sure they were long gone by the time we got there."

"So a crazed killer, another one, is on the loose in Magnolia Bluff," Magnolia Nadine said.

Tommy shrugged and drank coffee. "Looks like we might have two operating at the moment. One focused on Ember, and one... We're not sure what his game is."

"He's killing sinners," Billy Bob said.

"Good Lord," Caroline said. "That's all of us."

"Make that certain sinners," Tommy said.

"So which sinners is he after?" Magnolia Nadine asked.

"We're not exactly certain," Tommy said, and drained his coffee cup.

"Great." Magnolia Nadine's tone of voice dripped with disgust.

Tommy stood. "Gotta go, folks. Got a couple of killers to catch." He snatched a cinnamon roll. "Thanks, Harry." And disappeared out the door.

Within minutes, the meeting broke up.

When everyone was gone, Ember and I sat at my table.

"Well, Mister, what's the plan? I know you have one."

I smiled at that. "You mean the world to me, Emmy, so yes, I have a plan. For situations like this one, I have a special person I call. He's quiet, discreet, and efficient. And that's all you need to know."

"Are people going to die?"

"Not if I can help it."

"Good. I don't want people to die."

What I didn't tell her and won't be telling her is that Elmore makes his own decisions. And if he thinks the person needs to die, the person ends up dead.

37

TEXT FROM ELMORE. He's in town. We'll meet after dark so I can tell him what his job is.

In the meantime, he'll perform a surveillance check of our little world here.

With only one customer in the shop, I filled my pipe and ambled over to my bench that is on the Green across from the Really Good.

I got the pipe going, and Fergus sat down on the opposite end of the bench.

"Afternoon, Fergus."

"It is indeed, Mr. Thurgood."

"What have you been up to?"

Fergus laughed. "That's what God asked Satan just before He let him take everything away from Job."

"Is it now? Well, I don't mean to imply—"

"No harm done, Mr. Thurgood. It's only a story."

"Some people think it's real."

"And some people think the earth is flat, and we never walked on the moon."

"Very true."

"So what have *you* been up to?"

I laughed. "Not much." I pointed with my pipe. "Tending the store."

"That friend of yours is back."

"What friend?"

"The one who was watching Mrs. Fight and her detective."

"Huh. You saw him watching them?"

"People pay me no never mind. I'm like a ghost. I'm there, but no one sees me."

"Well, tell me this, who's trying to kill Ember?"

"Not who you think."

"Really? Who is it?"

"If your friend is any good, he'll find out."

"So it's not Oralene. That's a surprise."

"Wickedness comes from her, but not all wickedness. Be vigilant, Mr. Thurgood. I like my breakfasts."

He stood and shambled off across the Green.

The annoying thing about Fergus is that he's so darn cryptic, and when he isn't, he only gives you half of what you need or want.

So, someone else is after Ember. Doggone it. Two perps. As if one wasn't bad enough.

And that's when I heard the squeal of tires, and two shots fired.

38

I JUMPED UP, turned, and saw a car speed down West Main Street.

Standing next to her Cadillac was Mary Lou Fight, wearing a dark blue car coat and holding a gun in her hand.

I ran across the Green to her car.

"What do *you* want?" Her tone of voice was what you'd use on someone who just tracked dog crap across your ivory carpet.

"Are you all right?"

"No, thanks to you. Thank goodness I had this." She held up her small-caliber pistol. "Scared off your assassin. The coward. Just like you, Mr. Thurgood."

"Glad you're all right, Mrs. Fight."

I turned to go when a squad car pulled up and Officer Dick Schreiber stepped out.

"What happened?" he asked. "We got reports of someone shooting. Was that you, Mrs. Fight?"

"It was. I scared off that man's assassin."

"I'll be at the shop, Dick, if you need to talk to me."

"Sure thing, Mr. Thurgood."

I guess it pays to be on the Police Advisory Board. Getting a reprieve from Mary Lou Fight is something one doesn't turn down.

After checking traffic, I started across West Main when a monster Land Rover cut me off. The passenger door opened, and a voice commanded me to get in. Since I'd know that voice anywhere, I got into Scarlett Hayden's vehicle.

Before I even had my seat belt buckled, she'd given me a kiss, and started down the street.

"Afternoon, Scarlett. Cruising the neighborhood?"

"Don't be rude. I love you. The young boys are a thing of the past. That itch has been scratched."

"Glad to hear it. How's Stanton?"

"He's wonderful, Harry. Very wonderful. I just wish he was you."

"He's probably very glad he's not me. He probably prefers you to Ember any day of the week."

"What does she have that I don't? Be honest with me."

"What can I say? I like you both very much. It's just that I fell in love with her and not you."

"Pity poor old me."

"Old? You're not old. You're in your thirties."

She slammed on the brakes, which set off a flurry of horn honking, leaned over, and gave me what was probably the most passionate kiss I've ever experienced.

When she was done, she stepped on the accelerator and continued on down the street.

"What was that for?" I asked.

"You just made me feel alive. Thirties." She giggled. Giggled like a schoolgirl.

"I am so happy when I'm with you, Harry. Truly happy. I

know you have Ember and the children. But couldn't you give me an hour of your time each week? Just one hour?"

"I could, but I won't. You know that."

"Yes, unfortunately, I do."

"So where are we going?"

"Just a little drive."

"Mind if I ask you a personal question?"

"No."

"How much are you worth?"

"That's an odd question, because I know you don't care about my money."

"True. I'm just curious about how much I'm not caring."

"The resort is worth about twenty-five, thirty million. And I have around ten million in investments. The house is worth around a mil. Do I have enough money for you?"

"I'd still like you if all you had was a dollar."

"So how much money am *I* missing out on?"

"Oh, I don't know. Enough."

"Nope. Dollar signs, baby."

"Okay. Anywhere between one hundred and eight hundred million. Depends on the market."

"That's a very volatile market."

"It is."

"What kind of market?"

"Ah. My secret."

"Of course it is." She paused for a moment while turning around in the college parking lot. "What I wanted to tell you is your little wife and the mother of your children might be a bigamist."

"How so?"

"We don't know who she is. She has a story about fleeing an abusive husband and then getting sucked into the porn industry. But she never said she divorced the man. So the question naturally presents itself. Did she? Do you know?"

I have to say that was a kick in the head. Quite honestly, I'd never thought about it.

"I never asked, and she's never said."

"Be prepared. The rumor mill is saying she's a bigamist. Might be more turmoil, and there will definitely be more turmoil once Mary Lou gets wind of it. And she might have already."

"Thanks for the heads up, Scarlett."

"It's what we do for those we love."

She stopped the Land Rover in front of the Really Good.

"Take care, Harry, my love. You are so precious to me."

"I wish you well, Scarlett."

I exited the vehicle and watched her drive off.

That's all Em and I need. More crap from the past to haunt us.

39

FRIDAY, JANUARY 9, 4:32 PM

REECE SOVERN PUSHED OPEN the door of the Really Good. The bell above the door announced his entrance.

The man himself was at his table and looked up, a smile on his face.

As Reece approached, Harry stood.

"Hello, Reece. Want some coffee to go with your dessert tonight?"

"Thanks, but no thanks. I just stopped by to ask if it was true that you hired a hitman to take out Mary Lou."

"Oh, that. I wish it was true, but it's not."

Reece took a seat.

"You sure I can't get you a coffee?"

"I'm good."

Harry sat. "So that's what you stopped by to ask, if I tried to off Mary Lou?"

"Basically. Know anything about what happened?"

Harry told him what he knew.

"Didn't get the license by chance, did you?"

"No. The car looked like maybe it was a Pontiac."

"Pontiac? They stopped making those, what, fifteen years ago?"

"Something like that."

"Any idea as to model?"

"A big one. Bonneville, perhaps?"

"That would be a twenty-plus-year-old car. Well, we can do some checking and see if we come up with anything."

"Sorry I can't be more helpful. I was focused on making sure Mary Lou was all right."

"Oh, she's perfectly fine. Ornery as ever."

"I guess that's good to know."

Reece stood. "Thanks for the info. And next time? Hire a better assassin."

Harry laughed. "I'll get a union worker."

Once on the sidewalk, Reece pondered his next move. According to the young Reston girl, the family viewed Oralene as the leader because God spoke to her. Which was hogwash, but undoubtedly an effective control tool. Talking to them further was now out of the question. Lawyers were getting involved. He'd have to employ different tactics. But which ones?

He put his feet in motion and headed back to the station.

On the way, he debated who would be the target of those different tactics he wanted to employ. The weakest link appeared to be Lofton. Raylene had sounded like her sister: nobody did anything — it was God. Which probably meant she had fallen under Oralene's spell.

Samuel and Elisha denied culpability but were softer on the God part.

Maybe Harry can talk to them and get them to spill the beans.

It was definitely worth a try.

But back to Lofton. How to pry apart that weak link? That was the question.

Talking to him ain't gonna get anywhere. He already told us to talk to Oralene. And that's out of the question. She's not going to tell us anything. We need a confession or a piece of hard evidence. So how do I get either or both?

Reece walked around the back of the city hall and entered the police station. He greeted Bill Lynch, a retired officer who volunteered to man the reception desk several evenings a week, and continued on to his office.

He put his hat and coat on the coat tree by the door, sat at his desk, and studied the whiteboard.

They knew who the culprit was. Oralene was their Moriarty. And like that arch-villain, she was untouchable. At least so far. So who *was* touchable?

"Lofton's still the best bet," Reece murmured. "So how do we touch him?"

Reece leaned back in his chair and put his hands behind his head. He stayed that way for a minute or two and then sat up.

"We'll touch him psychologically. We'll put an open tail on him."

40

FRIDAY, JANUARY 9, 4:38 PM

MARY LOU FIGHT WAS FURIOUS. Someone had tried to run her down. Again! Who was it this time? Last time it was that deranged Effie Snyder. She'd spent years recuperating from that attack.

"Thank goodness my gun scared them off this time."

Who would have the audacity to try running her down again?

"Whoever it is, they are going to rue the day they were born."

She picked up her phone and dialed a number. When the voice at the other end answered, Mary Lou said, "I need you. Now."

———

Oralene was not a happy camper. Mother survived the attempt on her life.

I am thankful for Mother. She has given me and taught me so very much. But now she has become a stumbling stone. She is no longer useful. I must make other plans. It is my destiny to be great, and I must surround myself with those who will help me become great.

The question before Oralene, now that Mother was still in the picture, was who would help her achieve her destiny? Her siblings were becoming increasingly unreliable. And Lofton was now downright dangerous. A rebel. A rebel against God's anointed.

So who is there to help me in my hour of need?

After a moment, she smiled. She knew who would help her. And it would be so easy to gain his support.

———

We were busy getting ready to put the Really Good to bed for the night.

Graham had stopped in and picked up his dinner. He asked me what I knew about the attempted hit-and-run on Mary Lou. I told him; he thanked me, and left, saying he had to get the paper printed.

A little over a week into the new year and Magnolia Bluff was already racking up quite a list of murder and mayhem.

The murder of Patrice Bremen. The attempted murders of Tansy Truitt, Patrice's daughter, Ember, and Mary Lou Fight.

I don't know if the attack on me was attempted murder or just a game of cat and mouse with me being the mouse. What it showed, I think, was that Oralene was serious on making good on the threat to harm me and my family.

Yes, it is evil of me to think it, let alone say it, but I should've shot her in the alley the other night. The world would be a better place if I had. If wishes were horses...

In any event, this is shaping up to be another bloody year in quaint and scenic Magnolia Bluff.

What I don't get is Reece's preoccupation with the murder of Reverend Humphrey. As far as I'm concerned, it's high time he put that case back on the shelf and focused on our current crop of death and destruction.

I might have to make that suggestion to him. As a member of the Civilian Advisory Board.

In the meantime, I'll be conducting my own investigation. I can't sit on the sidelines. Not with someone after Em. And my talk tonight with Elmore will set the wheels in motion.

41

I ARRIVED home only to learn we had a dinner guest. Miss Tansy Truitt. From the squad car parked at the foot of the drive, I suspected something was up. Now I know it was Tansy's bodyguard, so to speak, keeping an eye on things.

Everyone was in the family room. And I do mean everyone. Ember, the kids, Clara, Tansy, Princess, and Wilbur.

Our guest was sitting by the fire with the animals. Clara was on one of the loveseats. Max was on the floor by Clara's feet playing with a toy car. Ember was holding Monette.

I scooped up Max, raising him high in the air. He squealed with joy, and I gave him a hug before setting him down so he could continue playing with his car. Then I kissed my darling wife and took my equally darling daughter into my arms and sat in my chair.

Ember performed introductions, after which I said, "Looks like you're part of the family, Tansy. Wilbur sits in no one's lap but Ember's, and there he is in yours. And Princess doesn't lay her head on anyone's leg except mine. So welcome to the family."

I was surprised to see her wipe her eyes before uttering a barely audible "Thanks."

"Tansy and I talked, and we're going to do a brief memorial service at the funeral home," Ember said.

"Mom wasn't religious, so a church funeral wouldn't be her thing."

I finished lighting my pipe. "Sounds good."

"We'll arrange it with Barron Schiff so everything's ready when the police release the body," Ember said.

"Barron will do a good job," I said to Tansy.

"Shall we eat?" Ember asked. "Jerri has everything ready for us."

We moved to the dining room, Clara staying with the children as she'd already eaten.

Ember got the food and set it on the table. A chicken pot pie, a kale and beet salad, and an apple pie.

"Must be nice to have a cook," Tansy said.

"It is helpful with both of us working outside the home," Ember said.

Having only Ember's previous descriptions of her, I was surprised at how well our guest looked. Her hair was combed. It was the color of a maduro cigar. She'd lightly applied her makeup. Her dress was a dark blue A-line with long sleeves and a paisley pattern in red, brown, and gold. Her shoes were dark blue high heels, but of a modest height. One would have no idea she was an indie pornstar by looking at her. There was actually a wholesome quality to her, even with her facial wound.

Ember said grace and then we passed the food around the table, starting with the salad, followed by the pot pie. Our guest getting first helpings.

"So how did you two meet?" Tansy asked.

"At the coffee shop," I replied. Looking at Ember, I added, "As I recall, you were my first customer."

"Could be. The shop was pretty empty back then."

"That it was. Anyway, when I saw Em, it was love at first sight. There was no doubt in my mind she was the one."

"Oh, wow. What about you, Ember?"

"Harry was, and is, very charming. He's a great conversationalist. And he is movie-star handsome. I always wanted to run my fingers through those blond locks. But I had a bad marriage and was very skittish about a romantic relationship. Plus, there was the church, and I felt I needed to maintain an image."

While Ember explained her side of our early relationship, my mind drifted back to what Scarlett had said. Was Em a bigamist? Did it matter? To me, no. To the good citizens of Magnolia Bluff, yes. Which meant we had a potential problem on our hands.

I heard Em say, "But he always thought I was worth the wait."

"Wow. That's so romantic."

"Not only is it romantic, it's true," I said. "I'd still be waiting if I had to. I'm very glad Jesus finally told her to quit procrastinating."

"Very funny, Mister. I wasn't procrastinating. I was waiting for His approval of you."

"If you say so."

Tansy laughed. "You two are funny. Not at all what I thought you'd be."

"How did you think we'd be?" I asked. Then quickly said, "Wait. Don't answer that."

Our guest laughed. "I don't know. Holier than thou. Stuck up. But you're really down to earth."

"We're just people," Ember said. "Although *I* have lightened up since we got married. I just don't feel like I have to prove anything anymore."

"I hope I can find a guy and have a relationship like yours."

There was a pause, and then she continued, "My mom wasn't a very good person. She used men. Only married them for their money. She was a wonderful mom to me, but kinda mean to everyone else. Do you think she might be in heaven?"

Ember put her fork down. "I can't answer that, Tansy. I have no idea what the state of her soul was. What I can say is this: I believe God is merciful to sinners. I don't think He wants anyone in hell. Does He give people a second chance? I don't know. What I do know is that how your mother will be remembered is now up to you. That she was a wonderful mother to you speaks volumes as to her inner character. Maybe you can write something up so Graham can put it in the paper, and that way the whole town will know."

"I'm not a good writer. Could you do it?"

"The perfect person is Monika Crow. I'll talk to her. She can interview you and then write up something fabulous."

"Really? That would be great. Thank you."

There was another pause, then, "Why are you being so nice to me?"

Ember smiled and reached out her hand to the young woman. "Because you need a friend, and I'm here to be your friend."

Tansy took Em's hand, tears streaming down her face.

My little Emmy isn't perfect. I've seen her get short with people. Even yell at one or two. Kind of like Jesus throwing the moneychangers out of the temple instead of turning the other cheek. But most of the time she is compassion incarnate. Like right now.

When their moment was over and we were all back to eating, Tansy asked, "Do you think they'll find who killed my mom?"

I said, "The police don't have any clues. Do you know something that might help?"

She shook her head. Then said, "I don't know. Maybe."

"Tell us," Ember said.

"We didn't think anything of it at first. Mom and me. After all, people were always sending us hate mail, or doing nasty things to us. Back in October, one of my high school classmates asked me out. I'm wearing a really nice dress, and when I step out of the house, he and his buddies have these big water guns filled with cow piss and they start shooting me. By the time I got back in the house, they were laughing and calling me all kinds of nasty names. I'm soaking wet, and my dress is ruined."

"That's awful," Ember said.

"Yeah. Welcome to small towns and small minds. Anyway, so when the notes started coming, we didn't pay them any attention. Just threw them away. But they kept coming. Always in purple ink. That's when Mom started getting worried."

"Didn't she go to the police?" I asked.

"Like *they'd* do something. My mom was a pariah. Me, too. No one, not even the police, wanted anything to do with either of us."

"Do you have any of the letters?" Ember asked.

"Maybe. I'd have to look. As I recall, Mom started keeping them after a while."

"How often did you get one?" I asked.

"It varied. Some weeks, just one. Others, five or six. Always, though, we got one on Sunday."

"So they weren't mailed," I said.

"No. Just put in the mailbox."

"See if you can find them," Ember said. "I'd like to take a look before you take them to the police. If that's okay."

"Sure. You're my friend. If you want, you can help me look."

"Okay. We should do it tonight. The sooner Sergeant Sovern has them, the better."

With that settled, and the main part of our meal eaten, I made coffee and we retired to the family room with pie, ice cream, and good, hot java.

The rest of the conversation was mostly girl talk. Which was fine. It gave me time to consider what Tansy had said. The killer had toyed with them, sending them notes for weeks. I suppose with the idea of building up fear and dread in the targeted victims.

Purple ink isn't overly common. You can get it for fountain pens, but who writes with fountain pens these days? I do. But that just means I'm part of the odd one percent.

The real question that needs to be asked is, does Oralene or any of the Restons write with a fountain pen?

That's a question I need to ask Jearlene.

42

FRIDAY, JANUARY 9, 10:09 PM

"So what do you think?" Ember asked.

Reece shrugged and repositioned his glasses. "They tell us someone had targeted Patrice Bremen. But not who."

"Maybe they do. Purple ink. Most likely from a fountain pen."

"Okay. But the handwriting... Obviously several hands were at work."

"How's that a problem? There's a gang. How many are into killing people?"

"This one."

"Right. Now, of all the people in Magnolia Bluff, what group is the most closely knit?"

"The Reston family."

"Precisely. All you have to do is get writing samples and find out if they have a bottle of purple ink."

"Easier said than done. There's a little thing called probable cause. Even Judge Jones would blink if we asked for a search warrant and only gave him speculation."

Ember stood. "Then you'll just have to get the information by some other means than a search warrant. Good night, Reece."

"Goodnight, Ember."

When Ember had left, Reece spread out on his desk the seventeen notes.

Nice paper. Very smooth. Yet, it has a bit of... What do they call it? Tooth? Yeah, tooth. Gives the nib some purchase.

Reece was surprised he remembered that. His dad had learned how to write using a steel dip pen and an inkwell. Unlike others of his generation, his dad continued to use the steel pens even after ballpoints were everywhere.

What was the shop he bought pens and ink at? Funny name, it was.

Reece woke up the computer from its nap and searched for pen stores in Texas. And there it was. Dromgoole's. Houston.

I may have to take a drive there and see what they can tell me about this ink and paper. That'll be tomorrow's project. A pleasant drive into the stinky, crime-riddled big city.

Reece couldn't help but laugh.

———

Having caught Eliška with her diary and having put the fear of God into the young maid, Oralene decided to play a trick on Mother. Because she knew from Eliška that Mother was the one behind the maid snooping in her things.

Oralene decided to write a fake diary and have the maid show that one to Mother.

"If I control the words she sees, then I have the power to manipulate her thoughts about me. Which means I will be the one controlling her. Perhaps I can even get Mother to do my bidding. If so, maybe I won't have to get rid of her."

———

Eliška knocked on her employer's bedroom door.

"Come in."

The maid entered.

"Any new entries?" Mary Lou asked.

"Yes, ma'am. I have copies." She handed the photocopies to Mary Lou.

"You're sure she doesn't know her diary has been found."

"Yes, ma'am. She doesn't know. I've been very careful." Eliška feared Mary Lou. But she was terrified of Oralene. Lying to Mary Lou would get her fired. Disobeying Oralene would get her dead.

"Very good. You may go."

Eliška curtsied, turned and left. Walking back to her room, she thought, and not for the first time, that the smart thing to do would be to buy a bus ticket and leave town.

———

Even though the air was quite chilly, I took Ember's electric moped and rode it to the church. From there, I walked to the Really Good and ascended the stairs to my old digs above the shop.

In my home away from home, I'll smoke my pipe, have a Corpse Reviver No. 1, and wait until it's time to meet Elmore.

43

SATURDAY, JANUARY 10, 2:00 AM

I'M SITTING on a bench in the park by the reservoir. The half-moon is floating among the millions of stars. Its light occasionally obscured by a scudding cloud.

The night air is chilly. The light breeze coming in off the water wafts the smoke from my pipe off to somewhere behind me. In spite of the wind, the water looks calm.

A dark shape slides onto the opposite end of the bench. My fingers tighten their grip on my revolver. A little snub-nosed S & W .38 caliber.

From where I'm sitting, the shape on the end of the bench could end up being meat if I were to pull the trigger.

I can't see the shape's face. It's obscured by a hoodie.

A voice, a man's voice, says, "The half moon is good, but the new moon is better."

I reply, "If you want to bang your shin on the furniture."

"Or conduct your affairs in private."

"Hello, Elmore."

"Hello, Harry."

I don't know his last name. He probably knows mine.

"You have some work for me," he says. A statement, not a question.

"Yes. Oralene Reston, now Fight."

"I know her. Terminate?"

"Only if necessary. I want to know every movement she makes, as well as the movements of anyone doing her bidding."

"Consider it done. Report daily?"

"Yes. Our usual arrangement for services rendered?"

"That works."

"Thank you."

"My pleasure."

The dark shape vanishes into the night. I've never seen Elmore's face. Safer that way. You can't tell what you don't know.

———

Oralene crept out of her bedroom. She was thankful she didn't have to tiptoe past Mother Fight's door. The one she wanted was across the hall and one room before Mother's.

She carefully crossed the dark hall until she reached the opposite wall. With her back against the wall, she edged towards the chosen door.

The wallpaper's slight texture rubbed against the palms of her hands. The carpet was soft on her bare feet.

She reached the door. The wood was cool to the touch. The grain, barely discernible to her fingertips.

Oralene prayed the door wasn't locked.

Her fingers grasped the knob and turned. The knob rotated, and with a slight push, she opened the door.

Oralene slipped into the room, and closed and locked the door behind her.

He was lying on his back. Visible in the nightlight's orange glow. His breathing was softly audible.

She opened the curtains, and moonlight fell onto the bed.

He stirred. Then came his voice. "What the devil?"

"It's me, Father, Oralene. Your daughter."

"What? Why are you here?" He sat up. "Is something wrong? Are you sick?"

"No, Father. Nothing's wrong. Everything will be all right. I've seen you looking at me. So I've come to satisfy you."

"Looking at you? Satisfy me? What the devil are you talking about?"

Oralene opened her robe and let it fall to the floor.

She was naked.

"I'm here for you, Father. It's what daughters do for their fathers."

44

SATURDAY, JANUARY 10, 9:36 AM

REECE DIDN'T LIKE city driving, so he let GJ drive the big, black unmarked SUV.

They left Magnolia Bluff early. Six o'clock early. Reece had brought along a thermos of coffee and four fried egg sandwiches for their breakfast. Coffee and sandwiches made by his darling wife, Hetta.

Their ETA at the pen shop in Houston was nine-thirty. A three-and-a-half-hour drive.

"You sure this is worth it?" GJ asked. "I mean, what can they tell us? It's paper and ink."

Reece explained the nuances of paper and ink. "Every paper is unique. We don't realize it because there's so much paper around we never think about it. The same with ink. They aren't all the same. Each ink is made to a different formula. Again, we never think about it because pens are everywhere. Think about it. Do *you* ever give two thoughts about the paper or pens you use?"

"No. They're just pens. And paper is paper."

"Right. But they aren't just pens. And it isn't just paper.

So we have notes written with liquid ink. Ink that was in daily use a hundred years ago. Long before ballpoints and gel pens. But it's ink that is used very little today. And then there's the paper. Even I can tell that those notes weren't written on a notepad purchased at Walmart."

"You are so smart, Sarge. They should've made you captain."

"Very funny. The city doesn't have enough money to make the job at all enticing. Besides, I wouldn't have you for a partner."

"Aw, shucks, Sarge. Thanks. I still think you'd make a great captain, though."

"I'm happy where I'm at."

"And I'm glad, because I like working with you."

"We make a good team."

"Yes, we do. So once we get the scoop on the ink and paper, then what?"

"Don't know. Depends on how big the scoop is."

GJ laughed. "Good one, Sarge. Hopefully, it's a really big scoop."

"Hopefully."

The conversation left the case behind and drifted to such topics as basketball, and if the Bulldogs had a chance at the state championship; the best 9mm round to stop a perp; and if they could stop at the art museum gift shop so GJ could get something for Burdette's birthday, she being the wife of GJ's cousin, Waymon.

And somewhere on the drive between Austin and Houston, Reece dozed off.

He was standing on the shore of a burbling stream, fishing rod in hand, when GJ's voice made the pastoral scene vanish.

"We're here, Sarge."

Reece pushed his fingers up under his glasses and rubbed his eyes.

"I was fishing," he said.

"I've never seen you fish."

"That's because our quiet little town keeps us hopping."

"Maybe someday you could show me how to fish."

Reece gave her a squinted sideways look, and said, "Maybe."

He opened the car door. "Let's go find out about paper and ink."

They exited the vehicle and entered the store.

Reece let his eyes roam the displays and racks of pens, ink, and paper.

A young man asked if he could help them.

"I'm Sergeant Investigator Sovern and this is Investigator Riggins. We're with the Magnolia Bluff Police Department."

They showed the clerk their IDs.

The young man glanced at the IDs and repeated his question.

Reece got out one of the notes. "You can help us by telling us about the ink and the paper."

The fellow took the sheet and studied it for a few moments, then walked over to a rack of tablets and ran his fingers over the samples.

"I just wanted to be sure," he said. "The paper is Rhodia."

"And what's Rhodia?" Reece asked.

"It's a French paper. Fairly popular. Good with a wide variety of inks and nibs."

"Is it expensive?" GJ asked.

"Fifteen dollars for seventy sheets. There are more expensive papers, and a whole lot more that are cheaper. I think it's a very good paper for the price."

"What about the ink?" Reece asked.

"That's more difficult. The nib looks to be a fine point, and that can alter the look of the ink, say, compared to a broad nib. I assume I can't keep this for a while."

"You assumed correctly. It's evidence," Reece said. He looked around, spotted a counter, and walked over to it. He laid out several more notes.

"Okay," Reece began, "don't touch. What do you think?"

"Whoever wrote those is sick."

"You get an A for stating the obvious. What about the color?"

"Whoever wrote those used the same ink for all the notes." He shrugged. "There are lots of purple inks."

"Really?" GJ said.

"We carry dozens."

"Wow," GJ said. "Can't imagine using purple ink."

The young man shrugged. "Some people like to be different. We sell lots of greens, browns, reds, even pink and orange."

"Pink ink?" GJ snorted a laugh.

The clerk smiled. "As I said, people like to be different."

"I guess," Reece said. "So no guesses on the brand of this ink?"

The young man looked around, called out, "Hey, Lily," and waved over a young woman.

She joined them and said, "What's up?"

"What ink is this?"

"At first guess, Poussiere De Lune."

"Yeah, kinda what I thought. Thanks."

"That person," she pointed to the notes, "is sick."

"Yeah, we know. Thanks, Lil." He turned to Reece. "Without comparing this to each of the purples we carry, Poussiere De Lune is our best guess."

Reece thanked him, collected all the notes, and turned to leave.

"Hey, Sarge. Why don't we buy a bottle and try it ourselves?"

"Sure, why not? What cheap fine-point pens do you have?"

"A Platinum Preppy for six bucks is the cheapest we have."

"I'll take one, a small bottle of the ink, and a pad of that paper."

"The pen uses a cartridge. You'll need an empty cartridge and a syringe."

"You have that?"

"Sure."

"Okay. Those too."

A few minutes later, they were back in the SUV.

"So now what, Sarge?"

"We start asking everyone on our list if they write with that Frenchy ink."

"That'll take…"

"Until hell freezes over."

45

SATURDAY, JANUARY 10, 5:08 PM

"WHAT THE HELL, Sergeant? You take a police vehicle into Houston so you can have some store clerk manhandle evidence?" Captain Davis Briggs yelled.

"I was pursuing more evidence regarding those notes."

"Right. Some ink called Pussy Da Loon and some fancy paper called Rodeo. And what did you find out?"

Before Reece could answer, Briggs raised his hand. "Wait a minute. Something this cockeyed... I'm smelling Thurgood and the little saint. Am I right?"

Briggs got up, walked around his desk, and stood towering over the seated Reece Sovern. "It was them. Wasn't it?" He walked behind Reece and stood on the other side. "Don't even answer. Because I *know* you've been talking to them."

The captain walked back behind his desk. "They're trouble, Sergeant. Trouble with a capital T. They conned you into wasting a whole day chasing down goddamn paper and ink. For Christ's sake, Sovern, what the hell is wrong with you?

When I was a detective, I detected. I collected evidence, studied it, and made arrests."

Briggs sat, then stood, leaned over his desk, hands planted on the desktop, and bellowed, "I want arrests. Get your ass out there and start making arrests. And leave Mr. Coffee and the Saint out of it. They're trouble. You hear? *Trouble.*"

He sat. "Get the hell outta here and get me some arrests."

"Yes, sir," Reece said, and beat feet back to his office, where GJ was drawing intricate patterns in purple ink.

Reece closed the door and went to his desk.

"Wow, Sarge. I could hear almost every word."

Reece sat. "Yeah. I needed earplugs. My ears are shell-shocked."

"It's not right. We're doing police work. The more we understand about the notes, the more we understand about the Bremen woman's killer."

"You know that. I know that. Even Briggs knows that. He's just pissed Harry and Ember are involved."

"He is kind of funny. Mr. Coffee and the Saint."

"I suppose. Not in the mood at the moment to appreciate the humor."

"Sorry, Sarge."

"Not your fault. So what do you think? And I like your doodle."

"Thanks."

Reece noticed a bit of color creep into GJ's cheeks.

"I'm not a forensics geek, but I think the perp used this ink, or one very similar, and this paper, and this pen, or one very much like it."

"I doubt we could track sales."

"You're right. This stuff is all over the place. I looked online, and the killer could've gotten these things anywhere."

"What we need is access to bank and credit card statements."

"We'd need a warrant for that, and who are we searching? There are too many suspects."

"Yeah. You're right. It's the perfect cover, isn't it? Too many suspects masking the real culprit."

"Pretty solid."

Reece pushed his glasses back to the top of his nose. "Still, we now know what ink, paper, and pen the perp used. We'll file that away. Nothing may come of it. And then again, everything may come of it."

46

I QUIETLY CREPT around the corner of the house. The night vision goggles showed my yard and the house in shades of green and black. In my hands was a twenty-gauge shotgun.

There, by the window, I spotted movement. In a moment, in the green night vision world my goggles presented me, I saw a figure turn and start walking away from the house.

I pumped a shotshell into the chamber and yelled, "Freeze!"

Of course the jerk started running. I took aim and squeezed the trigger.

The roar of the shotgun was loud in the stillness of the night. The screams of the person I had just shot made the shotgun sound like a whisper.

I walked to where he'd fallen. He rolled over and, before he could make any other movements, I put the muzzle of the shotgun on his sternum and pushed him flat against the ground.

"Those rubber pellets don't tickle, do they? You're going to have trouble walking for a few days."

"Go to hell, you bastard," he ground out between gritted teeth.

"Who are you working for?"

"Nobody."

"Nobody, huh? Why do I find that difficult to believe?"

"I don't know. Why do you?"

"Because I have never seen you before. And if we don't know each other, it means someone hired you. So who was it? And why?" I pressed the muzzle of the shotgun into his chest until I heard him grunt.

"If I pulled the trigger now, the rubber pellets would blow a hole in you the size of a dinner plate."

"You're no killer."

"And how do you know that?"

"I can tell."

"Can you now? Well, I can tell you know next to nothing about me. So, I'm going to ask you again, who are you working for? And just so you are aware, I have five acres here and a shovel. No one will ever find you. Well, I should say, no one will ever find your body."

I took my knife out of its sheath, which was on my belt. "See this knife? You sure you don't want to talk?"

At that point, he grabbed for the shotgun. And I gave him quite a nasty cut on his left arm. He cursed. But he did stop fighting.

"So you want to play rough, eh?" I backed away. He wasn't going anywhere soon. Not with his legs messed up from the rubber pellets. I put the knife away, got out my phone, and called Reece Sovern.

———

"Jesus Christ, Harry, what did you do to the guy?" Reece asked.

"I stopped an intruder on my property, and then defended myself when he attacked me."

"Stopped him?" GJ said. "Looks to me like you shot him from behind."

"It was dark," I said.

She thrust her chin at the goggles hanging around my neck. "Aren't those night vision goggles?"

"Yes, they are."

"Then you could see he was running away."

"Only if I were wearing them."

"C'mon, Thurgood," she said, hands on hips, "you expect me to believe you have night vision goggles and weren't using them?"

I shrugged.

GJ stepped over to the wounded trespasser. In a moment she came back. "He says you were wearing them."

"My word against his."

"Oh, for God's sake." She bowed her head and slowly shook it.

The ambulance pulled into the drive.

"So what's his name?" I asked.

Reece said, "Jasper Tillaway. Private dick from Dallas."

"If you find out who hired him, let me know."

"Maybe," Reece said.

"Maybe? What gives?"

GJ got in my face. "Don't want any vigilantism. That's what gives."

"You need a breath mint, Investigator."

"Go to hell, Thurgood." She stepped back and stood next to Reece.

"On a different note," Reece began, "he was apparently planting some kind of surveillance device outside your window there."

"Figures. I'm guessing Mary Lou hired him. If so, this would make the third PI she's hired."

"She's determined," Reece said.

"Like a pit bull," I added.

"I wouldn't insult the pit bull," he said.

"Gotta point there."

"You going to press charges?" he asked.

I watched the ambulance crew haul away Jasper Tillaway.

"Not at this time," I answered.

"Okay, then, I guess we're done here. C'mon, GJ, let's call it a night."

"Hope you have a calm rest of the evening," I said.

"I'll try to," Reece said. "Same to you."

GJ was probably flipping me the bird in her mind.

The surveillance system was good. Caught the guy the moment he stepped foot onto the property. Nevertheless, I'll check out the house in the morning to make sure no other presents were dropped off.

The main target is Oralene. Mary Lou is second string. Now, to update Elmore. Because it may be that Oralene hired this joker and not Mary Lou.

47

SUNDAY, JANUARY 11, 11:11 AM

I ALWAYS SIT on the last pew on the right. It just doesn't seem kosher that I sit up front with the faithful, because most days I'm hard pressed to admit categorically that there is a god. It's not that I don't believe. In fact, I'd very much like to believe. I think faith can provide a comfort to the soul that no godless philosophy can.

Nevertheless, I can't bring myself to set aside my disbelief. And so on most days I'm an agnostic.

This morning we were standing and singing the hymn "Be Thou My Vision."

I happened to notice Mary Lou Fight staring at me while we were singing the following lines:

> *Riches I heed not, nor man's empty praise,*
> *Thou mine inheritance, now and always:*
> *Thou and Thou only, first in my heart,*
> *High King of Heaven, my Treasure Thou art.*

It's somewhat difficult to smile while singing, but I did my best.

That she, Gunter, and Oralene were in the back of the church was a surprise. They almost always sit in the front. I guess Mary Lou felt I needed the evil eye more than Ember this morning.

My darling wife's sermon was on loving your neighbor as yourself. It was a good reminder as to how we need to trust each other if we want peace and tranquility this side of the pearly gates. I hope Mary Lou and Oralene were paying attention.

When the service was over, I joined Ember at the door to greet people as they left. The third family we greeted was the Fights.

Because other people were present, they were the epitome of Texas grace and culture. But I'm not from Texas.

I said, "Last night I had a talk with your friend, Tillaway. He was leaving gifts outside my windows. I didn't like them and will be returning them."

"I'm sure I have no idea what you're talking about," was Mary Lou's response.

I said, "*Au contraire. Vous savez de quoi je parle, vous ou Mademoiselle Fight.*"

Mary Lou's face revealed nothing. Nor did her words: "*Non, ce n'est pas le cas. Et même si c'etait le cas, je ne vous le dirais pas.*"

When everyone was gone, Ember asked me what Mary Lou and I said to each other.

"I said that she or Miss Fight did in fact know what I was talking about. She said, no she didn't, and even if she did, she wouldn't tell me."

"You're sure one of them sent that private detective?"

"Ninety-five percent sure. I can think of no one else who would hire a PI to spy on us. Besides, Mary Lou was too unemotional in her denial, and her response was childish. She hired that joker. Now that he's out of commission, she'll have to find someone else to spy on us."

"I hope she gives up. This hatred must be terribly taxing. A constant drain on her energy."

"I don't know. Maybe it energizes her."

"That's a scary thought."

"Yes, it is."

"Enough of Mary Lou. I want to get out of this robe and get something to eat."

"Any place in particular?"

"That noodle place in Austin."

"You get out of that robe and I'll let Clara know where we're going."

When Em was out of sight, I read the text from Elmore. It brought a smile to my lips. He'd placed tracking devices on all of the Fight's vehicles while they were at church.

Where, oh where, has Oralene gone? Oh, where, oh where, can she be? Now we'll know.

48

SUNDAY, JANUARY 11, 12:12 PM

GRAHAM HUSTON HAD FOLLOWED Jearlene Reston from her home to the First Baptist Church and waited patiently outside until the service was over. Graham diligently watched the people file out of the building, talking, shaking hands with Pastor Chris Hayes and his wife, Rhoda, and head for their cars.

At last his patience was rewarded. Jearlene and her children filed out of the church, she in the lead and Raylene bringing up the rear of the column.

Just like a military formation, Graham thought.

When the family was on the sidewalk and headed home, Graham broke into a trot until he was even with Jearlene, and then matched her stride.

She glanced at him and smiled.

He smiled back and said, "Hello, Mrs. Reston, I'm Graham Huston, editor of the *Magnolia Bluff Chronicle*.

"I know who you are, Mr. Huston, and I also know you are looking for a connection between my family and the murders."

Graham held up his hands. "Guilty as charged."

"Ask your questions. I'd rather you left me and my children alone, but I know you won't. So ask your questions. And once you do, I don't want you botherin' me and mine again."

He opened his mouth and then closed it. *This is a job for Monika. Woman to woman. A human interest piece,* he told himself.

To Jearlene, he said, "I'd like you to talk with Monika Crow. Tell your side of the story. Let the people of Magnolia Bluff get to know you. The real you. What do you say?"

"I don't want me and mine in her gossip column."

"No. Of course not. This would be a regular article. A human-interest story. Will you talk to her? Let her interview you? Maybe take a family photo?"

"You send her and I'll see."

"Deal. You'll like her. Monika's a fun person to be around. Thanks, Mrs. Reston."

Graham stepped aside and watched the squad of Restons troop past him.

Lofton gave him a glance and then quickly turned away. Samuel and Elisha ignored him. The five younger children looked at him with curiosity written all over their faces. And finally there was eighteen-year-old Raylene. Her dark honey blonde hair was curled and swirled around her face like a cloud. She caught his eye, and Graham thought to himself, *There's a man-eater if I ever saw one.*

After Raylene had passed by, he watched them troop down the sidewalk.

Hopefully, Jearlene will be more open to talking to a woman than a man. Who knows? Maybe we'll get a gem that will bust these cases wide open.

He turned to head back uptown and almost ran into Officer Dick Schreiber.

They both said, "Excuse me," and Graham watched the police officer follow the Reston family.

Well, I'll be… Reece is up to something. Wonder who he's put a tail on, and an open one at that?

49

SUNDAY, JANUARY 11, 12:32 PM

Reece Sovern tracked down Brandon Turner at his girlfriend's house. His truck was parked in the driveway. He didn't see Joyce's car and hoped it was in the garage.

Getting out of his SUV, he was halfway to the door when he heard Turner's dog start barking. And a couple moments later, Turner was out the door, hands on hips.

"What do you want?" he snapped.

Reece stopped. Pushed his glasses up and shifted the emerald green lonsdale to the other side of his mouth.

"And a good afternoon to you, Turner."

"It was until you showed up."

Reece, a big smile on his face, said, "Good to know. Was wondering if you'd had any insights. You know, about the cases I asked you to think about."

"And why should I be doing your work for you?"

"Didn't ask you to do my work for me. Just asked if you had any insights. You know, coming from the big city and all, where you had to deal with murder on an hourly basis. Not like us hayseeds. Just wondering, that's all."

"Why couldn't they have kept Kraus and sent you to Austin?"

"Because he was on loan, that's why. I'm sure, coming from the big city and all, you know what the word 'loan' means."

Turner shook his head. "I was going to tell you tomorrow, but since you're here, I'll tell you now."

"Hope it's something good."

"I checked with a few people, and Joyce did as well. Most of the information was hearsay. However, Joyce was told to talk with Henrene Boseman."

"GJ and I spoke with her."

"Well, maybe you didn't ask the right questions, Sergeant Investigator."

Reece shrugged. "Maybe we didn't. What did Joyce find out?"

"According to Henrene, there's a lot of gossip pointing the finger at the Reston family. And in particular, Raylene Reston."

"Interesting. Anything in particular?"

"Perhaps you should talk with Henrene yourself."

"Okay. Thanks, Turner. Appreciate the info. I'll put in a good word for you with the guys down at the station. You know, private dicks like yourself are always in need of official help. Enjoy the rest of your day."

"Don't worry. I will. Now that you're leaving."

Reece got back in his car, pressed the starter button, backed out onto the street, drove down a block, and parked.

He pondered his and GJ's conversation with the old woman. Either she had held out on them, or the information had come to her after their talk with her.

If she, for whatever reason, had held out on them, then

going back to talk with her would probably not get them anywhere.

So who can I send to talk with her that wouldn't arouse any suspicion? Probably not a cop. She'd know a cop was coming a mile away. Who would she trust?

Suddenly, Reece smiled. He knew who to ask. He'd ask Ember.

50

SUNDAY, JANUARY 11, 2:04 PM

WE WERE TALKING love on the drive back from Austin. Specifically, how we were going to love each other up when we got home.

But when I pulled into the driveway and saw the big black SUV, I knew our afternoon of adult gameplay had just vanished.

Princess greeted us at the door, and I gave my buddy a hug. She responded by licking my face, and then led us to the family room where a cozy little domestic scene greeted us.

Graham was holding Monette in his lap with one hand, and a glass filled with some type of amber fluid in the other.

Reece was on the floor playing trucks with Maximillian.

Clara was sitting on the loveseat opposite Graham and carrying on a conversation with the men.

When the men saw us, they stood.

"Graham, Reece," I said, "good to see you. What brings you to my humble abode?"

Reece snorted, and Graham laughed.

"Well, Mr. Got Bucks," Graham said, "if this is humble, I'd like to see posh."

"Figure of speech, Graham, figure of speech," I said. "Although you could check out the Huntington."

"Notice how he didn't blink at the name 'Got Bucks'," Reece said.

I shook hands with the men, Reece gave Ember a nod, and Graham, baby and glass in arm and hand, bowed.

Wish I'd taken a picture of that.

Ember and I sat in our chairs, Clara scooped up the children and departed, and the two men sat on the loveseats. Princess curled up at my feet, and Wilbur decided to occupy Em's lap.

"So what's going on?" Ember asked.

"Seems we both want to talk about the murders," Reece said.

"Cheery subject," I responded.

"For some," Reece said, then added, "Graham has an interesting story."

"Tell us your tale," I said to Graham.

"A few nights ago, I was out walking and thinking and ended up in the cemetery. Fergus was there, and we talked. Long story short, I'm convinced Fergus believes the Reston family is behind all of the murders."

"All the ones Reece is working on," I said to clarify.

"Correct," Graham said.

"Did he say why he believes the Restons are involved?" Ember asked.

"He believes they're cursed," Graham said. "His words were 'Bred in sin. Live in sin. Die in sin.'"

"Interesting," I said. "Just an opinion, though."

"It is," Graham replied, "but I'm willing to wager he's seen or heard something that gave him that opinion."

"Good luck getting it out of him," Reece said.

"There is that," Graham conceded.

"Nevertheless, his opinion does corroborate our current line of reasoning," I said.

"True," Reece said, "but so far that's pretty much all it is: reasoning. We have very little evidence. Hard evidence. Circumstantial evidence works, but again we need something to make it concrete. Not just some theory."

"If Fergus agrees with us, then it seems to me we're on the right track," Ember said. "And we well know that Oralene controls the family."

"That control might be slipping," Reece said. "Lofton virtually gave her up. When questioned, he kept referring us to Oralene. And the one young kid, don't remember her name offhand, told the school resource officer they had to do what Oralene said because God spoke to her."

"It comes back to Oralene as the mastermind," I said.

"And what started out as cleaning house in the family has expanded to the community," Graham said.

"That's what it's looking like," Reece agreed.

"And the monster gets to hide behind Mary Lou Fight," I said.

"What if she's now controlling Mary Lou?" Ember asked.

"That's a scary thought, Rev," Graham said.

"Opinions are fine and dandy," Reece began, "but I need facts. Cold hard facts. I need a crack so I can get in there and pry things apart. Because if I can't, these cases won't be solved."

And that's when the doorbell rang. I excused myself to

answer the door, Princess tagging along. I told her to sit before I opened the door. And when I did, there, standing before me, with a small suitcase beside her, was Mary Lou's maid, Eliška.

51

SUNDAY, JANUARY 11, 2:58 PM

"PLEASE," she said, although it sounded more like "Pliz." "You help people and I need help. Please help me."

I invited her in, got her suitcase and brought that in. Princess sniffed her feet and wagged her tail. Eliška patted her head.

"We're having a little party, and you might as well join us," I told her.

Puzzlement crossed her face, but she followed Princess and me to the family room.

Eliška and I stopped in the doorway. Princess went on to lay down by my chair.

"Hey everyone," I began, "this is Eliška. Eliška, that is my wife, Ember, and that fellow over there is Graham Huston, and I believe you're acquainted with Reece Sovern. This young lady is asking for my help."

To our new guest, I said, "Why don't you have a seat by Graham and tell us why you need my help."

I returned to my chair, Graham moved over, and Eliška sat.

She was wringing her hands, and I was concerned she might bolt, so I said, "It's all right. We're all friends here. Tell me what you need help with."

The young maid took a deep breath and began. "I'm scared, and I want to leave. Will you help me leave here? You help people. You're a good man, and I need help."

"I can possibly help you," I answered. "Why are you scared?"

"I think Miss Fight will kill me. She does not trust me. I know things."

"What do you know?" I asked.

"I know what she wrote in her diary, and I gave the information to Mrs. Fight. But Miss Fight caught me putting the diary back one day, and she started a new diary of made-up things in order to fool Mrs. Fight."

"What was in her diary?" Reece asked.

"Everything. Her life in the house with Mrs. Fight. Her thoughts about her family. Her thoughts about who needed to die."

"*Needed* to die?" Ember asked.

"Yes. The people in her family and the people in Magnolia Bluff."

"She actually named names?" I asked.

"No. It was... I don't know the word. She wrote things but didn't always put the name. Sometimes she gave people different names. But it is all there in the diary. She shall purify. She wrote that over and over."

"Purify what?" Ember asked.

"Everything."

"The world?" Graham asked.

"No, not the world. Her thoughts are not that big. Not

now. Her family and this town. These are what she will purify."

"How will she purify her family and Magnolia Bluff?" I asked.

"I remember what she wrote. She wrote it many times. 'God hates sin and the doer of sin. I am the Handmaid of the Lord. His beloved. I must destroy the sinner to please Him whom I love.' That is what she wrote and wrote that is what she is doing."

"We need that diary," Reece said.

"You will not find it. She moved it after she caught me with it and I told her that Mrs. Fight made me spy on her." Her eyes met mine. "Will you help me? I do not want to die."

52

SUNDAY, JANUARY 11, 4:02 PM

"I'LL HELP YOU," I said.

"Wait. Not so fast," Reece countered. "We may need this young woman's testimony."

Eliška visibly blanched.

"But her life could be in danger," Ember said.

"We may have to give her protection," Reece said. "But we will need to know where she is at all times."

"Were you followed here?" I asked.

"I do not know. I do not think so," Eliška answered.

"Doesn't matter," I said. "Oralene probably has this house under surveillance."

Eliška nodded. "I think she does."

"Who's helping her?" Graham asked.

"I do not know. She does not use real names."

"Code names?" I asked.

Eliška nodded. "Yes. Sometimes, I think they are that. Sometimes, she uses words to describe the person."

"So the diary is in code or symbolic language," I said.

"Yes."

"Don't think it will help you much, Reece," I said, "even if you were to find it."

"Probably not," he agreed. "Nevertheless, it's evidence. I could get a warrant and tear apart the Fight house looking for it." He turned to Eliška. "What does it look like?"

"It is a book with no words inside. The pages have no printing. She writes in the book."

"What color ink?" Reece asked.

"Usually purple. Almost always purple. Sometimes blue. A light blue like the sky. Sometimes a dark green."

"What size is the book?"

"About this size." She showed us with her hands.

"That's about six by eight," Graham said. "How thick?"

She spread thumb and index finger apart.

"About an inch," Graham said.

"What color is the cover?" Reece asked.

"Black with a gold design on the top, bottom, and sides."

"Can you draw the design?" Reece asked.

When Eliška nodded, Reece handed her his notebook.

She drew the design and handed it back.

"Are you going to get a warrant to search the Fight home?" I asked.

"Might," Reece answered. "But something that small will be difficult to find."

"She hid the book in the toilet tank. Now the fake one is there. I do not know where the real one is."

Reece nodded, but from the look on his face, he was lost in thought.

I said, "We have plenty of room here, Eliška. You can stay with us until Sergeant Sovern figures out what he needs to do."

"But I want to leave Magnolia Bluff. She will kill me."

"You'll be safe here," Ember said. "No one will get to you."

"But I will be a bother."

"No, you won't," I said.

"I could have Monika create a diversion," Graham said. "She could mention in her gossip column how you left Mary Lou's employment and headed off to parts unknown."

"That would be a lie," Eliška said.

"Bah." Graham waved away her comment. "People lie all the time. Far more than they ever tell the truth."

I repeated, "You can stay here until the good sergeant decides if he needs your testimony or not. Then once this is all over, I'll see to it you can go anywhere you want."

"I have some money."

I waved her statement away. "I'll help you. You asked for my help, and I said I'd help you."

"Thank you, Mr. Thurgood."

Ember stood. "Come with me. I'll show to your room."

The two women left.

Reece came out of his brown study.

"I'll have to talk this over with Briggs and Tommy. Searching the Fight home will be a big deal as they have a lot of clout. However, if we can get our hands on that diary…"

Reece let the last sentence hang, but we understood. That diary could possibly send a killer to jail.

53

I WAS LYING on my back in bed. Ember was snuggled against me.

After Graham and Reece left and supper with the family and our guest was over, Ember and I finally got our chance to love up each other.

"You know," Ember began, "doesn't it seem strange Eliška would come to you for help?"

"In what way?"

"She's Mary Lou's maid, privy to all manner of conversations in that house, was spying on Oralene for Mary Lou, and suddenly she shows up on our doorstep because Oralene supposedly threatened her. Doesn't that seem odd? Why wouldn't she talk to Mary Lou? Tell her that she got caught and Oralene threatened her?"

"Maybe she was afraid Mary Lou would chew her out and fire her. Or that Mary Lou wouldn't believe her. Or Mary Lou couldn't protect her."

"I don't know."

"Mary Lou has to be a harsh mistress. It's her nature."

"True."

"If you were in her employ and you screwed up, what do you think she'd do?"

"Fire me and give me a bad reference."

"Exactly."

"But what if this is all a lie? That Eliška is really working for Mary Lou to spy on us?"

"I suppose that's possible. But did you get that impression from her?"

"No, I guess not. Still, why you?"

"The enemy of my enemy is my friend?"

"I guess that's one explanation."

"But you're not convinced."

"I don't know. It just seems kind of odd, that's all."

"Well, tell you what. Talk to Clara and Jerri and ask them to keep an eye on her and tell you what they think."

"Then I'd be spying on her."

"Seems to me you either trust her or you don't. And if you don't, then you need to do something to learn if your lack of trust is warranted or not."

"That makes sense. Okay. I'll trust her until she proves untrustworthy."

"Glad we got that solved."

"Me too. Now do you think you're up for a second go-round?"

"Thought you'd never ask."

———

Oralene Fight stood on the sidewalk across the street from the house of Harry Thurgood and Ember Cole. Standing next to her was her sister, Raylene.

"The sinner has taken refuge with her kind," Oralene said.

"What shall we do?"

"Bide our time. I have not received a word from the Lord."

"Okay. So we just watch her?"

"Yes. We will act when the Lord reveals His will to me."

"Okay."

"Do you know what to do about Lofton?"

"He's a sinner. He was supposed to be our scapegoat but failed to do his duty."

"Yes. All because," Oralene extended her right arm and pointed her index finger at the house across the street, "of that man's lawyer."

"Yes. He convinced our brother not to do his duty."

"Lofton is weak. And now he dares to disobey me."

"He has committed grave sin by disobeying the Handmaid of the Lord."

"Yes, he has. You know what to do?"

"Yes. I shall obey the word of the Lord given through His Handmaid."

Oralene took her sister's hand. "Good. And when the time comes, the Lord will reach out and strike down all of these sinners. The first to go to Hell will be the traitor to Mother Fight."

"And then the Jezebel and her lover and the issue of her harlotry."

"Yes. She is Mystery. Babylon the Great. The Mother of Harlots and Abominations of the Earth."

Raylene's voice took on a chant-like quality. "And he is the scarlet-colored beast, having seven heads and ten horns. The one full of names of blasphemy."

"We will save Mama from out of their sinful grasp."

"Amen and amen. I will do all that the Handmaid of the Lord requires of me, for I am faithful unto death."

"And who is the Handmaid of the Lord?"

"Thou art the Handmaid of the Lord, my sister. I will do all that thou asketh of me."

And Oralene smiled.

54

MONDAY, JANUARY 12, 7:41 AM

HAVING GOTTEN the Really Good open for business, I paid Lofton Reston a visit. Hopefully, speaking *mano a mano*, he might divulge something of value.

I rang the doorbell. When there was no answer, I pressed the button again. This time the door opened.

"Oh, hi, Mr. Thurgood," Lofton said. "Mama's not here." He screwed up his face, unscrewed it, and said, "Isn't she at your place?"

"I'm sure she is. But I'm not here to see her. I'm here to see you."

A look tantamount to fear flitted across his face.

"You've nothing to be afraid of. Have you had breakfast?"

He shook his head.

"Grab your jacket and let's get something to eat."

"Oh, um, I suppose I can do that."

"Are your brothers and sisters in school?"

"Uh, yes, sir, they are. Raylene took them; well, Samuel and Elisha went by themselves, and she isn't back yet."

"Leave her a note or text her. We won't be gone long."

"Okay." He got his phone out of his jeans pocket, typed on it, and put it back in his pocket.

"He grabbed a jacket off the hook in the entryway, stepped out of the house, shrugged into the jacket, and locked the door."

We walked down to my car and got in.

"Spoon okay?" I asked.

"Yes, sir."

"Then the Spoon it is."

I started the car, and we were off. Five minutes later, I pulled into a spot three doors down. We got out of the car, walked to the diner, and made our way to a booth in the back.

The waitress took our drink orders and left menus.

"Order whatever you want," I said.

From the look on his face, I could tell eating out was a rare treat.

When the waitress brought our coffees, she took our orders. Biscuits and gravy, ham and eggs, and hash browns for Lofton. French toast for myself.

She left, and I asked the young man if he was working.

"No, sir. I haven't found a job yet. It's been hard since John-John..." He looked as if he was going to cry and quickly lowered his head.

I said, "Since your brother passed."

He nodded.

"I can only imagine. If you need help, ask me. Okay?"

His head moved up and down. Eyes glued to the tabletop.

Our food came, and that pulled him out of his funk.

We ate in silence for several minutes before I pushed the envelope a bit.

"Why does your family protect Oralene?"

The fork with its load of hash browns stopped in mid-air.

"What do you mean?" His eyes were focused on his plate.

"She killed your father, Purnell Tully, Reverend Humphrey, your brother, and probably Patrice Bremen. She is also the one most likely behind the attacks on my wife and Patrice's daughter, Tansy. So why protect her?"

"They died at the hand of the Lord."

The fork that had been poised in mid-air finally completed its journey.

"That's a load of cow dung, and you know it. You'd be in prison now, maybe even death row, if I hadn't intervened. So I'm curious. Why protect her?"

He swallowed his food and looked me in the eye. "We're family. All we have is each other. Everyone has always been against us. So we protect each other."

"That's not entirely true. Ember and I helped your family, and continue to do so, because we know what it's like to be alone and to have no one. No one who cares. We care, Lofton. So I ask again, why protect her?"

"We're family, Mr. Thurgood. Now I better get back home." He stood. "Thank you for breakfast. I wish you hadn't asked that question."

He turned and walked out of the diner.

"Well, Harry, I think you just screwed that up royal."

55

MONDAY, JANUARY 12, 10:04 AM

I GOT BACK to the Really Good to catch the tail end of the breakfast crowd. Although "crowd" might be an exaggeration.

The Niners came and went. The gossip was minimal this morning, with not much of interest happening even for the gossipmongers.

Then, there is usually a lull until the lunch regulars start to show up around eleven-thirty.

That downtime is the perfect opportunity for me to spend a few moments on the Green with my pipe. And today was no different. I got the tobacco in my bent bulldog lit and headed across the street to my favorite bench.

I hadn't been there more than a few minutes when I got a call from Clara.

"Oh, Mr. Thurgood, I'm so glad I got you. Something awful's happened to one of Mrs. Reston's children. She's gone to hospital and asked that I call you."

"Did she say which child?"

"No, sir, she didn't."

"Okay. Thanks, Clara. Did you call Ember?"

"No, sir. I will do so as soon as our call is finished."

"Very good. Thanks, Clara."

I headed back to the Really Good, told Jack I was off to the hospital and why, cut through the kitchen to the alley, and got into my car.

Burnet Medical Center is just south of town, by the college. About ten minutes or so from the Really Good. Traffic was light, so I punched it, and the Alfa got me there in seven and a half.

Once inside the facility, I inquired if they had a record of a Reston being admitted. The receptionist told me no. I thanked her and headed for the ER waiting room.

Our hospital isn't large. Probably has a dozen beds at most. However, because of some hefty donations, it sports some top-notch equipment.

In the ER waiting area, Jearlene was sitting alone; hands clasped, head bowed. I sat next to her and waited. After a minute, her head rose.

"Hello, Mr. Thurgood. Thank you for coming."

"Don't mention it. What's going on?"

"Someone knifed my boy, Lofton."

My heart sank. "Oh, dear. How is he?"

"I don't know. I got a call from the hospital. They said he'd been attacked and was in the ER."

"I'm so sorry, Jerri." I put my arm around her and pulled her into a hug. Her sobs were soft against my shoulder.

"We're cursed, Mr. Thurgood. We're being punished for our sin. My sin."

"I don't think so."

"Oh, yes. The sins of the fathers shall be visited—"

"No. Don't you believe in Jesus?"

She pulled away from me. "Yes. With all my heart. I've sinned, but I've prayed for forgiveness. That life is behind me."

"Do you believe you are a new creation in Christ? That the old things have passed away, and all things have become new?"

After a few seconds, she uttered a slow yes.

"Then you aren't cursed."

"But so much evil has befallen my family. How do you explain that?"

"I don't have to. And you don't either. This is a mega-testing of your faith. Like with Job, God must think you are up to the challenge."

"I didn't think you were a believer."

"I'm not. But you are, and I'm just reminding you of what you believe."

"I see. Well, thank you for reminding me."

"You're welcome. Em's not here, so I'm filling in."

She smiled at that. "Please forgive me, but you two are an odd couple."

I laughed. "Perhaps. But we work, and that's all that matters."

"I suppose so." She paused, then said, "I just don't understand it. Lofton is such a sweet boy. Who would do this to him?"

What could I say? Your psycho daughter is a killer? I don't think she'd believe me. So I told her I didn't know.

We sat there.

Waiting.

Waiting for news.

And while we waited, Ember arrived. She hugged Jerri,

kissed her cheeks, told her she loved her, and was there for her.

I moved over to let Em sit next to the grieving mother, which she did, and took her hands into hers.

They started praying, and I started thinking.

Why Lofton? Why did Oralene want Lofton dead? At this rate, she was going to kill everyone in her family.

How she could do that baffled me. Then again, she was without a doubt insane.

But why Lofton? What's he done? Or not done? Whichever it is, he's earned the wrath of his sister. If only he'd talked to me. But he didn't, and here we are.

My hope now is if he pulls through he might talk. Put aside family loyalty. Tell me who attacked him. If he doesn't, I see no future for the young man. At least none here on planet earth.

56

MONDAY, JANUARY 12, 12:28 PM

EVER SINCE EM and I were first tagged for being murderers some four or five years ago, the Really Good always sees an uptick in the number of people who come through the door when there's a murder.

Not sure why that is, unless the townsfolk want to see if the newcomers did it.

So with one murder and four attempted murders, our lunch rush was almost to the point where I had to start issuing numbers.

When Graham walked through the door, I was only mildly surprised to see him. He rarely comes in for lunch, but we have that murder and the attempted murders, and the *Chronicle* is coming out tomorrow, which means he probably wants something in addition to food. Something like information.

He sat on a stool at the counter.

I got up from my table, walked behind the counter, and stood before him.

"Afternoon, Mr. Editor, what will it be?"

"Bowl of chili with a side of information."

"What makes you think I'm serving information today?"

"Because you're always serving information, but only to your special customers. And I just so happen to be one of your most special customers."

"Pretty sure of yourself there, Mister. Aren't ya?"

"Yup."

I turned to the window opening onto the kitchen and called out, "One bowl of chili, Huston-style." Then I turned back to Graham.

"Huston-style? I have my own special chili?"

"Yep. Comes with extra information."

"Ha. Very funny. So what do you know?"

"About what?"

"Attempted murder number four."

"I suppose half the town's heard about it."

"At least that."

"Sorry to disappoint you, but I don't have anything to tell you."

"Nothing? I don't believe it."

I told him about my morning. When I was done, he sat there for a moment before speaking.

"Yeah, I'd say you missed the putt on that one."

"Gee, thanks."

He lifted his hands and shrugged. "Just agreeing with your own assessment."

"I know. I feel bad about that. Instead of helping him, I made things worse."

"Can't say about that. It was all pretty bad to begin with."

"True. Have you heard if he's going to live? I assume you stopped by the hospital."

Graham nodded. "I did. Looks like he's going to make it.

The blade missed his heart, but caused a lot of damage going in. He'll definitely need physical therapy."

"He needs to get away from that family."

"Or the family needs to overthrow the tyrant."

"There is that. And at the moment it's the best solution."

"Nothing else you can tell me?"

"Nothing. You might want to catch up with Em and see if she got anything from Jerri."

"Nah. Ember respects people's privacy. She's almost as bad as a priest with things said in a confessional."

I laughed. "She'll love that comparison."

"Well, it's true. And that's very commendable. People feel safe with her. And there's something to be said for that."

"Yes, there is."

Graham's chili was up. I retrieved the bowl and set it before him.

"Anything else?" I asked.

"Regarding the chili, no. Our discussion, yes."

"Okay. What else do you want to know?"

"What do you say about this? Patrice was stabbed to death. Her daughter and Lofton Reston were attacked by a knife wielder. However, Ember and Mary Lou don't fit that picture. Ember was shot at and attacked with a drone. Someone tried to run down Mary Lou for a second time. Perhaps we're dealing with two or three killers here. What say you?"

"Well, that's somewhere I don't want to go."

"Is it plausible?"

"Of course it's plausible. Even possible. Is it likely? I don't know. I don't want it to be, but, yeah, it could be likely. What made you think this?"

"Means. I was looking at the method of killing. And if we

bring in the young John Reston, Reverend Humphrey, and Purnell Tully, we have a trend. But Ember and Mary Lou don't fit. The *modus operandi* is completely different. Which, to my mind, says it's a different perp."

I shrugged. "Makes sense, Graham. I hate to say it, but it actually makes sense. We could have three killers on the loose."

"That's what I was afraid of. Three killers and we have no idea why they're killing."

57

REECE MADE himself at home at my table.

I was so engrossed in checking out paper product suppliers I hadn't heard the bell over the door ring.

"Sure must be some interesting reading," he said.

"You bet. Never thought descriptions of paper cups could be so riveting until I got into the coffee shop biz."

He chuckled. "No, thank you."

"My sentiments exactly. So what brings you in? Coffee?"

"Sure, I'll have a cup."

And before I could signal Estrelita, she was there pouring our sergeant a cup. She asked if he wanted anything to eat, and when he said no, she left.

He took a sip of the hot joe, sighed his satisfaction, and said, "Tried to talk to the Reston kid about the attack, but he wouldn't say anything to me. He say anything to you or Ember?"

"I haven't talked to him. Em might've."

He nodded, sipped coffee, and set the cup down. "Don't know what to do with that kid. He needs to talk."

"Has your tail picked up anything?"

"Nothing of importance. The kid hardly ever leaves the house. And before you ask, Oralene wasn't there."

"So, probably one of the other family members did it. But weren't the kids in school?"

Reece got out his notebook. "According to Mrs. Reston, Raylene walked Wendolyn, Jeb, Sinclair, Mary Jean, and Jacob to school. Samuel and Elisha walked by themselves. That was confirmed by Combs at the house and the school resource officers when they all reached the school. Combs also noted when Raylene returned home."

"Then it had to have been Raylene who attacked him."

Reece held up his hand. "The kid staggers out the front door and collapses on the lawn. Combs administers first aid and calls it in. When Schreiber shows up, Kristine asks him to check out the house. He does, and no one's home. Raylene must've slipped out the back while Kristine was keeping Lofton alive."

"That's annoying."

"Not as much as Briggs. He shows up and chews her up one side and down the other. Was even going to suspend her without pay for a week."

"You're kidding. He can do that?"

"Don't know. The chief stepped in and ended that talk."

"So Schreiber answers Combs's call for backup and finds an empty house."

"Right."

"Have you talked to Raylene?"

"Helen Beauregard did. The girl said she walked to the Piggly-Wiggly to pick up a few things for dinner. And one of the checkout gals told Helen she'd checked the girl out."

"Times?"

"The timeline generally fits the picture. But not one hundred percent."

"So her alibi doesn't eliminate her."

"Correct. It's possible she stabbed him. Left him for dead. And went to the store."

"I suppose she's saying someone stabbed him while she was gone."

"Correct. I'm trying to pin her shopping trip down to an exact time. The DA may have his investigator join us."

"That's what it will take. A few eyewitnesses who can speak to the time they saw her."

Reece nodded and drank coffee.

"I think we can be pretty certain that Oralene has corrupted Raylene."

"Yep," Reece said, and finished his coffee.

He stood. "Thanks for the chat and coffee. Gotta run."

"No problem."

I watched him leave.

There has to be some way to get Lofton to talk. Because if he doesn't, she won't miss the next time.

58

MONDAY, JANUARY 12, 2:49 PM

THE TEXT from Elmore was long. The information was valuable. Yet somewhat disturbing.

The question was what do I do with it.

If I give it to Reece so he can follow up on it, he'll want to know where I got it. And I won't be able to tell him. He'll get angry and try to bully me. I don't bully. And our friendship will suffer. What's worse, he might throw me in the jug as a material witness. I have nothing against Lorraine's grub, but I'd rather eat Jerri's.

If I keep the information to myself, do I act on it or not? If I decide to act on it, how do I do that? Without breaking the law, that is.

Which means it might be best to just sit on it and do nothing.

Of course, I could have Elmore solve the problem. That would be simple and efficient. But at this stage of the game, I'd rather reserve that option as the last resort.

I got up from my table and walked back to the kitchen.

Miguel was plating an order for the only customer in the shop.

My stomach was rumbling, and it was telling me it wanted chili. I grabbed a bowl, filled it from the pot on the range, and walked back out to my table.

The first spoonful was on its way to my mouth when Telford Whitacre walked through the door. When Gunter Fight turned him and his wife down for a loan for their tobacco shop, I gave them one. We've been friends ever since.

We exchanged smiles. He walked over, sat, and plunked a baggie down on the table.

"What's that?" I asked.

"Something I want you to try."

"A new experiment?"

"Yes. As you are aware, when that big European tobacco company destroyed Sutliff, we lost the source for many of the ingredients we use to make our own blends."

I nodded.

"So I've been experimenting with raw leaf."

"And this is one of your experiments?"

"It is, and I'd like your opinion."

"Okay. What is it?"

"Rough cut burley, lightly cased with molasses, to which I added a very small amount of bright Virginia for sweetness, and then lightly topped the whole thing with licorice and maple sugar."

"Sounds like Velvet."

"That was the inspiration."

"Why not just offer Velvet?"

"I'm not supporting that big European tobacco company anymore. It's my private boycott of an insensitive, monopolistic mega-corp that doesn't care about its customers, only their dollars. And they make Velvet."

"I see. That's going to take a lot of product off your shelves."

"Yes, it is. And when customers ask why I don't carry such-and-such, I'll tell them why and suggest a replacement."

"Well, bully for you." I picked up the baggie and looked at it. "I'll give it a try and let you know."

"Great. Suggest a name while you're at it."

"Will do. I hope you come up with subs for my favorites."

"Don't worry. I'm working on it."

He stood. I did as well. We shook hands, and he left.

I sat back down, opened the baggie, and examined the tobacco.

You and I, my new friend, are going to pursue a solution to a three-pipe problem.

59

MONDAY, JANUARY 12, 3:00 PM

THE REVEREND EMBER Cole sat in the room with Jearlene Reston. Her boy, Lofton, lay asleep on the bed. He was hooked up to half a dozen different machines, drip bags, and who knew what else.

Jearlene sat next to the bed and held her boy's hand. Her eyes were closed, and her lips were moving, but barely.

Ember assumed she was praying.

Who wanted Lofton dead? And why?

That is the question, Ember told herself, *why?*

She let her mind drift over the murders and attempted murders. What was the thread they all held in common?

After a while, Ember smiled. It made sense. At least for some of the murders and attempted murders. What about the ones that didn't make sense? Or did they, and she just didn't see the connection?

Pastor John Reston. Guilty of incest and adultery.

Purnell Tully. Guilty of adultery with Jerri and fornication with her daughters.

Reverend Adelbert Humphrey. Guilty of the sin of homosexuality. Not that Ember thought it a sin, but the killer did. At least that made the most sense given the brutality of his murder.

The young Pastor John Reston. Was he guilty of sin? And if so, what sin? *I'm going to take a wild guess here,* Ember mused, *and say he was following in his father's footsteps and having sex with the young women in his church. It's the only thing that makes sense.*

Patrice Bremen. The sins of adultery and fornication.

Tansy Truitt. The sins of adultery and fornication.

Myself. Former porn star. Guilty of adultery and fornication.

Every one of the murders and half the attempted murders has to do with sex.

So how do Mary Lou Fight and Lofton fit in? Are they guilty of some manner of sexual sin? I don't know. However, there's only one way to find out. Ask them.

———

Scarlett Hayden sat in her Land Rover. She was watching the entrance to the hospital.

When is that skinny man stealer going to come out?

She glanced at the scarf folded up on the console.

The plan was simple. Ask Ember for a moment of her time. Once she was in the car, crack her on the head with the bottle of gin in the door pocket, then strangle her with the scarf, and dump her body out in the country.

Best to keep things simple. Too elaborate and something's bound to go wrong. Like that damn drone.

———

Reece Sovern pocketed his cell phone. He'd just gotten from Ember her thoughts as to the motive behind the Bremen and Humphrey murders and the attacks on her and Tansy Truitt.

Plausible, he told himself. *And if true, all I need to find is the person who is obsessed with sexual sin.*

Of all the suspects in the case, only one fits the bill. Oralene Fight.

However, Oralene wasn't present when Lofton was attacked. But Raylene was. In spite of her claim to the contrary, she had to be the one. Kristine Combs hadn't spotted anyone hanging around the house. Only Raylene had left and returned. And at some point, had left again.

Reece dug through the file folder, found the picture of Raylene, and put it in his pocket.

Maybe Tansy Truitt will recognize her.

———

Scarlett watched Ember Cole leave the hospital. She started the Land Rover and put it in drive.

A black SUV stopped in front of the hospital entrance, and when it drove away, Ember was gone.

"No!" Scarlett slammed her hand against the steering wheel. "No, no, no. It's not fair. He's mine. Why won't she die?" She shook her fist at the sky. "Stop protecting her. He's mine, and I'm going to get him. You hear me? He's *mine.*"

60

MONDAY, JANUARY 12, 3:52 PM

EMBER HAD TEXTED Tansy to let her know she and Reece Sovern would pay her a visit, and the young woman was waiting for them when they arrived.

The first thing Ember noticed when the door opened was the absence of marijuana reek.

That's a good sign, she told herself.

The young woman wore slacks and a blouse. Which was quite a change from the previous attire she'd worn when opening the door. A light floral perfume scented the air instead of the body odor that had previously greeted her.

"Hello, Tansy. This is Reece Sovern. He's the sergeant investigator on the police force."

"I know. We've met. C'mon in. The place is decent. Pretty much like when Mom was alive.

For being millionaires, the place looks like any middle-class bunga-low. Money was apparently important to Patrice, but other than her car, you'd never know she had any.

Tansy led them to the living room. When they were

seated, she said, "So what's up? You want me to look at a picture?"

"Before you do, I'd like to repeat what happened when you were attacked," Reece said.

"I already told you."

"So you did," Reece agreed. "But if you tell me again, it will put your mind back in the scene."

Tansy rolled her eyes, but complied with Reece's request.

"I ordered a pizza for delivery. Smokin' makes me hungry. When the doorbell rang, I opened the door. That's when she threw the pizza at me and charged into the house, swinging her knife. It was a big mother, too."

"The knife?" Reece asked.

Tansy nodded.

"Go on."

"When she charged me, I tripped on the rug and fell. She was on me and cut my face. I hit her in the head and managed to push her off me, got to my feet, kicked her, and ran like hell for upstairs."

"How do you know the attacker was a she?" Reece asked.

"Well, she was wearing a hoodie and had the hood over her head. But when she stormed into the house, the hoodie slipped off, and she looked like a girl. At least I think she looked like a girl."

Reece nodded, and Tansy continued.

"I was halfway up the stairs when she caught me and cut me again. I kicked back with my foot, heard a grunt, and managed to get into the bathroom. I locked the door and called nine-one-one and apparently passed out."

"Thanks," Reece said. "Now I'm going to show you a picture. I want you to tell me if you recognize the person."

"Okay."

Reece took the photograph out of his coat pocket and handed it to the young woman. She looked at it and shrugged.

"I don't know. Maybe. It all happened so fast, and I wasn't in the mood to commit her face to memory, ya know?"

"Yeah, I know. Take your time."

Ember said, "Look at the photo, then close your eyes and replay the attack in your mind."

Tansy did what Ember suggested. After a few moments, she opened her eyes and said, "Maybe. She had long hair. It might've been blonde. Dark, though, kinda like in the pic."

She handed the photo back. "Sorry. I was half-stoned and then fighting to get away."

Reese nodded, putting the picture back in his pocket.

"How tall is the person in the photo?" Tansy asked.

"Five-seven, five-eight," Reese said.

Tansy tilted her head. "A little taller than me." She thought a moment, then said, "She might've been my height."

"Your door sill is higher than the porch," Ember said. "So that means she was probably taller than you."

"I suppose," Tansy replied.

When a moment or two passed with no one saying anything. Reece stood, and Ember followed suit.

"Thanks for your time," he said.

Tansy stood. "Sorry I wasn't helpful."

"Don't worry about it," he said.

Tansy walked them to the door, everyone said good night, and Ember and Reece left.

When they were in his car, Ember said, "She's it. Isn't she?"

"Probably."

"So how are you going to get Raylene to confess?"

"That's the proverbial fly in the ointment."

61

MONDAY, JANUARY 12, 5:01 PM

THAT WAS THE QUESTION. How was he going to get Raylene to confess? And if he couldn't get her to confess willingly, how was he going to trick her into confessing?

Reece had dropped Ember off at her home and then driven back to the station. He'd called Hetta, told her he wouldn't be home for supper, and then walked over to the Silver Spoon to grab a bite to eat.

He needed time to think.

The waitress set before him the Frito pie he'd ordered, asked if he wanted anything else, and departed when he said no.

He loaded his fork and conveyed the little bit of heaven to his mouth. While he chewed, he thought about Raylene's alibi.

She'd admitted she'd returned to the house, that Lofton was there, and that she'd left the house by the back door to go to the grocery store. She'd been noncommittal about the timing. Which meant if he could get definite times when she was seen out and about, he might be able to sink her alibi.

However, if he couldn't get definite times, he was sunk. Sunk on the alibi angle, that is.

He loaded his fork and conveyed it to his mouth. While he chewed, his mind shifted to Lofton. Now, that guy was one bad-luck magnet.

The family throws the kid under the bus and leaves him to take the rap for the murders of his father and the business manager. If it hadn't been for Harry Thurgood getting his lawyer to defend the boy, he'd be in prison right now. Maybe on death row. Instead, he was walkin' the streets.

However, in a different twist of fate, it now appeared he was the target of someone's anger. And that someone had to be his sister, Oralene. After all, they all knew she was the one pulling the strings. They just couldn't prove it. No one was willing to rat her out.

Not for the first time, Reece wondered about the hold she had on her siblings and mother.

Not much he could do about that. Unless someone was willing to spill the beans.

Lofton, though, might be persuaded to do so. He was the weak link in the chain. And being the weak link, had Oralene decided he needed to be silenced, using Raylene as her instrument of execution?

From the look of things, that's where the path was heading.

————

Oralene Fight was furious. She rounded on her sister, Raylene, the pointed finger on her outstretched arm aimed directly at her heart.

"You are a bungler, Raylene. The Lord's mighty wrath is turned against you."

"I did my best, O, honest."

Oralene grabbed her by the shoulders and shook her. "Twice. You failed *twice.*"

"I'm sorry, O. Truly sorry. It won't happen again."

Oralene pushed her sister away and turned her back to her. "You aren't worthy."

"No, O. Don't say that." The young woman buried her face in her hands and sobbed.

Oralene turned around. Her eyes scanned the park. It was empty, except for someone walking their dog at the opposite end. Then, those dark orbs settled on her sister.

Pathetic. Good for nothing except turning men's heads and having them pay attention to her.

Oralene's eyes narrowed as she took in the sobbing girl. *Maybe she'd been going about this all wrong. Maybe…*

She lifted Raylene's chin. The girl dropped her hands to her sides.

"I'm sorry, O. You're the Lord's Handmaid. I'm so sorry."

"The Lord is merciful. He hates sin, but is merciful. I will intercede for you."

Raylene's eyes grew large with astonishment. "Oh, thank you, O. Thank you. I tried. Honest, I did."

"I know." She pulled the girl to her. "What of Samuel?"

"Samuel? What do you mean?" Raylene's eyes searched her sister's face.

"Is he with us? Does he fear the Lord? Or is he another worthless man?"

"Uh, I think so. I think he fears the Lord."

"Good. Convince him. Tell him he's the instrument of the Lord. He must do this."

"O-okay. How?"

"You're a woman. Use your cunning. Use your wiles."

Raylene's face was a question.

"Go in unto him as a wife. It's what all men crave and will do anything to get."

62

MONDAY, JANUARY 12, 5:10 PM

WHEN EMBER WALKED through the door after Reece had dropped her off, her nose took in an array of savory smells. And she followed her nose to the kitchen.

There she found Eliška pouring apples into a pie shell.

"What are you making? It smells heavenly."

Eliška curtsied. "A shepherd's pie is in the oven. Clara showed me how to make it. Now I make apple pie for dessert. With Mrs. Reston at hospital, I thought I would help."

"That's very kind of you. You didn't have to, you know."

"You have been very kind to me. I want to show my gratitude."

"And you are very thoughtful. Is Clara in the family room?"

"I think so."

Ember left and found Clara playing with the children in the family room.

"Ah, Reverend. You are just in time. They are starting to get fussy."

Ember picked up Maximillian. "Okay, you, the chuck wagon is here."

Clara took Max and picked up at Monette, while Ember shed her jacket and unbuttoned her blouse.

She sat, and Clara handed the twins to her. When they began to nurse, Ember sighed. The experience was almost orgasmic.

"Pardon my asking, ma'am, but how long do you plan on nursing them?"

"Not sure. Maybe I'll start weaning in the fall. What do you think?"

"Not my place to say, ma'am."

"I'm asking for your opinion."

Clara thought for a moment. "They'll be almost two. That should be a good time to introduce solid food."

"Good. That's what we'll do."

"Very good, ma'am."

"That was awfully nice of Eliška to make supper."

"She wanted to show her appreciation for what you and Mr. Thurgood did by taking her in and agreeing to help her."

"It's what we do. We help people."

"Still, it was very nice of you to do so. Not many would have."

"Jesus says to love your neighbor as yourself. It's how we show the world we love God. And in loving your neighbor, it is how we do to others as we would have them do to us. We aren't to judge people. We are to love them."

"He did say we'd know people by what they do."

"Yes, He did. But that doesn't mean we judge them. We love even those who do bad things as we love ourselves. And we do to them as we'd like them to do to us, even though we know they won't."

"Not many do that, though."

"No, they don't. But that is how we Christians need to act towards others. And in doing so, we know all things will work for the good if we love God. Because if we love God, we're the called according to *His* purpose. Not ours. I'm a Christian. I love God. I treat others as I want them to treat me."

"Mr. Thurgood, pardon me for saying so, but he doesn't strike me as a man of faith."

Ember smiled. "He doesn't think he is, but by their fruits you shall know them. And Harry has a lot of good fruit."

"Yes, he does."

Princess, who'd been curled up next to Harry's chair, jumped up, and ran out of the room.

Ember laughed. "Speak of the devil. The master has arrived."

Harry entered the family room, his dog by his side.

"Were your ears burning?" Ember asked.

He gave her a kiss. "Were you talking about me?" He sat in his chair and petted Princess, who was next to him and kept looking up at him.

"She sure adores you," Ember said. "And yes, we were talking about you. Clara and I were extolling your virtues."

"Wow. Well, thank you. The smells in here are heavenly. What are you making?"

"I'm not making anything," Ember answered. "Eliška is. A thank you for our kindness to her."

"What a surprise. I think I'll check it out."

He stood, gave each of his nursing children a kiss, and Ember another one, and left.

———

I found Eliška in the kitchen.

"Smells good in here," I said.

"Thank you, Mr. Thurgood. Everything is almost ready."

"When you can leave, do you want to go back home?"

"You mean Chechia?"

"Yes."

"It is tempting. But I would like to stay here. In the States."

"Do you know where you'd like to live?"

"I was thinking of California."

"Any particular reason why?"

"I have read that the weather is perfect in California."

"That's pretty much true for Southern California. I've been there, and the weather is the best. I didn't care for all the people, and the political scene is crap. But the weather and scenery are wonderful."

"Then I'd like to go to Southern California. The people don't bother me, and I'm not into politics. But the weather and the scenery, that I would like very much."

"I'll make arrangements as soon as possible."

"Thank you. I wouldn't mind staying here. But…"

"I understand."

She looked as though she was going to say something else but didn't. She went back to cutting cubes of cheese, putting them on a plate. I waited. Leaning against the counter, hands in my slacks pockets.

After a minute or so, she said, without looking at me, "Mrs. Fight hates you and the Reverend."

I chuckled. "Tell me something I don't know."

She looked up. "I think Miss Fight… I think Mrs. Fight is afraid of her daughter."

"Makes sense. Oralene is a whole lot scarier than Mary Lou."

"I think Miss Fight is insane."

"Won't get a disagreement out of me."

"I'm afraid, Mr. Thurgood. I'm afraid they'll find me, even in California."

I shook my head. "No, I don't think so. They live in a small world. The world beyond Magnolia Bluff? It might as well be on Pluto. You'll be fine. Once you are no longer in our little hamlet, they'll forget about you."

"Mrs. Fight has a long memory."

"No doubt. But once you are no longer here, you are no longer in her world. And if you aren't in her world, for all intents and purposes, you no longer exist."

"I hope you are right, Mr. Thurgood."

"I am. Don't you worry."

She smiled. "All right. I won't."

"When will dinner be ready?"

"It is ready now."

"I'll round everyone up."

I left the kitchen and returned to the family room.

"Grub's ready," I announced.

On my way to the dining room, I got thinking it might be a good idea to see if I could persuade Mary Lou to leave the young woman alone and let her work for me.

63

REECE SOVERN COULDN'T SLEEP. He got out of bed, threw a robe on over his pajamas, and padded downstairs to the den. Pickett, his chocolate Lab, followed.

The house was quiet, save for the gusty wind soughing around the windows.

"We're in for a storm," he said to his dog.

Pickett looked at him, lazily wagged his tail, and lay down by Reece's chair.

He continued talking to his dog. "Those cases. I feel like I'm just not seeing the thread. That one loose thread that when I pull it, the whole thing unravels and I get to put cuffs on the killer."

Reece poured himself two fingers of Dagger Texas Bourbon and put the bottle back in the cupboard. He swirled the amber fluid, held the glass to his nose, held it up to the light, then took a sip.

"Mighty fine," he said to Pickett. "Too bad we can't share a glass."

He sat in his rocker-recliner and gently rocked while

sipping his whiskey and letting his mind roam over the details of the cases.

If Oralene was behind the murders of Humphrey and Bremen, then who did the actual killing?

If Raylene knifed her brother, Lofton, was Oralene behind that? And if so, why did she want the boy dead?

Reece sipped bourbon. If the motive was sexual sin, then how did Lofton fit in? Or was there a different motive for him? And if so, what was it?

Until now, Lofton had looked to be the weak link. The one most likely to talk. Except he hadn't. Not yet, at least. Family loyalty kept his lips zipped.

Reece raised his glass to his lips and sipped the amber fluid. Raylene, however, was perhaps the one who'd prove to be the weak link. Not finishing off Lofton before going to the store just might prove to be her fatal mistake.

———

Tuesday, January 13, 12:42 am

Gunter Fight sat in his oversized office chair behind the massive solid oak custom-made desk, which was the centerpiece of his home office.

He sipped the thirty-year-old Iron River Texas Pot Still Bourbon. Small batch. Three hundred dollars a bottle.

Twenty-five years. That's how long he and Mary Lou had been married. Husband and wife till death do us part.

He stared at his glass. "Except she hasn't been a wife for the better part of twenty-three years. Twenty-three years of sleeping alone in my own bed. No warmth. No love. And during that entire time, I was faithful. Until now."

He sipped whiskey.

Oralene. He hadn't wanted the adoption. But Mary Lou insisted. And what Mary Lou wanted, Mary Lou got.

At first, he'd been indifferent. But he was a man. And Oralene was a woman. A beautiful woman. A beautiful woman who exuded vitality and sensuality. He couldn't remain a stone. She stirred in him fires he thought had died out long ago.

And then she'd shown up in his bedroom. Naked. Offering herself to him. He'd wanted to say no. His mind wanted to say no. It was morally and rationally imperative to say no.

But that young, supple flesh begged to be touched. And reason fled. Driven out by the fire raging in his loins.

He touched. Oh, God, had he touched.

And she was a devil. A wild animal.

My God. I didn't know two people could do all those things. The feelings. The ecstasy is beyond telling. There're no words.

Saturday.

Sunday.

Monday. At his office. On his desk, no less.

The clock sitting off to his left told him it was very early Tuesday morning.

"I shouldn't. This should stop. But I feel so alive. All those years. I'd forgotten. Or maybe I just forced it from my mind."

He sipped bourbon.

"I should stop. No good is going to come from this. I should end it now."

He stared at the glass of whiskey. Then downed it in a gulp.

"She's waiting. She texted. And I've been delaying."

The glass was empty. Just like his life had been.

He stood.

"This will be the last time. She'll understand why it can't continue. I'm sure she will."

Gunter Fight left his office, headed for the stairs, and his last visit to Oralene.

64

WHILE EM WAS at her morning prayers, I headed for the kitchen to make coffee.

So imagine my surprise to find Eliška preparing breakfast.

"The coffee is ready, Mr. Thurgood."

"Wow. Thank you. I appreciate it. But you're going to spoil us. We might not let you go."

She laughed and deflected. "That is a very handsome suit."

"Thank you. What are you making?"

"Eggs, bacon, hash browns, and apple-filled kolaches. They are in the oven."

I assumed she meant the pastries, because she was in the middle of frying bacon.

"Do you know when Mrs. Reston will return?"

I sat in the breakfast nook, holding a cup of coffee in my hands. "No, I don't. But I'm not going to rush her."

"You are a good man, and Pastor Cole is a good woman. I don't understand why Mrs. Fight hates you."

"I don't either. In fact, it's a mystery to both of us."

"I know a lot of things, Mr. Thurgood."

"I imagine you do."

"She is wrong to want to hurt you. I will tell you everything I know."

"Do you know why Oralene wants her brother, Lofton, dead?"

"Her journal was very difficult to understand. English is not my native language, and her sentences were difficult to understand. I don't think even Mrs. Fight always understood the meaning."

"If I'm understanding you right, she wrote about Lofton in a kind of code."

"Yes, that is it."

"So she mentioned Lofton, but you didn't understand the meaning."

"Yes. That is how it was."

"Don't worry about it. I was hoping to find out why she wants her brother dead."

With the bacon fried, she started on the hash browns. "Mrs. Fight hired private detectives to follow you and the pastor."

"Yes. I know."

"Do you know that Mrs. Duvall is a spy? A secret member of the Crimson Hat group?"

"You mean Tipper?"

"Yes."

"No. I didn't know that. I don't think Em does either."

"She meets with Mrs. Fight two or three times every month."

And while I watched her make breakfast, she told me about Mary Lou's instructions to Tipper on how to undermine Em's position as pastor.

All I can say is I am amazed at the lengths a person will go to in order to get what they want.

Em joined us as Eliška was finishing her exposé on Tipper Duvall. Her comment was, "I'm not surprised. This explains a lot of things."

When breakfast was ready, Em and I insisted Eliška join us.

"I am just a maid. I cannot."

"No, you're not," I replied. "Not in our house. You are a guest. Please do Em and me the honor of sharing our table and the food you so graciously prepared for us."

She relented, and after Em said grace, that's when our guest dropped the bombshell.

65

REECE SOVERN and GJ Riggins sat in his office and stared at the labyrinthine lines connecting the various photographs on the whiteboard.

They sipped dark, rich Columbian coffee and took bites from the humongous cinnamon rolls.

"You know, Sarge, this gives me a headache just looking at it." GJ followed her statement with a bite of cinnamon roll. After she'd chewed and swallowed, she took a drink of her coffee.

"This is really good coffee."

Reece smiled. "Yes, it is."

She set the cup down and looked her boss in the eye. "This is Thurgood's stuff, isn't it?"

"It is."

She put the cinnamon roll down and pushed the coffee away from her.

Reece frowned. "C'mon now. You just admitted the coffee was good, and the way you've been eating that cinnamon roll, that too must be good." He shook his head. "You dislike the guy so much you won't even drink a free coffee and eat a free roll? I can't believe it."

"You and I both know that guy is a crook. He has to be. Look at his lifestyle. Look at his insufficient means of support. It doesn't add up. Then there's his street walkin' pornstar wife. I betcha a dime to a doughnut there's still somethin' hidin' in her closet. No, sir. I'm *not* supporting criminals."

Reece blew out a gust of air. "Yes, the accounting doesn't add up when it comes to Thurgood. But we have no proof the guy's a crook. None. Innocent until proven guilty."

"I don't care. Thanks for thinking of me, Sarge, but I will not support his establishment. Mrs. Fight, no matter what we think about her, she's right on this one."

An enormous sigh rolled out of Reece.

"You're mad at me," GJ said, almost with a pout.

"Not mad. Peeved."

"Peeved?"

"Yeah. Peeved. Annoyed. Irritated. Displeased."

"Ah, Sarge. C'mon. Don't be mad at me. You know I can't stand it when you're mad at me."

"I'm not mad. I'm just not happy that you have this irrational dislike of Harry Thurgood. Yes, I'm willing to admit something's not kosher about him. But he is a generous guy and a genuinely nice guy."

"That's fine, Sarge. And I'm sorry I don't share your opinion, but I don't."

"Objection duly noted." He pointed at the board. "Now what are your thoughts about that mess of spaghetti over there?"

"It's the craziest mess I've ever seen."

"Ain't that the truth."

"And one of those Restons is at the bottom of it. And don't forget Harry Thurgood is supporting that family."

"Yeah, so? Doesn't mean *he's* responsible."

"Just sayin'."

Reece slowly shook his head. "In any event, there's probably a Reston involved. Maybe more than one. The question is which one and how do we catch him or her."

"We could start with that Joetta. Heard tell, though, she's expecting again. So she's probably off the hook."

"Right. Which leaves as most likely Oralene, Raylene, Lofton, and possibly Samuel and Elisha."

"We've been thinkin' Lofton was the weak link."

Reece nodded. "Right. But he's not talkin'. So maybe he's not so weak after all."

"Maybe not. Samuel and Elisha are minors. So questioning them going forward will be a hassle. And don't forget Thurgood employs both of them."

"Forget Thurgood. What's more important is they weren't cooperating when we pulled the family in."

"Oralene's all lawyered up. So we won't get anywhere with her."

"No, we won't. Which leaves Raylene."

"Too bad we didn't put a tail on her like we did Lofton."

"You're right about that. But we only have so many officers. We can't put a tail on everybody. Besides, at the time, we thought the boy was the better bet."

"We could put one on her now. An open tail, so it gets on her nerves. Always being followed. Always being watched."

Reece thought for a moment before speaking. "That's a good idea. You just earned your paycheck for the week."

"Thanks, Sarge." She paused. "Um, you're not mad at me, are you?"

"No, I'm not."

"Oh, wow. Thanks. I don't like disagreeing with you. I don't want Thurgood to come between us. Ya know?"

"He won't. See if the DA's office can help us with an investigator to tail Raylene."

"On it, Sarge. Hopefully, the pressure will make her crack."

66

I WATCHED the big Cadillac stop in front of the Really Good.

Double parked.

Emergency lights flashing.

The car door opened, and Mary Lou Fight exited.

My only thought was, here comes trouble.

She entered the shop. Her eyes turned right. Then they turned left. And finally stared straight ahead.

I was in her line of sight.

The face remained impassive. But I could swear her eyes glowed. Just like the monster in a horror movie.

Her right arm rose. The index finger stabbed in my direction.

The imperious voice said, "You!"

I smiled. "Hello, Mary Lou. You here for a cup of coffee or tea? I have a very good Highland Ceylon for you this morning."

Her arm snapped to her side. "You kidnapped my maid. I want her back."

"Apparently, she didn't like the working conditions and came to me asking for help."

"You stole her from me. She's under contract. And the service duration has not been fulfilled."

"I'll buy her out."

"I don't want your filthy money. I want my maid. And if you don't return her, my lawyer will file a suit against you."

"I don't think it will go anywhere, seeing that I'm willing to buy her out."

"Very well. Since you are not willing to restore my property, I will see you in court."

She made an about-face and strode from the shop.

I watched the Cadillac drive away.

One of the old-timers, Marie Jordan, who was eating breakfast, said to her table companion, "Did you hear her call her maid property? Do you think she knows slavery ended a hundred and sixty years ago?"

Alice Green, the table companion, shook her head and said, "That woman."

That woman indeed. I'm glad the confrontation is over. I've been dreading it ever since Eliška rang our doorbell. Now I can let Stanton Lauderbach know I'm willing to buy out the contract, and he can say as much to Mary Lou's attorney. End of story.

———

Thirteen minutes after Mary Lou walked through the door, the Niners began filing in.

Graham, Chief Jager, Reverend Billy Bob, Caroline McCluskey, Magnolia Nadine, Telford Whitacre, Brandon Turner, and my lovely Emmy.

They sat around the tables while Estrelita and I served pastries and coffee.

With coffee cups filled and hands reaching for the sweets, I took a seat between Em and Telford.

"I'm surprised to see you here, Brandon," Caroline said.

"Well, this gathering is a source of information, and a PI needs to have his fingers on the info pulse," he responded.

Tommy Jager, mouthful of cream cheese kolache, managed to get out, "You'll get info. Little of it helpful."

"Don't listen to him," Graham said, "because plenty of useful information is shared here. You just have to sort out the useless."

"And that I'm pretty good at," Brandon said.

Tommy nodded. "Cop instincts."

Brandon flashed him a thumbs up.

"How's the Reston boy doing?" Billy Bob asked.

"He's recovering," Ember answered. "He'll probably need physical therapy; otherwise, the prognosis is that he should make a full recovery."

"How's Mary Lou's maid working out?" Graham asked.

"That was a surprise," Magnolia Nadine said.

"You just missed the Queen Bee," I said.

"Mary Lou was here?" Caroline asked.

"Yep. Gave me what for in no uncertain terms. Accused me of stealing Eliška."

"Did you?" Tommy asked.

"No. She came of her own accord."

"She's afraid for her life," Em added.

Magnolia Nadine nodded. "Bet it's that no-good Oralene."

Ember nodded. "Yes."

Graham jumped on that. "Can't you arrest her, or something, Tommy?"

Tommy shook his head. "On what grounds? That people think she's evil?"

"It's too bad you can't," Telford said, taking a bite out of his cinnamon roll.

Tommy looked at Brandon. "See what I mean?"

Brandon chuckled.

Tommy drank coffee. "Whatever happened to innocent until *proven* guilty? Just because we don't like someone doesn't mean we hold them to a different standard."

"Amen," Ember said.

"Let me add mine as well," Billy Bob said.

"Many a time I wished we could," Brandon said, "but a just legal system has to have rules, and ours says innocent until proven guilty."

Holding his cinnamon roll in mid-air, Telford said, "But don't you all suspect her to be involved in a significant number of murders in Magnolia Bluff? And if so, why isn't there any proof?"

"She's our Moriarty," I said.

"Don't know what that means," Tommy said, "but I can say that we do have our eye on her and when she slips — and they all do at some point — we'll be there, handcuffs at the ready."

The bell over the door jingled, and the table went silent.

Standing in the doorway was Oralene Fight.

67

TUESDAY, JANUARY 13, 9:21 AM

"GOOD MORNING," Oralene said. "Pastor Cole, may I have a word with you in private?"

Em stood. "Sure. Where?"

"Is my car all right with you?"

"Yes, that's fine."

Em grabbed her purse and followed Oralene out the door.

She'd seen the look Harry had given her, but she wasn't afraid of Oralene. For in her prayers that very morning, Jesus had told her she had nothing to fear from the young woman.

Ember got in on the passenger side of the double-parked Caddy, while Oralene got behind the wheel.

"Where are we going?" Ember asked.

Oralene started the car. "Nowhere. Just driving."

"Okay. What's on your mind?"

The young woman drove north on East Main, swung around the courthouse where West Main joined East, and continued north on what was simply called Main Street.

"Mother Fight is very upset that you have given refuge to her maid."

"I'm sorry she's upset. But Eliška doesn't wish to work for her any longer."

"She is under contract."

"Is that so? I'm sure something can be done about that."

"Your…" Oralene hesitated a moment, then continued, "husband told Mother Fight he'd buy out her contract."

"There shouldn't be a problem then."

"There's always a problem with Mother Fight."

Ember said nothing, but thought, *That is very interesting. Sounds like there's a bit of discord in the Fight household.*

Oralene continued, "I suppose her lawyer and your lawyer will sort it out."

"I suppose."

There was a lull in the conversation as the Cadillac sped out of town past LouEllen's Lounge just inside the city limits and Ciara's Garage just outside.

Main Street became State Highway 28 North to Killeen and Fort Worth.

When the car was a couple of miles outside of town, Oralene spoke. "Will you keep a secret?"

"Generally. But it depends on what it is."

"It's Raylene. I think she's not well."

"How not well."

"Mentally not well."

"Has she seen a doctor?"

"No."

"You should take her to see Dr. Kurelek."

"Is he good?"

"Yes, I believe he's good. Very good, in fact."

"I'm worried about her."

"Mike will assess her and then prescribe therapy, or medicine, or both."

"She's delusional. Is he good with delusional people?"

"I don't know for sure. I think so. But the best thing to do is to talk with him."

"She says she has visions, and in the visions she's told to hurt people. People who are sinners."

"Hurt them? How? How hurt them?"

Oralene didn't answer right away, and Ember wondered why she was telling her this.

"Do you believe in demons, Pastor Cole?"

"You mean as counterparts to angels?"

"Yes."

"I don't know. They are mentioned in the Bible. But that may just be metaphorical. To convey a spiritual truth."

"Do you receive visions?"

"Not regularly."

"But you have."

"Yes. I've seen Jesus in my visions."

"I'm a prophetess. I receive the word of the Lord. And I believe Raylene may have been seduced by a demon. Perhaps even possessed."

"I see. So you think a demon is telling your sister to hurt people?"

"Yes."

"She might just be delusional. For the most part, I think we are our own angels or demons. You need to take Raylene to talk with Mike Kurelek."

Oralene said nothing, and after a moment or two Ember continued.

"Why are you telling me this? You threatened my family. You killed your father and Purnell Tully—"

"The Lord struck them down. In the midst of their sin.

Just like the Israelites who were destroyed while the quail was still in their teeth."

"That's old hat. No one believes it. Is Raylene your new scapegoat?"

Oralene slammed on the brakes, and the Caddy came to a halt, tires squealing on the pavement. Right in the middle of the highway.

The young woman turned her head and looked Ember in the eye. And Ember swore those eyes were red as blood.

When Oralene spoke, her voice seemed to come from a sepulcher. "I know you, Ember Cole. How dare you accuse the Handmaid of the Lord? She's extended you the olive branch, and you mock. Remember, O false servant of the Lord, the wages of sin is death."

Ember opened the car door and jumped out.

Oralene drove on down the highway.

What did I just witness?

She tried opening her purse to get her phone. Her hand was shaking, as if she had the palsy and wouldn't respond.

68

TUESDAY, JANUARY 13, 11:02 AM

EMBER KNEELED in the sanctuary of her church. In the middle of the center aisle, facing the communion table. On the back wall hung the large wooden cross.

By chance, or was it providence, Sheriff Buck Blanton had seen her standing by the side of the road. He pulled over and gave her a lift back to town.

When asked what she was doing alone, out in the middle of nowhere, she'd said, "Fighting demons."

Buck's perpetual grin had faltered for a second or two. But he'd recovered and said, "Looks like you won."

Ember had looked him in the eye and said, "Maybe."

At her request, he'd taken her to her church. He asked no more questions, and she'd said nothing more.

Now, with arms outstretched, palms facing heaven, she prayed. And her prayer was simple. "Help me, Lord."

How long she kneeled there with arms outstretched, reciting her prayer like a mantra, she didn't know. But when she opened her eyes, there was nothing but white light. It was as though the universe had vanished.

The voice that came to her was soft and gentle. A father talking to his frightened child.

"I am with you. Nothing can harm you."

She felt a hand gently touch her cheek.

"You know what to do, my child."

The voice continued to repeat the sentence until it faded away and her ears could no longer hear it.

———

I found Em lying on the floor of the sanctuary at Saint Luke's. She was asleep.

Buck had stopped by the Really Good and told me how he'd found her standing by the side of the road.

When his inquiring eyes met mine, I shrugged, thanked him, and beat feet to the church.

I gently touched her cheek and said, "Emmy, it's Harry. Wake up, sweetheart."

Her eyes fluttered open, and I helped her sit up.

Sitting on the floor, she hugged me, kissed me, and told me what had happened after she left the Really Good.

When she was finished, I said, "That's one heck of a story."

"You don't believe me."

"*Au contraire, mon amour.* I do believe you. I'm just not sure what to make of it."

"I'm a Christian. I believe Jesus talks to me. I also know that we can never fully comprehend God and the world in which He lives. Are they demon possessed? Are they insane?"

"I can't answer the first question. I'm still pondering

whether God exists. As for the second, I'm inclined to say, yes, they are."

"Maybe I just imagined Oralene's change."

"I don't know. When it comes to the spiritual and mystical, you're miles ahead of me."

"Jesus said I know what to do."

She wrapped her arms around me and laid her head on my shoulder. "But I don't, Harry. I don't know what to do."

I held her tight. "You don't *think* you do. Maybe stop looking for the answer and just let it come to you."

She pulled away. "You are so wise, Harry Thurgood. Is it any wonder why I love you."

I stood and helped her to her feet.

"Well, Mister, I guess I have work to do."

"Good. What is it?"

"To treat my neighbor as myself."

69

TUESDAY, JANUARY 13, 1:08 PM

EMBER PAID a visit to Lofton Reston at the hospital. She encouraged his mother to go home and get some rest.

Reluctantly, Jerri Reston did so. "But I'll be back in three hours," she said as she left.

Ember gazed at the sleeping form. *Now, I have three hours with you, young man, and you are going to tell me your story.*

————

Elmore sent me a text with an update on his activities. He'd not only been shadowing Oralene and Raylene, he'd been digging into the family's past. And from what he'd found out thus far, there was nothing savory about the Restons. They were corrupt and rotten to the core.

Even Jerri Reston. Although I truly believe after the death of her husband and Tully, her lover, she'd reformed and gotten her act together.

But prior to their appearing in Magnolia Bluff, the family cut a swath of thieving, underage sex, and hucksterism from the Texas Panhandle to Arkansas, and from Oklahoma to Louisiana. All that besides the incest, fornication, and adultery going on within the family.

However, since coming to Magnolia Bluff, things had changed. Three of their own had died, and they'd decided to settle down and give up the traveling evangelism show.

But the bad apples were still around. They'd gone nowhere. And were still causing the entire barrel to rot.

And the rottenest apple of the bunch was Oralene.

Thus far, that young woman was untouchable. Thus far. In the meantime, there was Raylene. If enough branches could be pruned, it might finally be possible to get to the trunk and put an end to it all.

———

Oralene parked on the street in front of the house where her family lived. The house owned by Harry Thurgood, who charged her Mama cheap rent in order to help the family.

Someday, she'd have to do something about that. In the meantime, she had more pressing matters to attend to.

She'd planted the seed that Raylene was mentally unstable. Now she needed to set things up so Raylene would be the scapegoat. She'd have to be set up so that she'd get caught and then all the murders could be pinned on her.

Once those crimes were "solved," the police would no longer look in her direction. And if she could persuade Father Fight to get rid of Mother, everything would be perfect.

While they couldn't be man and wife in public, she could certainly take care of his needs in private. And as long as she satisfied his man needs, she could make him dance to any old tune she played.

Men are so simple. Give them plenty of sex, keep their bellies full, and let them do their thing — and they're content.

She'd had to convince Father Fight earlier today that he did in fact want to keep seeing her. He insisted he couldn't. But after she got through servicing him, he relented.

A man rarely gives up good sex unless it's to fill his belly.

Her plan was simple: keep Father Fight happy and get Raylene to incriminate herself. Do those two things and she would be ready for the next step in her plan.

She had her hand on the door handle of her car when a Magnolia Bluff police car parked on the opposite side of the street from the house.

What are they doing here?

She decided she didn't want to find out, started the car, and drove off.

———

Lofton Reston opened his eyes.

"Hello, Lofton. How are you feeling?"

"Oh, hi, Reverend Cole. Uh, I don't know. I guess I'm okay. It hurts, but they give me stuff, so it doesn't bother me too much."

"That's good. Your mom is home getting some rest. I'm going to sit with you until she comes back."

"Oh, okay. Thank you. Is she okay?"

"Your mom?"

He nodded.

"Yes. Just tired. Been praying for you non-stop."

He nodded and closed his eyes. Ember watched a tear roll down his cheek.

"Do you feel safe going back home? You can stay with us until the police find who did this."

"Uh, I don't know. I…" His voice trailed off.

"Your mother would be there with you most of the day. We'd love to have you as our guest."

"I don't know. I'll think about it."

"Do you know who did this to you?"

He shook his head.

"The police know it was only you and Raylene in the house." Ember winced inside a bit at the lie.

"No, she wasn't there."

"But she was. The police know when she arrived, and they know she left before you came out of the house seeking help."

"She didn't do it."

"Who did then?"

"I don't know. I was attacked from behind."

"But only Raylene was in the house with you."

"No. She left, and someone came in the back door. The police couldn't see them."

"They have surveillance cameras watching the back door. No one entered." Another lie. *Forgive me, Lord. Please forgive me.*

"Oh. But I, I don't know who attacked me. My back was to them."

"You don't have to protect her. Oralene told me she thinks your sister is mentally ill and needs help."

"She did?"

"Yes. She told me this morning."

"Uh, I don't know." He closed his eyes, licked his lips,

opened his eyes, and studied Ember's face.

"She really told you that? O?"

"Yes, she did."

"What about Mama? Is she safe? Does she know?"

"I don't know if she knows. As for if she's safe, I don't think Raylene will hurt her. The question, though, is why does she want to hurt you? That's the part I don't get. Did you do something to her?"

"No. At least I don't think so."

"Why do all of you do what Oralene tells you to do? That's very puzzling to me."

"No, we don't."

Boy, he said that awfully fast. Ember reached over and took Lofton's hand in hers. "I'm going to tell you something that I've only told a few people. Can you keep a secret?"

"Uh, sure. I'll keep your secret."

"Jesus talks to me. Actually talks to me. Just like I'm talking to you."

"He does?"

"Uh-huh. He tells me when people are lying. He does this so I can help them make their lives more holy. And you know what?"

"What?"

"You're lying. To me. Your friend."

"No, I'm not. Honest."

"You don't have to defend Oralene. And you don't have to defend Raylene. They've done wrong, and Jesus wants them to come back to Him."

Lofton was silent for the longest time.

Ember decided to nudge him. "And Jesus wants you to come back to Him, as well. His heart aches for you and your sisters. Come back to Jesus, Lofton. And help me bring your sisters back, too."

"But O is the Handmade of the Lord. He speaks to her, and she does His bidding."

"She says she is. However, I have my doubts it's God speaking through her."

"No. You're wrong. O is the Handmaid of the Lord. She only does what God tells her to do, and we follow her because God's chosen her."

"Remember what Paul told the Corinthians? 'Even Satan transforms himself into an angel of light.' Our adversary is clever, and, sad to say, we are so easily deceived. Even I have been so deceived. But only when I strayed from the side of Jesus. When I let go of his hand."

"No. No. O is good. She walks with God, and He talks with her."

"Okay. Then that leaves me no choice."

"No choice? To do what?"

"Challenge her to a duel. Just like in the Old Testament."

"We'll each pray to our God to send fire and brimstone down on whichever of us is the false messenger."

"What? That doesn't happen today."

"No, it doesn't. Well, maybe instead of fire and brimstone she'll get hit by a car. *That* would be more modern."

A brief laugh came from Lofton.

"You're thinking that won't happen either. And you're probably right. But what I can do is issue the challenge this way: if I'm not speaking the truth, God will force me to resign from Saint Luke's. And if your sister isn't speaking the truth, the police will arrest her for the murders of your father, Purnell Tully, Reverend Humphrey, and Patrice Bremen, as well as the assault on Tansy Truitt. And since I know Reece Sovern is getting ready to do so, even as we speak, I know your sister is deluded and is a servant of Satan."

Lofton's eyes were wide open. Ember knew she'd just hit the ball out of the park.

He didn't say anything. Just stared at her.

Now I wonder how long it will take for this to get back to Oralene? And please, Lord, forgive my lies. Is it so different from when you didn't turn the other cheek and used violence to purify the temple?

70

REECE SOVERN FINISHED READING the report and set it on his desk. Sergeant Hans Winkler and Officer Peter Johnston had canvassed the entire area from the Reston home to the Piggly Wiggly. They'd gotten verification from the store's security camera and from Judith Tressel. Such as it was.

The security camera footage was grainy, and the time-stamp was off by an hour. The person could have been Raylene. The person could've also been someone else.

Mrs. Tressel recalled seeing a young woman with blonde hair, wearing a black jacket, walking toward the grocery store. When shown the picture of Raylene, Mrs. Tressel shrugged and said it could have been her. But wouldn't swear to it.

Reece dropped the soggy stogie into the wastebasket. He got another one out of the drawer and sank his teeth into it.

I think we need to pay Lofton another visit. And after him, Raylene.

He got up. Grabbed his hat and coat, and walked over to GJ's desk.

"C'mon. We're talking to Lofton and Raylene."

"Okay, Sarge."

She grabbed her jacket and followed Reece out the door.

———

Reece removed his hat. "Reverend. Lofton. Hope you don't mind if we join the party."

"Lofton and I were having a pleasant chat," Ember said. "But if you don't mind, I need to use the lady's room."

"By all means," Reece responded. "We'll keep Mr. Reston company."

Ember left, and Reece took her chair. GJ stood at the foot of the bed.

He set his hat on his knee.

"Well, young man," he began, "how are you feeling?"

"Okay. It hurts, but they're giving me something for the pain."

"Good. Have they told you when you start rehab?" Reece asked.

"No, they haven't." Lofton paused a moment and then asked, "Have you arrested Raylene?"

"Not yet," Reece said. "Do you think we should?"

"No. She's sick and needs help."

"How is she sick?" GJ asked.

"In the head."

"How do you know that?" GJ responded.

"Reverend Cole said O told her that this morning."

"That's very interesting," Reece said. "How does Oralene know this?"

"I don't know. She's the Handmaid of the Lord. Maybe He told her."

GJ snorted, but Reece said, "Maybe He did. I'll talk to her about it."

"Reverend Cole said you have cameras watching the back door of the house and no one entered."

Reece kept his face deadpan, GJ, though, had to turn around so she didn't give anything away. She pretended to cough.

"She said that, did she?" Reece said.

"Yes, sir."

"I'm going to have to talk to her. She's not supposed to be telling our secrets."

GJ turned around. "So why did your sister attack you?"

Lofton's eyes slid from Reece to GJ and back to Reece.

"C'mon, Lofton, protecting them isn't going to do anybody any good," she said. "Tell us what you know."

At that point, Ember returned, and by the look on the boy's face, Reece knew the moment had passed with the interruption.

He stood. "It's up to you, young man. No one else needs to die, including you." He put a card on the small stand next to the bed. "My number's on that card. I'll be waiting for your call."

GJ preceded him out of the room, and they walked out to the big black SUV.

"He was going to tell us, wasn't he, Sarge?"

"I think so. Poor timing on Ember's part."

"Maybe it was intentional."

"Nah. Coincidence."

"You always tell me there are no coincidences."

"So I do. This is the exception that proves the rule." But in all honesty, Reece wasn't so sure.

71

TUESDAY, JANUARY 13, 3:57 PM

WHEN JERRI RESTON returned to the hospital, Ember decided it was a good time to do the favor Reece had asked of her.

The drive to Henrene Boseman's house took ten minutes. During that time, Ember mused on Eliška's breakfast bombshell. And it was a doozy. A potentially deadly doozy.

Ember replayed Eliška's statement in her mind.

Mrs. Fight has evidence that you, Reverend Cole, are still married to the husband you left.

She also replayed Harry's comment.

It doesn't matter to me if you are. I love you. But the good folk of our town will have an issue. Which means we need to get ahead of this. And for that, my dear, you can leave everything to me.

She'd asked what he was going to do. His response was a laugh and the assurance he was thinking about it.

There was a part of Harry's life that was hidden behind a heavily barred door. She didn't like not knowing. But she also realized he was not going to tell her, or anyone, about that part of his life. And she'd grudgingly accepted that about the man she loved. Even though she didn't like it. They'd agreed to leave their past in the past.

But Harry's secret life wasn't actually in the past. It was in the present. And she suspected it had something to do with his money. But what about his money? She had no idea. All she could do was hope and pray it wasn't illegal.

Right now, however, Harry's mystery paled in comparison to her own.

Jake Butterman. Star linebacker for the Shelby, Ohio, Rockets football team. Wasn't good enough to get a college football scholarship and ended up working in his father's hardware store.

Alice White. Cheerleader. Married Jake right after high school graduation. With the last college rejection, Jake took his anger out on her.

And after a year of abuse, I left him. But didn't divorce him.

———

Ember sat on the sofa in Henrene Boseman's living room. In spite of her protest, Henrene was in the kitchen getting tea and snacks.

Ember's mind was too preoccupied with Reece's request to pay much attention to the comfortable, homey room. Her mission, should she choose to accept it, and she had, was to get from Henrene the information on the Restons, and in particular Raylene, that Henrene had told Joyce Blackstone.

Why didn't Brandon just give the information to Reece? Those two very much need to get over the pissing contest. It's not helping anyone or anything other than their egos.

Henrene entered carrying a tray with a teapot, cups and

saucers, milk and sugar, cookies, and a decanter. She set it on the coffee table between the sofa and the two rocking chairs.

"How do you like your tea, Reverend?"

"A splash of milk would be nice."

"I have blue corn bourbon if you need a little fortification."

Ember laughed. "Some days I do, but today is not one of them."

"Good for you, then."

Henrene poured tea, added milk to Ember's cup and a stiff shot of blue corn to her own.

"I don't need any fortification," Henrene said. "I just like the taste."

"When I was a drinking gal, I didn't care what it tasted like. All that mattered was how fast I got lit."

Henrene sat. "Know what you mean. Went through that phase myself. Grew out of it. Thank goodness."

The women sat there for a moment drinking tea. Ember nibbled on a Russian tea cake.

Then Henrene spoke. "So what's on your mind, Reverend?"

"I just thought I'd pay a visit. Now that Reverend Humphrey is gone, I need to check up on the seniors in the congregation."

Henrene smiled. "You sure it has nothing to do with what Mrs. Blackstone and I talked about?"

Ember hoped the surprise didn't show on her face. *Dang. She's good.* Out loud she confessed, "Okay. You got me. Yes, I'd like to know what the two of you talked about."

"Glad you didn't try to prevaricate. I suppose Mr. Sovern put you up to this."

"How did you know?"

"I didn't. But now I do. Before it was just a guess. It's common knowledge that Mr. Turner and the sergeant don't get along. It's also common knowledge Sergeant Sovern gets help from folks."

"All investigators do."

"Yes, that's true. Let's just say he *depends* on other folk."

"He's getting better."

"Good to hear. We need better in this town."

"Yes, we do."

"Now that we got that out of the way, what do you want to know?"

"The scuttlebutt about the Restons."

"Mrs. Reston works for you. Are you sure you want to know?"

"Yes. Jerri works for us. But what you tell me won't affect my relationship with her. She's a sinner saved by grace. I believe, since her husband died, she's made a complete turn-around with her life."

"That's good to hear." Henrene drank tea and took a bite out of her oatmeal raisin cookie. When she'd swallowed, she said, "Mind you, this is just gossip. Mostly. Very little has credible corroboration."

"Okay. Good to know."

"The current Reston family got its start in Oklahoma. Although the late husband may have another family or two out there."

"Wow. That's a scary thought."

"Those men have trouble keeping it in their pants. And there are plenty of women who don't want them to."

"Sad, but true."

"It is. But that's life. The pastor and his missus stole and conned their way from Oklahoma to Arkansas, using the revival meeting as a cover, and often they were barely one step ahead of the law."

"How do you know this?"

"As I said, I don't *know* it. Someone's cousin tells a friend, who tells their sister, who mentions it to another cousin. That sort of thing. Since they came to town, talk's been brewin' and growin'. Penny Jo Prettyman's friend's sister was with Pastor John every night for the week that the revival show was in her town. The show left, and the sister finds out she's pregnant. That's just one of the stories that are continually showing up."

"Oh, my. I didn't know."

"And the wife, Mrs. Reston, wasn't any better than that scalawag of a husband. There are those who believe half the children aren't Restons. If you get my drift."

Ember nodded.

"And then they show up here. The end of the line. At least for some of them. Everything was a con. Betty Ripple, who volunteers with animal control, said the snakes had their venom sacks removed. The snake handling was a stunt."

"Which means someone made a change."

"That's right," Henrene affirmed. "Which is why the old man's death was a murder."

"So where are Oralene and Raylene in all of this?"

"Mrs. Fight's ne'er-do-well has a very strong personality. As she got older, she gradually took control of the family. Creating a modicum of order in all the chaos. All that prophesying crap and speaking in tongues was just part of the con. But the family apparently came to believe Oralene truly had the gift. And using sex, she pretty much controlled that Tully fella, as well as her father."

"And now she's learning from the Queen Bee," Ember said.

"Mary Lou isn't doing her any good, that's for sure."

"So Raylene is just Oralene's puppet?"

"That's about the size of it. But you've seen her. She's stunning. And apparently that Oralene is using her sister's bodily charms to expand her circle of influence outside the family."

"Oh, that's not good."

"No, it's not. Jeanne Thorn's forbidden her son to see Raylene. But apparently he sneaks out at night to meet up with her."

"So why did they kill Patrice Bremen?"

"Well, the talk is she was a sinner and there's no room for sinners in Magnolia Bluff."

"But we're all sinners."

Henrene shrugged. "Something to think about, isn't it?"

"So how do we stop them? Gossip isn't proof of anything."

"True, it's not. But there's usually a kernel of truth somewhere in the story."

"But a kernel isn't cold, hard facts. It's a niggle. Perhaps a nudge. But it's not proof."

"No, it's not."

"And Reece needs proof."

"They're all guilty of something. Mr. Sovern needs to focus on Raylene. She's pretty, but not overly bright. That's my opinion. She'll slip up, and he needs to be there when she does."

"I think he already knows that."

"Good. Tell him to carry on."

"I will." Ember stood.

"Not so fast, young lady. We need to talk about you."

72

TUESDAY, JANUARY 13, 4:31 PM

"ME?" Ember said as she sat down.

"Yes, you. The storm is brewing, and you'd best be prepared."

"Oh." Ember paused, and then said, "I'll have that fortification now."

Henrene chuckled. "Help yourself, dear."

Ember took hold of the decanter and poured a slug of bourbon into her empty teacup, downed the contents in one gulp, grimaced, and poured another couple of fingers, before returning the decanter to the tray.

Henrene had a smile on her face. "You tossed that first one off like a real pro. Ready?"

Ember nodded.

"Good. You've said you left an abusive husband. Did you divorce him?"

"No, I didn't. Once he was out of my life, I did my best to forget about him."

"Did you?"

"Pretty much, yes."

"And it probably wouldn't have ever been a problem if you hadn't hooked up with Mr. Thurgood."

"I suppose you're right."

"But you did, and now Mary Lou Fight thinks she finally has the ammunition that will get you out of the pulpit."

"How so?"

"She supposedly not only has proof you're still married to the husband you left, but she's trying to get him to come to Magnolia Bluff."

"Seriously?"

"That's what the sounds on the wind are saying."

"Oh, dear." Ember picked up her teacup and tossed off the contents in one gulp. After the grimace passed, she asked, "And you're sure about this?"

Henrene laughed. "Honey, I'm not sure of anything. It's just what's floating around town. But you can bet your last dollar that if the talk is about something Mary Lou's going to do, it's a sure thing. She uses those Crimson Hats to spread terror to her intended victims."

"I can't believe she'd bring Jake here."

"Believe it, my dear. She wants you out in the worst way, and she will stop at nothing until you are gone. You've thwarted her thus far. So I hope for your sake you have something good up your sleeve, because you're going to be needing it."

"Harry said he'd take care of it."

"How's he going to do that?"

"He said he's thinking about it."

"You better hope he thinks fast. Because with this information, Mary Lou is going to move like lightning."

"I suppose so. Because if Jake didn't divorce me, I'm a bigamist. And that means I'm in a world of hurt."

73

THE BELL over the door tinkled. I looked up from my iPad to see Graham Huston enter the shop. He was the only customer.

He headed over to my table. "Well, Harry, I suppose you've heard the news."

"What news is that?"

He sat. "The news coming from Fight Towers. That Mary Lou is finally going to have her way. You and Ember are leaving town."

"News to me. We aren't going anywhere."

"Can I quote you on that?"

"Sure. What's this about, anyway?"

"Seems Ember is still married to the guy she left."

"Oh, that bit of gossip. Eliška told us this morning Mary Lou thinks Ember's still married to her ex."

"So he is the ex?"

"Actually, Ember has no idea. She just left him. She assumed he filed for divorce and moved on. It's what his parents would've wanted. They wanted grandkids in the worst way."

"According to Mary Lou, that's not the case. He's still carrying the torch for his high school sweetheart."

"How touching. Where are you getting all this? Surely not from Mary Lou."

"I haven't gotten any of the information personally. Monika has. This is the stuff of which gossip columns are made."

"She's not putting this in the paper, is she?"

"That's the plan."

"You're the boss, Graham. As a favor to me, will you not publish this? I'm checking it out to make sure it's legit."

"Okay, Harry, as a favor to you, I'll sit on it. Monika won't be happy, but that's life. We don't always get what will make us happy."

"Thanks, Graham. I appreciate it."

"Now to get me some supper."

———

When Graham left, I flipped the sign to closed. While Jack, Estrelita, and Miguel cleaned up from the day, I took the stairs to my apartment above the shop. I needed to be alone for a few minutes.

I texted Em to let her know I might be a bit late getting home.

Sitting in my rocker-recliner, in the quiet of my former home above the coffee shop, I smoked my pipe, drank Drambuie, and considered what to do about Em's and my problem.

Worst case scenario, she was still married. Solution? I move back here until she gets a divorce.

However, with Mary Lou involved, she could make it difficult for us by paying him to make it difficult. Solution? Make it worth his while not to make it difficult.

Then again, it could be they aren't married. Nevertheless Mary Lou could still create waves. Enough waves to swamp the boat, by having him say Em's story is a lie and she just abandoned a loving and caring husband. That might even be more insidious.

By the time my pipe was smoked out and the glass empty, I decided the only answer was to see how much money would buy him off. Which meant I'd be in a bidding war with Mary Lou.

I texted Elmore and told him we needed to talk.

In a couple of minutes he called, and I explained the pickle Em and I were in.

At the end, he simply said, "What do you want me to do?"

"Buy him off."

"Limit?"

"Five hundred thousand."

"That's a lot of money."

"It is. Hopefully, you can convince him less is more."

"Okay. Five hundred K being tops."

"Yes."

"What if he won't deal or wants more?"

I took a deep breath and slowly let it back out. "Then use your discretion so that he's no longer a problem."

"Consider it done."

"Good. I'll get you the details, such that I have, within the hour."

"I'll leave as soon as I get them. Anything else?"

"No. That's all."

I ended the call. Elmore would fix the problem for us. Now it was down to Em's ex. Would he deal or not?

74

REECE SOVERN PRESSED the button and heard the faint sound of door chimes from somewhere in the house. He waited ten seconds and pressed the button again. The door opened.

"Hello, Elisha," Reece said. "Mind if we come in? We'd like to talk to your sister, Raylene."

"She's not here."

"Can you tell me when she'll be back?"

"Nope. She didn't say."

"GJ, check with Officer Johnston and see why he isn't following her."

"Uh, she left by the back door."

"Oh, she did, did she?"

"Yes, sir."

Reece decided he'd try Ember's bluff. "GJ, check the surveillance cameras we have watching the back door. Because if you're lying to us, young man, I'm going to arrest you for obstructing justice."

He watched the fear sweep across Elisha's face and waited.

In a second, the boy said, "Oh, wait, I think I hear her. Just a minute."

The door closed, and Reece motioned for GJ to head around back. He watched her run around the corner.

The door re-opened. "Uh, she's here," Elisha said, as Raylene joined him.

"What can I do for you?" she said. Her voice was all peaches and cream.

"We'd like to talk to you. May we come in?"

"I only see you."

Reece retrieved his phone, tapped a text, and put the phone back in his pocket. "My partner will be here in a minute."

And in less than that, GJ was by her boss's side.

Reece said, "Now I'm a we. May we come in?"

"Or you can talk to us in the car." GJ hooked her thumb towards the unmarked SUV.

"What do you want to talk about?" Raylene asked.

"You," Reece said.

"Me?"

"Yes, you. Now we either come in, or you come down to the car with us, or I arrest you for obstructing justice, and because you're a material witness and a flight risk, you'll be sitting in jail for a long time. Your move."

Raylene shrugged. "Okay. Come in."

Reece and GJ entered. Elisha closed the door, while the investigators followed Raylene to the living room.

She sat in the center of the sofa, her hands folded in her lap. Elisha stood at one end of the sofa. Reece sat in a chair facing the young woman, GJ standing next to him.

To Elisha, GJ said, "You can leave now. We want to speak with your sister alone."

The boy looked at the girl, who sat watching the investigators, and then back at GJ, who hooked her thumb towards the door, and said, "Beat it."

After a long moment of hesitation, during which GJ took out her handcuffs, Elisha left.

Reece studied Raylene for a moment. She appeared rather nonchalant. Save for the white knuckles of her tightly clasped hands.

He asked, "Okay, young lady, how are you?"

"I'm fine. This is the day the Lord hath made."

"Yes, it is," he replied. "How's Oralene?"

"I don't know. We haven't talked."

"You sure?" GJ asked. "Because we can ask Officer Johnston."

"My hand on the Bible, Oralene and I have not spoken to each other today."

"Now we're paying you a courtesy call," Reece began, "because a person has come forward who claims to have seen you at the Cozy Corners Motel the night Patrice Bremen was murdered. What do you say about that?"

"Nothing."

Reece decided to re-phrase the question. "Were you there that night?"

"No."

"Do you have a twin?" GJ asked.

"No." After a moment, Raylene giggled. "It would be great fun if I did."

"Oh, I'm sure," GJ said.

"So where were you that night?" Reece asked.

"Here. Mama doesn't let us go out alone at night. Everyone will say I was here."

"I bet they will," GJ said.

"So you say you were here," Reece said, "and that your mother doesn't let you go out at night alone. But you could've gone there with Oralene or someone else. So who was with you?"

"Nobody. I wasn't there. I was here."

Reece stood. "Very well, young lady, that's your story, is it?"

"It isn't a story it's the truth."

"Don't go anywhere for the next couple of days. I'm putting together a lineup to see if our person can identify you. If the person can, then I'll arrest you and charge you with murder."

GJ said, "If you tell us the truth now, it will go better for you in the long run."

Raylene stood. "I didn't kill anybody. But God's sure been busy."

"We'll see ourselves out," Reece said.

When they were in the car, GJ said, "That was some story you came up with. Think it will work?"

"Don't know. Although I have my doubts. But we'll see after she gets fingered in the lineup and I arrest her."

"Aren't you skating on thin ice, Sarge? No one saw her at the motel."

"True. But she doesn't know that. If I can play out this hand without anyone exposing my bluff, we just might be able to get her to confess."

75

ORALENE WAS WAITING in the alley behind the Really Good. She answered her phone.

"O, the police are onto us. They were here and said someone saw me at the motel."

"What do you want me to do?"

"I don't know what to do or say."

"You say and do nothing."

"But they're going to arrest me. The person will point me out, and it will be all over."

"For you, possibly. That's why it is best if you say nothing. As the sheep before its shearers is dumb, so you need to be. It is the word of the Lord."

"But I don't want to go to jail."

"Perhaps you are the one who is worthy to be the scapegoat."

"Scapegoat? No, O, I'm not the scapegoat. That's Lofton. They should be going after him, not me."

"Perhaps the Lord has changed His mind."

"No, O, please. I can't go to jail. There's sin there. The lesbians. They'll make me serve their lusts. No, O, please."

"We must wait upon the word of the Lord."

Oralene heard her sister's sobs.

"Go to bed. I will pray to the Lord for a word."

Oralene disconnected the call. She was smiling.

The Lord's plan is coming together. It is as it was with David and Uriah the Hittite. Raylene is my Uriah. She will save me and our family. But because she is family, I will get him to help her, and it will be well.

————

Reece Sovern got off the phone. His niece, Julie, had agreed to be part of the lineup. She made number seven. With Raylene, there would be eight. A police buddy of his over in Fredericksburg had agreed to be the eyewitness.

Everything was set. They'd pick Raylene up at ten tomorrow morning.

He hoped that once identified as being at the motel the night Patrice Bremen was murdered, the girl would confess. If she didn't... Reece still hadn't come up with a contingency plan. Hopefully, he would by tomorrow.

————

Time to go home. I grabbed my hat and coat, put them on, checked to make sure the snub-nosed thirty-eight was in my pocket, and descended the stairs.

I left the shop by the alley door, making sure the alarm was set, and locked the door behind me.

Halfway to my car, I noticed a person dressed in black,

standing by the driver's door. My hand reached for my pocket.

"Hello, Oralene," I said.

She pushed the hood of her cloak back. "Hello, Mr. Thurgood."

I stopped about ten feet away from her. "What do you want?"

"I've come to ask a favor."

"You want a favor from me?"

"Yes, sir."

"What favor?"

"The police are going to arrest Raylene. I'd like you to hire that lawyer to defend her."

"And why would I want to do that? Why can't you hire him?"

"Mother Fight will not spend the money, and I have none of my own."

"Okay. So why do I want to?"

"Because if you agree to hire the lawyer, I will convince Mother Fight not to confront your wife before the church that she's a bigamist."

"What makes you think Mary Lou will listen to you?"

"She will. Just leave that to me."

"You're pretty sure of yourself. How do I know you can deliver?"

"I can deliver. What's more, I will make sure Mother Fight stops her campaign against you and your wife."

"That's a pretty tall order. I don't think you can do it."

"I can. I know secrets about Mother even Eliška doesn't know. If Mother doesn't listen to me, I can deliver them to you and you can persuade her to stop."

Well, well. The protégé was learning fast. She was willing

to throw Mary Lou under the bus to get a good lawyer for her sister. Blood's thicker than adoption.

Should I agree to her request? I had no guarantee she'd carry through on her end. But perhaps I did...

"All right, Oralene, I'll hire Stanton to represent your sister if she gets arrested. In return, you'll call off Mary Lou from harassing Ember and me."

"Thank you, Mr. Thurgood."

"One more thing. If you don't carry through, I'll tell Stanton to drop your sister as his client."

"I will carry out my part."

"Then we have a deal."

"Thank you, Mr. Thurgood. Raylene will be relieved. She's scared to death of the sinners in prison."

"I can imagine."

Oralene pulled the hood over her head and walked down the alley, vanishing into the gloom of the night.

I didn't actually hold out much hope that my pact with the devil would work.

If it did, great.

If it didn't, I had Elmore.

76

OUR SUPPER WAS HISTORY. A delicious repast of beef stew with dumplings.

We were all in the family room. A fire was burning in the fireplace. Em and I were sitting in our chairs. I was drinking coffee and Em, tea. We were also smoking our pipes.

The children were in their playpen. Clara and Eliška were in their rooms. Princess was curled up at my feet, and Wilbur was in front of the fire, sleeping on the hearthrug.

I told Em about my meeting with Oralene.

When I was finished, she said, "It sounds too good to be true."

I drank coffee, puffed on my pipe, and said, "It does at that. However, if she doesn't make good on her promise, I'll have Stanton withdraw."

She set her cup down. "Hopefully, Oralene cares enough about her sister and has the power to convince Mary Lou."

"I'm confident Oralene cares about her sister. I'm not convinced she can pull it off with Mary Lou. But I'll be very happy to be proven wrong."

"I hope this is the end, Harry. That some good will come from this tragedy by getting us out from under Mary Lou's thumb and end the strife at the church."

"One can hope."

I walked over to the patio doors. The sky was dark. Scudding clouds blotted out stars as they swept along. I pulled the curtains closed and returned to my chair.

Maybe. Maybe after all these years we'll finally have peace in our adopted home. Maybe.

————

Reece Sovern was sitting in the den. His man cave. The meatloaf and baked potato were giving his stomach a feeling that all was well in the world.

He turned on the TV and settled in to watch hockey.

Tomorrow he'd hopefully get that confession out of Raylene and wrap up at least one of these murders.

If she didn't confess, he wasn't sure how to play it. He couldn't hold her or arrest her. He had no actual evidence.

The Restons were too good. And that Oralene... Untouchable as a red-hot charcoal briquette.

But if he could chip away at the family, then perhaps he could deprive her of soldiers, so to speak.

It's a thought, and the only one I have that might have a chance of working.

————

Oralene sat in the overstuffed chair in her bedroom. The room was dark. She liked it that way.

Tonight, if all went well, the police would be satisfied.

And if they were satisfied, they'd stop poking around, and if they stopped poking around, she'd be safe.

Not that she'd done anything wrong. In the past, the police put a stop to sin. Not anymore. They were now the tools of sin. The tools of the corruption that had infected city governments all over the country.

Now, she and those like her who were sick of sin had to hide in the darkness of the night in order to root out the infection. The blight that was sucking the godliness out of the land.

Raylene was the scapegoat. Lofton had proven unworthy.

The word of the Lord had come to Oralene, and Raylene was the one the Lord had chosen to carry away sin from her family. She and the boy she'd wooed, a boy bent on satisfying the lusts of the flesh, would turn away the ones wanting to do her family harm. To do her, the Handmaid of the Lord, harm.

77

TUESDAY, JANUARY 13, 8:31 PM

EMBER WAVED to Officer Kristine Combs as she walked past the patrol car.

Tansy had called asking if she minded coming over. She wanted to order a pizza, but was scared to have it delivered.

Ember told her she understood and would be right over.

Walking up the walk, she texted Tansy she'd arrived so the young woman would know who was ringing her doorbell.

Tansy let her in, and the two women hugged.

"Did you order?" Ember asked.

"Not yet. Hang your coat there in the closet."

Ember did so and followed her friend into the living room.

"Thanks for coming over, Ember. I'm still spooked by the whole thing."

"You're very welcome. And don't worry. Everything will be fine. You aren't alone. Plus, I have pepper spray and my gun."

"You carry a gun?"

"Harry insists. Because we've had threats."

"Wow, who'd want to threaten you?"

"Someone in town who's used to getting their own way and isn't."

"That's sick."

"It is. But some people are sick, and that's just how it is."

"I guess. Sad world."

After checking whether Ember wanted anything, Tansy called in her order.

When the call was over, Tansy said, "I have some news to tell you."

"Sounds like it's good news. Tell me."

"I've decided to give up porn."

"That's wonderful! What made you decide to do that?"

"I got thinking about what I really wanted in life, and I looked at you and Harry, and I saw how happy you are, and well, I guess I want that for myself. And I'm not getting it doing porn. I'm just using up my body and for what? What's going to happen when I'm old? I have nobody. I have money. But what I really want is to be with the man I love, have his children, and to be happy."

Ember hugged her and kissed her cheek. "That is so wonderful. You won't regret it. What are you going to do instead?"

"What I told you before. I'd like to get married and have a family. It's only me now that Mom's gone, and I don't want to die alone. I don't want to be by myself."

"A family is nice to have when you get old. And even when you aren't old."

The two women laughed over that.

Ember continued, "But what about a job until you find that special guy?"

Suddenly Tansy stiffened. "Did you hear that?"

"Sounded like glass breaking."

———

The baseball bat caught the corner of the driver's door window, shattering it into a thousand tiny cubes.

Officer Kristine Combs reached for her pistol. The heavy end of the bat connected with her head, and the lights went out.

———

Ember took the can of pepper spray out of her purse and tossed it to Tansy. Next came the snub-nosed revolver. She felt the tension making the palms of her hands slick and tightened her grip on the weapon.

Tansy called 911.

Ember pointed to the other end of the living room, where they would be far from the door, where they could hunker down behind a couple of chairs.

Tansy nodded, and the two women took up positions behind the chairs.

There was the sound of wood splintering in response to a heavy thud. Then the crash of the door giving way.

In a minute, a tall and stocky figure moved into the room carrying a baseball bat.

Ember assumed the person to be a man from his size. A hoodie obscured his face.

Behind him, another person entered, smaller. Light glinted off the object the person was carrying. That person was also wearing a hoodie.

Ember said, "We're armed. Go away or we'll shoot."

A booming voice yelled, "Die, slut," and he charged towards the chairs.

Ember leaned around the chair and pulled the trigger. The roar was loud in the room, and her ears ached.

For a moment, the man stopped and looked rather puzzled, then he raised the bat, and Ember pulled the trigger again and again.

Her ears were ringing from the reports.

She watched the man sway for a second or two before he fell over backwards, hitting the floor hard.

The other person was screaming, "Don't shoot. Don't shoot."

She threw her knife to the floor, and her hands shot above her head.

Ember felt sick. She knew that voice. It belonged to Raylene Reston.

78

I ARRIVED at Tansy's home just seconds behind Reece Sovern.

Two ambulances were in front of the house along with two MBPD cruisers in addition to Reece's unmarked SUV.

I watched paramedics load Kristine Combs into one of the ambulances.

Inside, I found Em in the living room. She was talking to Sergeant Hans Winkler. Tansy was talking to Officer Logan Ytzen.

Raylene Reston was in handcuffs and under the watchful eye of Investigator GJ Riggins.

Forensics people were taking pictures. The paramedics were waiting to take the body of Jesse Evans to Austin for autopsy.

I hung out in a corner until Hans finished talking with Ember, then I made my way over to her.

"Harry, I'm so glad to see you."

"You all right?"

"I don't know. I killed that boy. They tell me he was

Raylene's boyfriend. He was a senior in high school. A member of Star of Bethlehem Foursquare Gospel Tabernacle. Just a boy, Harry, and I killed him."

I took her in my arms and hugged her.

Tansy joined us.

"You want to come home with us?" I asked her.

"Do you mind? I'd rather not be alone."

"Don't mind at all, that's why I asked."

"Thanks. Let me grab a few things."

"I'll come with you," Ember said, and left with Tansy.

Reece sauntered over. "Okay, Harry, I have to ask, are you calling Stanton?"

"I will be. Oralene asked me to."

"Would you do me a favor and not do so until I text you?"

"Sure."

"We're taking her down to the station now. I'm hoping she confesses to the whole thing."

"That would be nice."

"And I don't want Stanton getting in the way."

"I understand."

"Thanks, Harry."

Reece walked over to GJ, and they took Raylene away.

Hopefully, she'll turn on her sister and we can put the entire Reston nightmare to rest.

Graham Huston showed not long after Reece left.

"I missed the whole thing," he said.

"Not much to miss."

We stepped aside and let the paramedics take the body away.

"Who's the dead one?"

"Apparently, Raylene's boyfriend. Some kid from the Foursquare church."

He rolled his eyes. "Those folks are just as nutty as the Restons. A match made in heaven. Who shot him?"

"Em."

"Ember shot him? Wow. How's she doing?"

"Don't know yet. I don't think it's fully hit her."

"Better have her talk with Kurelek. She'll probably need his therapeutic hand to help her through the emotions."

"Good point. Thanks."

"Don't mention it."

Ember and Tansy joined us.

"Hi, Graham," Em said.

"Evening, ladies. Ember, I was just telling Harry you should probably talk to Kurelek. Killing someone's really tough. It doesn't leave you, and you need to learn how to cope with it."

"Thanks, Graham. I'll do that."

"You ladies ready to leave?" I asked.

They nodded.

"Join us?" I said to Graham.

"Sure. Why not? You have a bottle of Blue Corn, right?"

"I do. Just for you."

"Good."

We headed to my car.

I hope Raylene spills the beans, and Reece gets to arrest Oralene as well. Then again, if wishes were horses...

79

FOUR MONTHS LATER.

Magnolia Bluff Chronicle

Mary Lou Fight Dies in Boating Accident

This past Sunday, Mary Lou Fight was killed in a bizarre boating accident on Burnet Reservoir.

Her husband, Gunter Fight, told the *Chronicle* that his wife told him she was taking the cabin cruiser out for a ride on the lake. She needed some time alone.

"She seemed preoccupied," Mr. Fight said.

Witnesses said the boat seemed out of control when it hit the dam at the south end of the reservoir at high speed.

Magnolia Bluff police are investigating.

The funeral will be held at St. Luke's United Methodist Church as soon as police release the body.

EPILOGUE

THE DEATH of Mary Lou Fight overshadowed the trial of Raylene Reston, robbing Stanton Mirabeau Lauderbach, Esq., of the limelight.

Even in death, Mary Lou cast her shadow over the town of Magnolia Bluff.

I can't help but wonder if her death was in some way connected with Oralene's assurance to me that her adoptive mother wouldn't bother Em and me anymore.

One has to wonder about that. At least I do.

Reece wasn't able to get Raylene to confess. He told me later he tried six ways to Sunday, and she wouldn't budge. Just sat there mumbling, "As a sheep before its shearers is dumb."

Finally, her mother and Oralene intervened, demanding an attorney for the girl. And that's when Reece sent me the text.

But knowing who the culprit was, Reece and the DA were able to gather evidence and put together a case. Raylene was charged with First Degree Felony for the murders of Patrice

Bremen and the Reverend Adelbert Humphrey, as well as assault with a deadly weapon of Tansy Truitt.

Raylene's trial lasted only three days, and the jury took but two hours to reach a verdict. She was acquitted of all charges by reason of insanity. It was one of Stanton's finest performances. He said so himself.

Judge Jones, however, committed the young woman to two years of inpatient treatment and five years of outpatient.

What all of this means for Em and me, I'm not sure. Oralene has been quiet. She's the new queen of the New Order of the Crimson Hats, and I don't think that bodes well for anybody. Although the Hats, too, have been quiet. But all of this is undoubtedly the calm before the storm.

With Mary Lou gone and Oralene keeping to herself, Eliška accepted my offer of employment as our housekeeper and cook on the weekends, when Jerri has off. Em and I are very happy to have her working for us. She's a good worker.

Elmore tracked down Ember's husband and for one hundred and fifty thousand dollars persuaded him to file for divorce and not bother us.

The entire town turned out for Mary Lou's funeral. And perhaps the biggest surprise of all, Gunter and Oralene insisted Ember conduct the service.

One thing I thought strange, though, was Gunter seemed to always be holding Oralene's hand or have his arm around her waist. Rather odd that.

Then again, this is Magnolia Bluff, and lots of strange things happen here.

Magnolia Bluff. That quiet little family-friendly town in the Texas Hill Country. The best place to call home. Even if murder waits in the wings.

AFTERWORD

I hope you enjoyed *Death of a Porn Star*.

If you did, please leave a review where you bought the book and on your favorite social media sites. Your review is like word of mouth advertising. And it is pure gold.

Enter my World

Enter my world and you'll find that murder was never so good. Just click, tap, or scan the QR code below.

There's nothing like a good old-fashioned slow burn murder mystery. The quirky characters. The eccentric sleuth. The bumbling police detectives. The nefarious villain. And of course, the leisurely pacing until we reach the exciting climax.

If you are new to the Magnolia Bluff Crime Chronicles, then

Death of a Porn Star is an excellent entry point into the series and into my world.

In addition to my books in the Magnolia Bluff Crime Chronicles, I write the Justinia Wright Private Investigator Mysteries, which are an homage to Nero Wolfe and Archie Goodwin. You'll discover exciting stories, eccentric and quirky characters, and wicked killers. And if you like Magnolia Bluff, you're sure to like Justinia Wright's Minneapolis.

So just click, tap, or scan the QR code to enter my exciting world of mystery and mayhem. You will get a free copy of *Vampire House and Other Early Cases of Justinia Wright, PI* and you'll get my monthly email of news and curated contact. The game is a foot!

ABOUT THE UNDERGROUND AUTHORS, THE MAGNOLIA BLUFF CRIME CHRONICLES, AND TALES FROM CAR 4488

A Co-op of Authors

The late Caleb Pirtle III organized the Authors Marketing Cooperative in mid-2020. The purpose was to harness the collective reach of a dozen authors to promote each other's books.

But writers like to write and it didn't take long for the co-op to come up with the idea to put together a member collection of short stories to aid the joint marketing efforts.

Beyond the Sea: Stories from the Underground was published in April 2021. (Pick up a copy from Amazon) And with the publication of the story collection, the co-op began calling itself the Underground Authors.

Little did the authors realize that with the publication of *Beyond the Sea* things were about to change and change in a way they couldn't even imagine.

Magnolia Bluff Crime Chronicles

In May 2021, coming back from an online writers conference, CW Hawes proposed that the Underground Authors write a multi-author series. After a flurry of emails that sketched out the broad picture, the important landmarks and the main characters each writer would use in his or her books, the Magnolia Bluff Crime Chronicles was born.

The series revolves around the goings on in the small (fictional) Texas Hill Country town of Magnolia Bluff. The lives, loves, and deaths that happen in our town are chronicled by each author. A dozen different perspectives on life in Magnolia Bluff, Texas. That beautiful and peaceful little town on the shore of Burnet Reservoir, where murder waits in the wings.

We are now in our fifth year and Magnolia Bluff has taken on a life of its own. For the writers and readers, the town has become a real place.

We are now in our fifth year and Magnolia Bluff has taken on a life of its own. For the writers and readers, the town has become a real place.

We are amazed at the wonderful reception the series has received. It's exciting to know that we have something that is a little bit unique in the world of crime fiction. Perhaps the only multi-author crime fiction series published today.

I hope you enjoyed this chapter in the ongoing saga that is Magnolia Bluff. If this is your first visit, I hope you come back for more. And if you are a return visitor, thank you for once again making the trip to our favorite small town.

Tales from Car 4488

In 2025 Joe Congel and CW Hawes proposed the possibility of writing a new multi-author series.

Several of the Underground Authors liked the idea, deciding they wanted to try their hand at something new. After much discussion, Tales from Car 4488, a portal fantasy series, was born.

This new series will feature a variety of genres tied together under the portal fantasy umbrella, and all linked together by the mysterious subway Car 4488 and portal gatekeeper Arman.

Tales from Car 4488 launched in 2026 as the Underground Authors begin a new phase in their ongoing creative and entertainment endeavors.

COMING TO MAGNOLIA BLUFF IN APRIL

Coming out towards the end of April will be *Dead and Then Some* by Marjorie Swift Doering. I read an advanced copy of the book and this is one exciting thrill read.

To whet your appetite, below is a sample of *Dead and Then Some*. Enjoy!

1

8:22 AM – Friday, August 8th

Catching a nap at 32,000 feet proved to be as difficult for Ray Schiller as it was anywhere else. Still, he sat in the aisle seat beside his wife with his eyes closed while his fourteen-year-old son stared out the window, looking for a break in the clouds.

There was nothing below but white fluff for as far as the eye could see. Joey's absentminded tapping on the glass had already been going on for three minutes.

The sound was getting on his parents' nerves.

Gail Schiller turned the page of a book she'd brought along to help pass the time. The uninspired storyline left her wishing she had chosen differently. "Joey, would you stop doing that, please?"

"Doing what?"

"Quit tapping on the window."

The tapping became quieter but didn't stop.

Gail counted to ten. "Joey, that's really annoying. It's probably bothering other passengers too."

"I doubt it. It's so darned early, just about everyone's sleeping."

Ray Schiller brought his seat fully upright. "Joey!" His tone had the stopping power of a large caliber handgun. The tapping stopped instantly, replaced by a complaint.

"I thought flying would be fun. This is boring. No movies, no Wi-Fi, nothing—not even anything to eat or drink."

"This is an economy flight," Ray told him. "When you fly 'economy,' you give up those things."

"Jeeze," Joey grumbled, "couldn't we have paid a little more?"

Ray turned and looked at him from his aisle seat for several seconds without saying a word. "You know," he said at last, "we could have. We could have flown First Class for that matter, but since we're only staying the weekend, I booked this early flight so we can spend a few more hours with your sister. It's about priorities, not the amenities. Anyway, we'll be landing before too long. Now, sit back and relax."

From two rows behind them, Ray heard someone quietly clapping. An appreciative acknowledgment for having asserted his parental authority? Maybe something else entirely. Ray didn't know—didn't care. It didn't matter to him. He wasn't a man who felt a great need for others' approval.

Joey settled back in his seat, still bored, still annoyed.

Knowing Ray was wide awake behind those closed eyes, Gail set her book aside and spoke to him in a hushed voice. "Ray, you will make a genuine effort to get to know Dave while we're there, won't you?"

His eyes remained closed. "Of course. What kind of question is that?"

"It's just that each time I bring him up, you change the subject."

"Only because I know very little about that particular topic. Don't worry. While we're in Magnolia Bluff, I intend to learn everything I need to know about David Aiken."

Gail sighed. "Hon, he's our son-in-law, not a murder suspect. We're going for a visit and to see their house, not for you to interrogate him."

"Who said anything about an interrogation?"

She shrugged. "It's the way you said it, I guess. Anyway, I haven't heard you say it in so many words, but I get the feeling you're not crazy about Dave." Gail put a hand on his arm. "As long as you're sort of trapped here for the moment, tell me—am I wrong?"

He opened his eyes. "Gail, look, I'm not sure how I feel about him yet. Krista meets this guy and wham-bam—they get engaged before we even get a chance to know him. We had no say-so—no input. Nothing. That's my little girl we're talking about. Dave Aiken came along and all of a sudden 'poof'—they packed up and got married all the way across the country—Magnolia Bluff—Texas Hill Country for God's sake. Why clear down there? In the blink of an eye, that guy put a couple thousand miles between us and our daughter."

"It was fast, but not as fast as you make it sound," Gail argued. "And roughly speaking, it's only fourteen hundred miles or so. I checked."

"What difference does it make? He might as well have taken Krista to the moon."

Gail tapped her lips with the side of a raised index finger and patted his hand. "You're making too much of it, Ray. It's not like we have to travel by covered wagon, and she's not on another planet. This flight is only what—about two and a half hours? That's not so bad."

"The distance is the least of it, babe," Ray argued. "Krista jumped into this awfully fast. Before making a lifelong commitment, a person should take their time—really get to know the other person."

"Like we did, you mean?"

He chuckled under his breath. "Never mind about that. I just expected Krista to be more levelheaded than we were."

"It's worked out for *us*."

He reached over and squeezed her hand. "It has—major rough patches and all—still in love, still together. But marriage is such a major decision. I thought when the time came, Krista would take time to really think it through."

"She's an adult... a smart adult. We have to trust her judgment. Besides, at this point, it's spilled milk, right?"

"I suppose so." He ran a hand through his hair. It was the color of wet sand, thinning with white strands scattered around the temples. "I didn't want to come out and say it, but you don't think Krista's pregnant, do you?"

Gail's chest rose and fell. "I admit that's crossed my mind, but if that was it, she would have told me by now."

"Are you sure?"

"I'm her mother, for heaven's sake. I'd feel hurt if she didn't," Gail confessed.

"If it was Laurie who'd done this, I wouldn't be as worried. Krista, though... She tends to get too caught up in her emotions."

"You're right." Gail grinned. "Laurie's tougher than Krista. More skeptical. Nothing gets past her—just like you. I always knew she'd wind up in law enforcement like her dad. Given enough time, she'll probably become a detective like you did too."

An ever-present concern overshadowed the pride in his eyes. "I sort of hoped Laurie would decide to do something else—*anything* else. Law enforcement is a tough road to hoe —even harder for a woman. She'll do fine, though." He looked at Gail and gently stroked her cheek with the side of his thumb. "I miss the job, but I'm glad I quit when I did. It was time."

She leaned closer. "It's been four years and some nights you still wake up in a cold sweat."

"Some on-the-job experiences stick with you forever. That's the price cops have to be willing to pay." He patted Gail's hand and moved on. "I hope Laurie makes it through without too many of her own 'Velcro' memories. Right now, though, it's Krista I'm more worried about. There's the age gap for one thing."

"Ray, Dave is only twenty-six, or maybe it's twenty-seven; I can't remember. Krista's about to turn twenty-two. Their age difference is more like a small crack than a gap."

"Okay, so he's *not* a cradle robber. I'll give you that."

"Good. Also on the plus side, Dave's a professional with his own business. I looked it up. It takes eight years to become a veterinarian. To accomplish that, Dave must have a lot of ambition and determination. He must be very intelligent besides."

"And don't forget," Ray scoffed, "it means he probably likes animals."

Gail's eyebrows arched. "Hey, don't make light of that. That says a lot about a person."

"You're right, babe; it does, actually. At least he's not likely to have grown up pulling the wings off butterflies or dismembering cats."

"Oh, for heaven's sake."

"Hey, there are more of those sick bastards out there than you'd think. Anyway, that still leaves a whole range of other possibilities on the table."

"Honestly, Ray, you're impossible."

"I'm keeping an open mind—considering all the possibilities."

Gail reopened her book. "All right, fine... as long as the one about Krista having made a good choice is still on the table."

2

8:29 AM – Friday, August 8th

The audible movement upstairs wasn't as fast-moving as Krista would have liked. Hurrying to the staircase, she brushed a few wayward strands of honey-blonde hair from her cheek and tilted her head toward the second floor. "Dave! We're going to be late. Let's go, let's go, let's go!"

"I'm comin'. Take it easy. " A plastic Piggly Wiggly grocery bag thumped rhythmically against her husband's leg as he rushed down the steps at a breakneck pace.

"What do you have in there?"

"My razor, shavin' cream, aftershave... " He reached the bottom step and pivoted past her toward the first-floor bathroom. "I thought I'd better clear up some space for your dad. He's gonna need room for his stuff while they're here."

"Good thinking."

The contents clanked and clunked as Dave doubled his lanky body over and tossed the bag into the narrow cabinet under the bathroom sink. He made a mental note to be careful the next time he opened it up as the toiletries toppled forward as he slammed the cabinet shut. "Are we ready to go?"

"I guess." She forced her shoulders back, surveying as much of the first floor as she could see from where she stood. "I don't know. Maybe we should have waited until we got a few more things done before we invited my folks to see our place."

"That's not what I meant, but it's too late to rethink that now." Dave saw small, familiar 'parentheses' form between her eyebrows. "Quit worrying; it'll be fine." He scooped her into the curve of his arm, coaxing her outside to his 2013 Ford work truck parked out front. "C'mon. We'd better get a move on, or they'll land before we even get to the airport."

He opened the door of the 4-door SuperCrew cab for her as Krista's head turned toward the Cruze parked alongside. "Maybe we should take my car."

"We've already talked about this, Krissy." He gave her a boost into his truck.

She cringed. Did he think she needed the assist—that she was so big she couldn't hoist herself inside on her own?

The taunting from a particularly loathsome grade school classmate years earlier had created Krista's nagging insecurity. He had called her 'Pudge' one day. She hadn't replied, but her crimson blush told him he'd struck 'gold.' He weaponized the nickname for years afterward. The memories turned the piddly ten pounds she continually battled with into a lasting personal issue.

Dave drove down their gravel driveway, the wheels of his truck spitting up dust and stones. "There's no need to go snubbin' my F-150," he told her. "Shovin' your folks and brother into that Chevy Cruze of yours would be like jammin' a pimento into an olive. My truck might not look great, but it's roomier. Ridin' with their luggage in their laps might be a tad uncomfortable."

"They're only staying the weekend. How much luggage could they have?"

"Prob'ly more than your Cruze can handle. You really want to chance it?"

She crossed her arms and stared out the side window. Her tone turned testy. "You've already made the decision. Whether I like it or not, there's no point in us discussing it anymore."

He chuckled.

"What's so funny?"

"You... gettin' all sulky."

Krista's blue eyes narrowed. "That amuses you?"

"No. It's just this side of annoyin' actually." Smile lines lit up his narrow face. "What I get a kick outta is gettin' to add a new 'tell' to my list."

"What are you talking about?"

"You know… a 'tell.' Like in a card game—a subconscious mannerism like a guy blinkin' a lot every time he has a good hand, or maybe he clears his throat whenever he's bluffing. A 'tell.'"

"Okay, I get it." She thought about it for a second. "So, what are *mine*?"

"Uh-uh. Oh, no. Once someone finds out what their 'tells' are, you're screwed. It's over. You lose your advantage." He looked at her playfully, arching a dark eyebrow. "We've been hitched for seven months already, so maybe you've noticed. Do I have any?"

"Any 'tells'?" Her grin mirrored his own. "Darned right you do."

"You gonna share?"

"No way."

"There you have it." He gave her one of his slightly lopsided smiles. "Anyway, there's no need to go gettin' all edgy over this visit from your folks. They raised you. They *have* to approve of how you turned out." He focused on the road again. "Me, though… I'm fair game, and truth be told, your father scares the hell outta me."

"What?" She stared at him, eyes wide, mouth open. "Why?"

"I don't think he likes me."

Krista shook her head. "What makes you think that? You've only met twice—once right after we got engaged and then at our wedding."

He bobbed his head. "Yeah. I s'pose, to be fair, I oughta give it the entire weekend to decide if he *really* hates me."

She laughed. "Now you're just being ridiculous."

"Are you sure about that? When he looks at me, I feel like

I oughta be wearin' a lead vest. It's like he's scannin' me with X-ray vision or something."

"Oh, that." She waved the comment off with a dismissive hand gesture. "You're talking about 'the look.' That's just a holdover from his detective days. Laurie and I used to get that a lot. 'Why were you late getting home? Where have you been? What were you doing? Who were you with?' I suppose that worked on the job… not so much with us, though. To us, he wasn't *Detective* Schiller; he was just *Dad*."

"*Your* dad, not mine. He gives off some pretty intense vibes—like he's not someone you wanna mess with."

"He isn't, but don't let that scare you. Honestly, Dave, I don't think you have anything to worry about. My dad's a fair man. Reasonable too… for the most part, anyway. Once the two of you get to know each other, you'll see. Just relax and be yourself."

"I'll give it my best shot." He paused, thinking. "I guess what kinda spooks me is those ice-blue eyes of his. I half expect to see lasar beams come shootin' outta them. Maybe if I don't look him directly in the eyes…"

Krista slugged him in the arm.

He reacted with an exaggerated, "Ow! What was that for?"

"Avoid looking him in the eyes and you might as well be a dead man walking."

"Yeah, you're right. Eye contact's a must—like two dogs sniffin' each other's butts."

"Really?" she groaned. "Did you have to turn that image loose in my head?"

"It's what came to mind—shop talk. Sorry."

"Veterinarian or not, that's still gross."

"So noted."

3

8:49 AM – Friday, August 8th

Krista's eyes welled with tears as her parents and brother come through the gate. She hadn't realized how badly she'd missed them. Since the wedding, things had been moving so fast, she'd had little time to dwell on their absence.

The entire Schiller family had undergone a major change four years earlier. Her father had retired from the Minneapolis Police Department and sold the house in Eden Prairie. He, her mother and brother had moved two and a half hours away while she and Laurie remained in the Cities to pursue their own direction in life.

The connection hadn't been broken then; it hadn't been broken now. They continued to talk with one another as often as before, and yet somehow, the new, still greater physical separation from her family made Krista feel... She couldn't find the right word for it. A little melancholy, maybe, she decided.

Weaving their way through a slew of other deboarding passengers, Ray, Gail, and Joey caught sight of Krista and met her in a tangle of group hugs and a hail of kisses.

She blinked her tears into submission. "Mom, Dad, Joey, hi! Oh, I'm so glad you're here! How was your flight?"

Their greetings and comments overlapped her own.

Gail hugged her a third time. "You look wonderful! Ray," she said, looking pointedly at her daughter's slim midriff, "doesn't she look terrific?"

"Absolutely," he agreed.

"Hardly. I'm two pounds heavier than you saw me at our wedding."

"Well," he said, "wherever you've got them, they look good."

Gail planted another kiss on her cheek. "You'll take them off again, Krista, like you always do. You have to expect to gain a little weight... you're a chef, after all."

"A sous-chef, Mom."

"We're blocking the path," Ray said. "Let's go grab our bags." He led the way. "Your husband couldn't make it, Krista?" he asked.

"No, Dave is here, Dad. He's circling the parking lot. He's waiting for me to phone him once we head outside so he can come pick us up in the pickup zone."

"So, he left his furry clientele to fend for themselves today?"

"The animals are fine, Dad. Dave has his people looking after them."

The entire gaggle of Schillers dodged past assorted bags and their meandering owners.

"His people?" Ray said. "How many employees are on his payroll?"

"Just two, but they're very capable."

Reaching the baggage carousel, Ray reached out and snagged Gail's suitcase and one of his own. He pointed down the way. "Joey, there's yours. Go get it."

"Okay."

Ray picked up the prior subject where they'd left off. "So, how's Dave's business doing? Making ends meet, or are you struggling to keep your heads above water?"

Krista tried to keep the exasperation out of her voice. "Dad, Dave's just getting his business started up. He's only been back in Magnolia Bluff for seven months. You can't expect miracles."

"I only ask because I'd like to know he's taking care of you."

"We're taking care of each other, Dad. I have a job too, don't forget."

"I know—the restaurant outside of town that you told us about." Ray bobbed his head and looked her in the eye. "Still, there might come a time when you'd rather not have to hold down a job. Once you start a family…"

Stretching on the balls of her feet, Gail put her lips to his ear and whispered, "Ray, you're setting a new land record for wearing out one's welcome!"

Krista wrapped an arm through his. "Don't worry, Dad. Dave and I will be fine. We *are* fine. Things are a little tight right now, but we're doing okay, and things are only going to get better. Dave's very good at what he does. Word is starting to get around." Starting toward an exit, she pulled out her cell phone, laughing. "The first thing I learned here in Magnolia Bluff is that, good or bad, word gets around about *everything*."

BOOKS BY CW HAWES

CW is a multi-genre author. The books below are portals to his many exciting worlds. And no AI was used in the writing of these books.

Justinia Wright Private Investigator Mysteries

Justinia Wright is the PI with panache. These slow burn mysteries, written in homage to Rex Stout's Nero Wolfe, are sure to satisfy your craving for intriguing puzzles, quirky characters, and wise-cracking humor.

Vampire House and Other Early Cases of Justinia Wright, PI

Festival of Death

Trio in Death-Sharp Minor

But Jesus Never Wept

The Conspiracy Game

A Nest of Spies

When Friends Must Die

Death Makes a House Call

To Right a Wrong

The Nine Deadly Dolls

Ripples on the Pond

Christmas with the Wrights

Minneapolis's Finest

Jack in the Box

Sauerkraut Days

Magnolia Bluff Crime Chronicles

Tense slow burn mysteries set in our favorite town in the Texas Hill Country.

Death Wears a Crimson Hat

Ten Million Ways to Die

Who Mourns Elektra?

Death by Moonlight

Death of a Porn Star

Pierce Mostyn Paranormal Investigations

The X-Files meets Cthulhu. Pierce Mostyn does battle with inter-dimensional monsters bent on the destruction of humanity.

Nightmare in Agate Bay

Stairway to Hell

Terror in the Shadows

Van Dyne's Vampires

The Medusa Ritual

Demons in the Dunes

Van Dyne's Zuvembies

In the Shadow of the Mountains of Madness

The Rocheport Saga

A post-apocalyptic adventure series in the style of cozy catastrophes such as *Earth Abides* and *Day of the Triffids*. Join Bill Arthur as he strives to build a new and better world on the ashes of the old.

The Morning Star

The Shining City

The Divided City

The Troubled City

By Leaps and Bounds

Freedom's Freehold

Take to the Sky

Decopunk

Alternative history adventures in a world where World War II never happened and swing is still king.

From the Files of Lady Dru Drummond

The Moscow Affair

The Golden Fleece Affair

Rand Hart Adventures

Rand Hart and the Pajama Putsch

Tales of the Macabre

For the horror lover in you.

Do One Thing For Me

Metamorphosis

What the Next Day Brings

Ancient History

Anthologies

Enjoy CW's stories in these short story collections.

The Phantom Games

Beyond the Sea

Overmorrow

Arachnapocalypse! The Anthology

Once Upon a WolfPack

You can find all of CW's books at Amazon. Just tap, click, or scan the QR code.

ABOUT CW HAWES

CW Hawes is a multi-genre author because he's a multi-genre reader.

He's penned works in a variety of genres, including:

The Justinia Wright Private Investigator Mysteries

Five novels in the Magnolia Bluff Crime Chronicles series

The Rocheport Saga: A Post-Apocalyptic Steam-Powered Future

The Pierce Mostyn Paranormal Investigations

And assorted alternative history/decopunk, science fiction, and horror offerings.

CW is enjoying his retirement writing, walking, playing chess, and enjoying the art of doing nothing.

He hasn't met a doughnut or a pizza he doesn't like, is something of a tea snob, and rocks out to Handel and Vaughan Williams.

You can reach him at his website, on X, and also Facebook. Just tap, click, or scan the QR codes below.

His website:

His X account:

His Facebook page: